BLOOD AND ASH

BLOOD AND ASH

MANUEL PEREZ

First Printing: 2016

ISBN
Paperback: 978-0-9975072-0-1
Hardcover: 978-0-9975072-1-8
Digital: 978-0-9975072-2-5

Manuel Perez
252 Summer Street
Somerville, MA 02143

www.bloodandash.com

CONTENTS

CHAPTER 1
SHADOW BURN

The furious storm that had been pounding New York City for the past few hours had subsided to a light rainfall. It was late, and the streets were empty. The neon lights of closed stores flickered in pools of water covering the asphalt. A beat-up red sedan sat parked down a lonely alley. The window was cracked open, and the gray puffs of smoke that oozed out were slowly dispersed by the drizzling rain.

Steam poured out of a manhole farther down, creating a fog that obscured the visibility at the alley's end. A lone figure emerged from the mist, his boots making ripples in the puddles as he walked, destroying his reflection with each passing step. His long dark cloak floated barely out of reach of the water's surface.

The man in the car lifted his arm and used the edge of his coat to wipe away the condensation that had collected on the interior of the windshield. Between the swaying of his windshield wipers, he saw a figure approach. As his heartbeat quickened, he lifted his shaking cigarette to his lips. Given his frail condition, he really shouldn't be smoking at all but needed something to calm himself down. He inhaled deeply and wheezed as he exhaled.

When the man in the cloak reached the car, he pulled his hand from his pocket and knocked on the driver's-side window. Using an old-fashioned hand crank, the man inside slowly rolled down the window. He looked out, but between the rain and the height of the man outside, he was unable to make out the figure's face.

"Are you Aleister?" the man in the car stuttered.

"Yeah, that's me," replied the figure in a British accent.

His voice was firm and confident, reassuring the man in the car that he had made the right decision to meet with him. He let out a sigh of relief.

"I almost didn't think you were going to show up. Do you really think you can help me?"

"I've helped many men like you, men with much deeper and darker issues. It all depends on how far you're willing to go," said Aleister.

"Thank God. I didn't know what I was going to do. I mean—"

"First things first," interrupted Aleister. "Did you bring what I asked for?"

"That old case...yes, of course." The man reached over and rummaged through a pile of items on the seat beside him.

"You have no idea how important that 'old case' is," replied Aleister.

At that moment, a shadow loomed over the already-darkened alley and was soon followed by something falling from the building above. It smashed into the roof of the sedan with a force that crushed and flattened it. Glass exploded from all sides of the car, sending Aleister flying into a brick wall behind him. Blood poured down the sides of the vehicle. The man inside was killed almost instantaneously.

Aleister was in tremendous pain and clutched his side as he brought himself to his feet. A few drops of blood ran down his arm and dripped to the ground. An inhuman-looking figure stood before him on the now-flattened roof of the car. The creature was more than six feet tall and hunched over, its pale-white skin glistening in the falling rain. Instead of eyes it had two holes of pure darkness that stared at Aleister. With a terrifying howl that pierced the air, it exposed its razor-sharp teeth.

"Yeah, this is not good," said Aleister.

*

A siren roared as a police cruiser headed to the crime scene. Detective Nicholas Valle sat in the passenger seat. As he exhaled from his thick Cohiba cigar, the smoke billowed through the slight crack in the window like a tornado seeking its last breath before its eventual dissipation. He had been sound asleep only twenty minutes earlier, but they needed him for this case. Valle specialized in cases that would drive most detectives straight into the nuthouse. This was his calling—to solve cases that other detectives couldn't even wrap their minds around, and according to the reports, this one was a doozy.

Detective Valle was a forty-five-year-old man of average height and build—well, if you consider a slight beer belly average. His hair was gray but speckled with black. Every day he wore what appeared to be the same suit: black pants, a white dress shirt, a red tie, and a worn yellow jacket. But his most distinctive characteristic was his bushy mustache, which looked as if it had been teleported straight out of the 1970s and onto his upper lip.

The driver of the cruiser was Detective Ethan Kent, a relatively young cop in his midthirties. Kent's auburn hair was cut short, and he was well groomed. He was relatively fit and dressed in a simple navy-blue suit. When he had first become partners with Detective Valle almost a year ago, the stench from Valle's cigars was almost unbearable. Now, much like a man who'd been working in the sewers for many years, Kent had acclimated to it. However, this didn't stop him from wearing looks of annoyance and disapproval whenever Valle smoked in the car.

As they got closer to the crime scene, the flashing red and blue lights of parked police vehicles, as well as spotlights atop cameramen's shoulders, lit up the area. Crowds of news crews and curious onlookers leaked into the streets. Kent honked his horn a few times to part a sea of reporters as he drove up to the cordoned-off alley. After he parked, the two detectives made their way to the scene. He lifted a strand of the yellow tape that sectioned off the area, allowing Detective Valle to duck underneath, then followed him in. Valle didn't waste any time and immediately addressed the police officers already on the scene.

"So who here wants to give me the lowdown?" he asked.

A young female officer, who had been conversing with some of the other cops on the scene, turned around. She was wearing a standard-issue dark-blue uniform with a silver badge over the left of her chest. A peaked cap covered most of her light-brown hair, which was pulled back into a neatly braided bun.

"I will," she answered. "I'm Officer Cameron. I was first on the scene and was in charge until your arrival."

"Pleased to meet you, Officer Cameron. I'm Detective Valle, and my partner over there is Detective Kent. Now please walk me through the scene."

"Well, over here we have the vehicle," she said, pointing at a red sedan with its roof smashed in. "As you can see, it appears something fell from one of the buildings and crushed the driver inside."

"What fell?" asked Valle.

"So far we haven't been able to find any objects in the area."

"That doesn't make any sense," he said. "Whatever crushed the car must have weighed hundreds of pounds. Are you telling me someone just dragged it away?"

"No, sir," she replied. "Even if someone managed to drag whatever fell away, we would have found scuff marks on the ground. Whatever caused this seems to have vanished."

"Nothing simply vanishes," said Valle. "Double-check the roof of the car and scrape it for clues. Send absolutely everything to the lab. Whatever fell must have left something behind."

"Yes, sir," she replied.

"Anything else unusual?"

"Well, there's this," she said, pointing up at the wall behind the car.

The dark outline of a tall, deformed-looking man appeared to be etched into the brick.

*

Aleister rose to his feet as the creature raised one of its grotesque arms toward the sky. The air crackled around its hand, and a dark-green energy was drawn into the beast's outstretched fingers. With a flick of its wrist, the creature hurled a glowing ball of emerald flames at Aleister. As if in slow motion, Aleister rolled out of the way.

Aleister reached into his cloak and removed a black rod with a bright golden gemstone on its tip. In a swift motion, he swung it outward. The bar extended itself to almost two feet in length. He held it above his head and pointed it directly at the creature.

In a hissing voice, the beast said, "Where is the boy, Aleister? You can't hide him from us!"

Aleister shrugged. "What boy?"

The creature growled and once again drew in green energy around its clawed fingers. Aleister quickly chanted in an arcane tongue, "ᗯᏗᏜᏆ (MA-RIM)." A bolt of green plasma emerged from the creature's other hand and flew toward him. But this time, just before it struck him, a field of glowing golden energy formed around the tip of Aleister's outstretched rod to block the incoming attack. The green energy pushed hard against the shield, forcing Aleister to press his feet up against the wall behind him to withstand its might.

"How much longer do you think your pathetic field can last, mage? The boy belongs to us! Tell us now, or we'll end your life right here!" spewed the creature.

"We'll see about that," responded Aleister as he dropped his shield and turned his body sideways to dodge the attack.

The green energy smashed against the brick wall behind him, resulting in a brilliant explosion so intense that it caused a giant cloud of smoke to fill the spot where he once had stood. The smoke was so thick that the creature lost sight of Aleister. It jumped down from the car and moved its head around as it sniffed the air in search of him. When it thought it had found his scent, it tore into the mist with its claws, but it found only emptiness.

A glowing golden aura grew in strength from within the cloud. The beast snarled as Aleister chanted, "ᏋᏆ ᏕᎰ (KI-NAS)." The golden aura turned into a concentrated beam then shot toward the creature. A brilliant energy engulfed it, and an intense yellow light filled the alley. The creature screamed in agony, and then it was gone, leaving only its shadow burned into the wall behind it.

*

"What the hell is that?" asked Valle as he looked up at the wall.

"This is why we called you, Detective Valle," replied Officer Cameron. "I've never seen anything like it. It looks like pictures from the aftermath of the Hiroshima bombings. I remember them from high school."

"Found something!" yelled Detective Kent, who'd been examining an area on the other side of the flattened sedan.

Detective Valle and Officer Cameron glanced over in his direction. Detective Kent emerged from behind the car and lifted something into the air. It appeared to be a solid ebony scroll case engraved with Nordic runes. He carefully carried it over to his partner and held it in front of him.

"Well, don't just stand there, Kent. Open it," said Valle.

"You know…something tells me that isn't the best idea," Kent replied. "I get a weird feeling just holding this thing."

Sarcastic expressions came over the faces of Detective Valle and Officer Cameron as they simultaneously stared at him. Though neither spoke a word, their expressions said, "Seriously?"

Valle extended his open hand. "Well, then, hand it over, son. I'll do it."

Kent hated it when Valle called him "son." It infuriated him, but he felt even uneasier about holding the case, so he handed it over without argument. As Valle held the case, he too felt something strange. Though the case didn't move, a slight energy pulsed through his glove and into his fingers. Not dissuaded, he gripped one end with his other hand and slowly tried to pry it open. Then all at once the case flew open. Hundreds of tiny pieces of parchment spilled into the air and onto the ground.

"Damn it!" yelled Valle. "Someone get those!"

Kent and Officer Cameron hopped into action. They quickly gathered the pieces from the wet pavement and even managed to catch a few in the air. Meanwhile, Valle resealed the case to prevent any further pieces from escaping. Within a few minutes, they had collected all the pieces and placed them into two small plastic bags. Valle emptied the rest of the case's contents into a third bag. They each slowly lifted their bags into the air and held them up against the light of a streetlamp.

Valle raised an eyebrow. "They're all blank."

"So are mine," replied Kent and Officer Cameron in unison.

Valle stashed his plastic bag in his left suit pocket while at the same time removing a cigar from his right. After placing the cigar in his mouth, he reached back into his right pocket to retrieve his lighter. He rotated the cigar slowly as he lit it and puffed it to life. Then he inhaled deeply and seemed to hold his breath for a few moments. Finally he exhaled several large puffs of gray smoke.

"Well, this keeps getting weirder," said Valle.

CHAPTER 2

BRILLIANT ASHES

Ashley Drake had just entered his senior year at MIT in Cambridge, Massachusetts. Since his first name wasn't a typical boy's name, he always introduced himself as "Ash," and that was how most people knew him. He was a handsome though somewhat lanky kid, with shoulder-length dirty-blond hair and light-blue eyes. Though he was nearsighted, he rarely wore his glasses and often walked around with everything in the distance in a slight blur.

On paper, Ash was studying mechanical engineering, but he spent far more time feeding his addiction to playing video games than going to class. Fortunately for him, he also was quite brilliant and always managed to pass his classes with a minimal amount of effort. To him video games were an escape from an otherwise ordinary and uneventful life into worlds in which he was a hero embarking upon a great adventure. He had no idea what he wanted to do with his life after college or in general.

BLOOD AND ASH

Ash had moved around a lot as a child and, despite being somewhat shy, had learned how to quickly make new friends, and MIT was no different. However, at the same time, he had become so used to people coming in and out of his life that most of these relationships weren't deep, and he had few close friends. He was never very social and often relied on others to pry him away from his books and video games to do nearly anything.

He lived in a small, unique dormitory on campus called Bexley Hall, which sat along the Charles River. It was a maze of staircases and hallways that connected suites of rooms. The dorm had both single- and double-occupancy rooms, and this was Ash's first year living in his own room. He shared a suite with two other guys he had just met but hardly spoke to.

Before moving to Cambridge, he had lived in California. His parents had divorced when he was fourteen, and he'd spent most of his teenage years moving from place to place along the West Coast with his mother, Kimberley. Ash never heard from his father again after his parents separated, and he never missed him. He had his mother, and she was all that he needed. They eventually settled in San Clemente just before he started his junior year in high school.

San Clemente was a small surfing town snuggled against the ocean, and whenever he told people where he was from and they saw the way he looked, they assumed him to be the type of person who was at home on the beach or in the water, but this wasn't the case. He'd always been a somewhat geeky kid who preferred escaping into the fantasy worlds of comic books and novels; they always seemed more interesting than his life.

He had a particular fascination with a genre known as steampunk. It was a mixture of science fiction and fantasy based on an alternate version of the world, with nineteenth-century-inspired aesthetics and technology. It was both retro and futuristic, both of which Ash loved, and contained spellbinding, beautiful machines with exposed gears running on steam power. He found the designs and fine details of this world so intriguing that it was one of the things that had inspired his attraction to the field of engineering.

Outside of the imaginary realms of books and video games, his life was in a bit of a rut. Every day seemed the same as the last. He'd get up, go to class, come home, read, play some video games, then go to bed. He was caught in a never-ending repeating pattern that would one day at best replace school with work. His view of life was even reflected in his unchanging wardrobe, which was pretty much the same every day: jeans and a black T-shirt. For as long as he could remember, he never felt he was doing what he was supposed to be doing and longed for something more. He just didn't know what that was.

It was Friday night. While many MIT students would be going to a party or one of the many bars in town, this was a big gaming night for Ash. In his favorite game, *Knightmage Online*, his character was an elven mage named Rath10n, and tonight he would be joining the rest of his guildmates on a raid to take down Malphas, the demonic prince and ruler of the Bloodcrown Keep in the northern region of Kalmar. At 8:30 p.m. he donned his gaming headset and sat down to play. Many hours of caffeinated beverages and mouse clicking lay ahead of him.

Hours passed as the guild made its way through the digital dungeon. It was now one o'clock in the morning. Suddenly a strange, faint voice whispered in his head.

"What did you say?" Ash replied, thinking it was one of the other people in the game.

"No one said anything, buddy," replied one of the players.

Thinking nothing of it, Ash continued to play. The guild had entered into the chamber of Malphas's guardian, Lilith, a half-dead witch queen with the ability to control some of the characters and conjure pools of boiling acid on the ground. This was an extraordinary difficult battle and required a high degree of coordination among all the players. The raid leader, who was playing a female dwarven cleric named Harl3y, addressed the guild.

"Okay, let's buff up," said Harl3y in a high-pitched voice. "Tanks, get ready to pull on my mark. Are we ready?"

Though Ash had no idea how old Harl3y actually was in real life, her voice sounded like that of a twelve-year-old girl, which he always found a little disturbing.

"Yup."

"Yes, ma'am."

"Hells yes."

"Let's rock out!"

The characters that were designated as tanks marched forward. Their job was to engage and occupy Lilith's attention while the other characters attacked. The battle was long and arduous, but despite a few fallen comrades, the guild was doing extremely well this evening and was about halfway through when the voice came again. Though it was still faint, this time Ash could tell it was that of an older man, and he could make out the words.

Ash, you are needed, it whispered.

Right after he heard this, his monitor flickered then went completely blank. With increasing brightness, the outline of a white rectangle slowly emerged in the center of the screen.

*

For a moment, Ash was no longer in his room. He stood in pure darkness with a door far off in the distance. Light poured out from its edges, creating a bright, illuminated rectangle.

I need you to wake up, said the voice.

Confused and disoriented, Ash replied, "What?"

You've been asleep, Ash. Within you are untapped power and potential, said the voice. *You're needed, and we're running out of time. Walk through the door, and we can begin. I can't make you do it. You must make this choice on your own.*

Even though the whole thing felt like a dream, and he was pretty sure he had inadvertently passed out while playing *Knightmage Online*, an uneasy feeling came over him. The dream was too vivid, too real, and the man's voice was somehow familiar, as if he'd heard it before but couldn't remember who it was. Despite these feelings, something inside him compelled him to make his way toward the door. With each step he took, the door seemed no closer than the last. His vision began to blur as he forced himself forward.

Don't fight to get to the door. You'll never make it, said the voice. *You have to let yourself go.*

The blurriness continued, and then there was darkness.

*

"Rath10n, what the hell are you doing?" yelled Harl3y through Ash's headphones. "Get out of the damn acid! You're going to wipe us!"

Ash was back in his room, staring at his screen, and yup, Harl3y was absolutely right. His character, Rath10n, was standing right smack in the middle of a pool of acid. Ash quickly gripped his mouse and attempted to move his mage, but it was too late. The guild had wiped, and the yelling ensued.

"What were you thinking?"

"Pay attention!"

"We almost had it!"

"Damn you, Rath10n!"

The gamers vented their anger and aggravation. The banter continued until Harl3y finally jumped in.

"Rath10n, we needed you on this," she said. "What happened?"

"I'm sorry. I don't know what happened. I kinda blanked out. I think I might need a break," replied Ash.

"Damn it!" exclaimed Harl3y. "Okay, everyone take a break. Be back here in five."

After rubbing his eyes, Ash took off his headset and placed it next to his keyboard. Then he sat there and stared at his monitor for a few moments, watching as some of the remaining characters moved around on the screen. While he was prone to daydreams and more than once had passed out on the couch while playing video games as a teenager, nothing like this had ever happened before. Though he didn't feel ill, he thought perhaps he was running a hallucinatory fever and put his hand on his forehead; his head, however, didn't feel any warmer or colder than usual. Deciding to chalk it up to exhaustion, he let out a long sigh, slowly pushed his chair back, and stood up.

He walked out of his room and down the hall to the shared kitchen area. The hallway was unlit, but the kitchen was illuminated by the light of streetlamps creeping through the window. Ash put his hand on the handle of the fridge, paused for a second, then opened it. He reached in, grabbed another bottle of soda, and closed the door. On his way back to his room, he unscrewed the cap and guzzled the drink. Though he was far from tired, he thought the caffeine might help him stay alert.

Back in his room, he sat down in his chair and rolled it toward his desk. He grabbed his headphones and put them on. After taking another swig from his soda, he placed it to the side of his mouse. He shook his head a few times to try to clear out any remaining thoughts of his recent hallucinations, but the remnants of the dark room with the glowing door still lingered.

A few minutes later, Harl3y came back on and said, "All right, guys and gals, hopefully everyone—that means you too, Rath10n—is ready to roll this bitch!"

On the next attempt, the guild executed its attack flawlessly and successfully defeated Lilith. They celebrated and bragged among themselves for several minutes before moving on to the next portion of the dungeon. The guild slowly cleared its way to the final boss. It was close to three in the morning when they reached the entrance to Malphas's lair.

"This is it, guildmates, the last and final boss of the evening," said Harl3y. "I know this guy has given us some trouble in the past, but I have a strong feeling this is our night for victory!"

Harl3y was obviously a wee bit optimistic this evening. Ash and his guild had been playing this dungeon for several months. Each and every attempt they had made against Malphas had ended in utter failure.

As Harl3y reviewed the battle plan, Ash's senses started to fade. Her voice washed out into a whisper, and Ash had to strain to hear anything. The room grew dim, and he could barely see the screen in front of him. Beneath his fingers, he no longer could feel his keyboard or mouse. Finally there was nothing but darkness and silence. Then the voice came again.

We're running out of time, it said.

*

Ash awoke the next day with an aching head. He felt as if he'd been on an all-night drinking binge and was now desperately trying to reconstruct exactly what had happened, but nothing came to him. He didn't even know how he had managed to make it to his bed. After pulling himself up, he sat for a moment and rubbed his face a few times. Then he glanced at his computer. The entire screen was black, but strangely his monitor was still on.

He walked over to his computer and moved the mouse around to see if his cursor would appear, but nothing happened. Next he tapped a few random keys, but still nothing happened. Still feeling partially asleep, he glanced at his alarm clock, wondering what time it was; it was 7:07 a.m.

He looked back at his computer to find the inner edges of the monitor glowing brightly. The glow intensified until the entire screen was illuminated and the room was filled with white light. Ash lifted his arm to shield his eyes. He slowly stepped backward from the screen. Then suddenly it went dark, but the afterglow of the light was still burned into his vision, as if he'd been staring at the sun.

When Ash's vision returned, he saw a moving black-and-white pixelated image on the screen. From the details he could make out, it was an older man with a light-colored beard; the upper portion of his face was covered by a dark hood.

The man's lips moved. "I hope you're feeling okay. I'm sorry I can't be there in person. I know this must all be very strange for you. I imprinted what I could into your memories last night."

"Imprinted? What are you talking about? Who are you?" asked Ash.

"I wish I had more time to explain, but they're already tracking us, and I can't risk your safety. You're too important. A package will arrive for you in a few moments. It'll have to suffice for now until I can throw off their scent and make my way to you," replied the man.

"What are you talking about?" Ash asked again loudly. Then, as it slowly dawned on him that he was having a full-blown, very loud conversation with his computer, he lowered his voice and repeated, "What are you talking about?"

"They're coming now! I have to go!" said the man, as his image slowly dissipated, leaving Ash staring at a blank computer screen.

Ash closed his eyes, put his face in his palms, and took a deep breath. When he opened his eyes again, his screen was displaying a gigantic "Disconnected from Game" message. Behind the message, he saw an open chat window with an unending list of angry words from his guildmates. He sighed and looked over at his dorm-room door; somehow he felt a presence approaching.

He went to the door and quickly pulled it open to see if anyone was there. With his hand ready to knock, a well-dressed middle-aged man in an all-black suit and wearing horn-rimmed glasses stood before him with a package tucked under one arm and a clipboard under the other. There were several odd things about this situation. First, it was far too early in the morning for anyone to be out delivering packages. Second, Ash lived on the fourth floor of his dorm, and packages were always collected at the front desk. Third, how did Ash just feel that the man was there? And fourth, who delivers packages in a tailor-made suit?

"Good morning, sir," said the man. "I apologize for disturbing you at this early hour. The young lady downstairs was kind enough to let me in. I'm told that you would be Mr. Ashley Drake. I have a package for you."

"Yes, I'm Ashley Drake," replied Ash, sounding bewildered.

"Excellent. Sign here, please," said the man, as he pulled out the clipboard and handed it over.

"Aren't you kind of well-dressed for a deliveryman?" Ash asked, as he signed his name at the bottom of a form.

"We service an exclusive clientele, Mr. Drake. And someone wanted to be very sure that you received this exact package at this exact location at this exact time," replied the man as he took the clipboard back.

The man started to hand over the package to Ash, who just stood there with a look of astonishment. He slowly took the package into his hands, almost as if it were a robotic response.

"Have a good rest of your day, Mr. Drake," said the man, before he headed down the hallway.

Ash closed the door and meandered over to his desk. He set down the package in front of him. This was by far the strangest start to a day he'd ever had. It was so strange, in fact, that something in the back of his brain was desperately trying to convince him that none of it actually was happening and perhaps he was still dreaming.

He sat and stared at the package for what seemed like hours, trying to come to grips with what was going on. Even if he had dreamed the rest of it, this box sitting in front of him was very real. It was wooden and had two latches on the side that held its top in place. There were no postal markings or addresses on its surface. He slowly undid the two latches, and the top separated from the base. As he opened the box, a thought raced through his head. He felt like an explorer who had just reached the end of a great adventure and was about to discover a treasure that had been hidden away for ages.

The inside of the box was laced with black velvet. A letter sealed with a mulberry wax stamp bearing the letter *W* lay atop four burgundy velvet bags. Ash removed the letter from the box and broke open the wax seal. He carefully unfolded it and read the handwritten letter:

BRILLIANT ASHES

Ashley Drake,
Within this box are the tools you will need to unlock your abilities.
I will join you as soon as I can.
—W

Ash put the letter to the side and dug through the rest of the box's contents. He opened the largest velvet bag first. To his surprise, inside was a pair of virtual reality goggles. He had only read about them online, but these were sleeker and much more high-tech in appearance than anything he'd ever seen. A slim, glossy, black visor with silver trim ran across the front of the glasses and was connected to a small pair of over-ear headphones with a single adjustable head strap along the back. The next bag contained some sort of disc player. It was made entirely of metal and bore no manufacturer's mark. The third bag contained what appeared to be a wooden disc case. The case opened effortlessly to reveal a disc constructed out of some kind of shiny black rock. The last bag contained a single clear, smooth gemstone about the size of a large marble.

He became excited by the thought that perhaps he was destined for something greater, and this device was the key that would pull him out of his ordinary, repetitive life. It didn't take him long to decide he was going to try this thing on. He plugged the goggles into the metal box then searched for where to insert the ebony disc. Though he couldn't find an obvious "eject" button, he noticed a thin, discreet slot along the side about the width of the disc. He slipped the disc into the slot. When it was about halfway inserted into the metal box, the rest of it sucked itself in. A flicker emanated from the goggles then slowly died down.

"All right, here we go," he said out loud as he put the goggles on his head.

At first all he saw was darkness. Then the headphones over his ears made a quiet humming noise, and a dim red line appeared on the horizon. The red line glowed brighter and brighter as it moved up and down. Ash realized it was scanning his eyes.

Suddenly he found himself in an old medieval room. The walls were made of stone blocks, and huge tapestries hung on all sides. The illustrations on the tapestries were out of focus, and no matter how hard he tried, he couldn't discern what they were. The room was otherwise bare, with no visible doors or windows, yet it somehow was illuminated. As he looked down, he noticed he was sitting in a white circle that was etched into the ground. Along the edges of the circle were symbols that he didn't recognize. The resolution and detail of the virtual reality were astonishing; Ash tried to find the pixels in the image but was unable to do so.

A monotone voice echoed in his ears: "Blessed initiate identified. Starting program."

The circle surrounding Ash suddenly glowed, as if it were being illuminated from a light source underneath the ground. Then the light slowly pulsed in and out, as though it were following the rhythm of his breath. Around the edges of the circle, the symbols rotated clockwise around him, at first slowly then faster and faster until they turned into a blur of light. Even though he thought this was a simulation, he felt as if some sort of energy were building and surrounding him.

A figure of pure light materialized a few feet in front of the circle. At first the being was so bathed in bright-white light that Ash could only discern a few features and was barely able to make out the shape of a person. An enormous set of glowing wings unfolded from the figure, filling the room from edge to edge. Then, as if a vacuum were pulling the light into the being, the figure of a female angel slowly emerged.

The angel's long auburn hair seemed to dance in the air like a slow flame swaying in the breeze. Her skin was pure white, and each of her facial features was etched to perfect distinction. She wore an impossibly long white robe with a shorter red cloak draped over her shoulders. Both swayed in slow motion. Her eyes were self-illuminating and appeared as bright-white gems.

With a sweet voice she said, "Greetings, initiate. I'm Elysium. I'm here to guide you through your training. I've also been designed to answer some basic questions. You can call for me at any time merely by saying my name. Do you understand?"

Ash, frozen for a moment in awe, finally responded, "Yes."

"Good. Then let's begin with the basics. First I'll explain what magic is."

He had more than a little trouble believing what he'd just seen and heard. While his comics and video games were filled with mystical elements, he had found nothing in the real world that made him believe such things actually existed. Yet the dark room with the bright door, the old man on his screen, the strange deliveryman, the package, Elysium—all of it was adding up, giving his mind just enough doubt to accept what she had to say.

"It'll be easiest for you to think of magic as a pyramid, formed by the mind, body, and soul," Elysium said, conjuring an inverted silver pyramid before her. "At the bottom we have the soul," she continued, as a glowing symbol appeared below the bottom corner of the pyramid. "The soul is connected to the universe and acts as the fuel for all your arcane abilities. Every being is born with a certain amount of energy. That energy can be used either consciously or subconsciously to influence the world around each individual. This energy can deplete over time with the use of spells but will always replenish itself."

Another glowing symbol appeared above the top-left corner of the pyramid. "Next we have the mind, which is often erratic and unfocused. It wanders from thought to thought throughout the day. It's driven by and connected to the soul. The mage uses the ancient tongue in the form of mantras to bring focus to the mind, allowing it to communicate directly with the energies of the soul."

A ball of cyan light emerged at the bottom of the pyramid, glowed more intensely, then split into two. One part remained at the bottom, while another traveled up the left side of the pyramid, leaving behind it a trail of energy. As they separated, the light at the bottom slowly changed to blue, and the ball traveling upward changed to green. When it reached the corner of the pyramid, it stopped and pulsed for a few seconds before the light faded from the image.

"Finally we have the body or, more aptly put, the physical," said Elysium, as a glowing symbol appeared above the top-right corner of the pyramid. "The body too is connected and driven by the soul. For a person to draw magical energies into the physical universe, these energies must pass through the body. A mage generally will employ a gem or wand to direct the energies."

Once again, a ball of light appeared at the base of the pyramid. This time it was magenta. After splitting in two, one of the balls rose up the right side of the pyramid. It changed from magenta to red, while the light remaining at the bottom changed to blue. A trail of illumination was left behind it until it reached the corner of the pyramid. The light pulsed for a few seconds then faded from the image.

"A mage uses his conscious mind, focused by a mantra and directed by his wand, to bring the pure energy of his soul into this world and change the reality around him. With the proper training, nothing will be beyond your abilities," Elysium explained, as another glowing white ball appeared at the base of the pyramid.

This time the luminous ball split into three parts. One remained at the bottom, while the other two traveled up the left and right sides of the pyramid, creating a flaming path of energy as they ascended. As they traveled upward, the light on the left changed to green, and the ball on the right changed to red. When they reached the corners of the pyramid, they paused for a second and pulsed with energy. Then they continued along the top edge of the pyramid on a path to meet at its center. When the two collided with each other, a brilliant flash of yellow light appeared.

"Do you understand?" she asked.

Elysium was asking the wrong question. Did he understand it? Yes. It seemed like a simple description based on additive color mixing. Did he believe it? That was the real question. Well, he was still doubtful of that part but was definitely intrigued enough to continue listening.

"I think so," he replied.

"I can answer any questions if you need clarification."

As Ash was pondering a proper question to ask, his mobile phone beeped from outside the simulation. He must have just received a text message. He was hoping it was from April, a girl he had been flirting with in class and had invited out for brunch earlier in the week.

"I'll be right back," said Ash, as he removed the helmet from his head.

He looked down at his phone. The message read, "Hey, Ash. Sorry, but I can't make it to brunch today. Something came up. See you in class."

This was the second time April had canceled at the last minute, and it was becoming very apparent that she had no interested in hanging out with him outside of school. With a look of disappointment, Ash sat there for a few moments, staring at his phone. He wondered why he had such trouble with girls. They always wanted to be his friend and nothing more.

He sighed and responded to the message: "All right, see you in class."

Ash felt more than a little disheartened and rejected, but as he gazed at the virtual reality helmet, these feeling were replaced by a piqued interest in continuing his exploration of this fascinating new world he had just discovered. He smiled as he enthusiastically put on the visor. Within a few moments, he was back in the medieval training room. In a glimmer of light, Elysium emerged, hovering before him.

"Greetings, Blessed initiate," she said. "Do you wish to continue your program where you left off?"

As he sat before this angel, fully immersed in the vivid virtual reality, some of his previous doubts crawled away from his conscious mind. Just as he was partially starting to accept what was going, a thought came to him.

"Elysium, I have a question first," he said.

She nodded. "I've been designed to answer some basic questions. Please ask."

"Why was I chosen to receive this training?"

"Initiates are selected and approved by members of the council."

"Okay…what can you tell me about this council?"

"I'm sorry. You don't have the required privileges to access information regarding the council."

Ash felt a little uncomfortable with her response. He didn't get the impression that she was hiding anything from him but rather thought that her responses, no matter how lifelike she seemed, were automated. She appeared to be some sort of sophisticated artificial intelligence, more than likely constructed by these mysterious council members. He wondered who they were, what their intentions were, and whether they could be trusted. But did the answers to any of these questions even really matter? What was he going to do? Go back to his ordinary, repetitive existence and pass up what might be the most amazing opportunity of his life?

He sat in silence, until Elysium again asked, "Do you wish to continue your program where you left off?"

He put his questions and any lingering hesitations aside and replied, "Yes."

"Next in your training, you'll learn the words to use in mantras."

She spread her arms in front of her with her palms facing up. A large leather-bound tome materialized, floating above her hands. As if she were commanding it by her will, it slowly opened and the pages turned. Eventually the pages stopped; apparently she had found what she was searching for.

"The words you'll use to focus your mind are special," she said. "They're from an ancient tongue that can communicate directly with your soul and the universe as a whole. These words are very precise and powerful. While mortals will be able to hear them, few if any will be able to pronounce them."

"The ancient tongue can't be taught using any known traditional methods of instruction," she continued. "In fact some believe it can't be taught at all and can only be remembered. This program will make use of various brain frequencies that will alter your state of consciousness to allow an easier imprinting of the ancient tongue into your mind. You should make sure you're comfortable and will be undisturbed for several hours, as you'll lose consciousness during this process. The imprinting isn't easy and will take several sessions to complete. Do you wish to begin?"

Ash lifted the bottom of his visor so he could partially see his room. The effect of being in two worlds simultaneously caused him to feel slightly dizzy and a little woozy, as if he had just stepped off a slowly spinning amusement-park ride. He gave himself a few moments to regain his sense of balance. Then he took the disc player from the table and stumbled over to his bed. After lying down, he pulled the visor back over his eyes.

"Let's do this," he said eagerly.

Elysium waved her hands, and the book vanished. She spread her arms out to her sides, her palms facing Ash. Both her hands glowed with a bright white light. The light grew and grew until it encompassed all of Ash's vision. Then, in a blink, everything turned to darkness.

"We'll be shining light and transmitting the imprinting through your closed eyelids," said Elysium. "Make sure they're closed. Please confirm when you're ready."

"I'm ready," Ash told her, then closed his eyes.

A low-frequency tone emerged in his ears. As the sound slowly intensified, light flashed before his eyelids. The tone and the lights synchronized and settled into a pleasant frequency and rhythm. A vibrato resounded in the tone, and he felt increasingly relaxed as his brainwaves navigated from beta to alpha.

The frequency of the sound and lights changed several times until Ash eventually fell into a dreamlike state. His mind drifted, and then he felt as if he were rapidly coming in and out of a daydream. He saw himself in different places with different people doing different things. For a moment he was a child again, riding in the car with his mother down a seemingly endless stretch of road. The ocean was out the window on his right. A calm breeze carried the fresh scent of salt water through the window. Next he was in class. His professor was handing out midterm exams. Ash totally had forgotten there was a test and hadn't studied. Then he was in a bathroom looking at himself in the mirror. He was wearing medieval chainmail covered by a royal-blue tabard. He glanced down at the sink. It was overflowing with water, dripping onto the floor. Then slowly all thoughts faded, and his mind became clear and empty.

Glowing symbols emerged in front of him, floating in the distance then rapidly hurtling toward him. They appeared to be heading straight for the center of his forehead. As they struck his head, he heard them echo in his mind, but it was more than that. He was learning their pronunciation and deeper meaning. This continued for several hours.

When Ash finally awoke from his trance, he removed the helmet from his head and rushed over to his desk. Any lingering doubts were now completely gone. What he had experienced was very real. He felt compelled to write everything down so he wouldn't forget any of it. The truth was that when one was imprinted in this manner, there was no need to write anything down. The transferred knowledge was just as if one had studied another language over a period of years, but faster. Once mastered, a language was yours to keep.

Ash opened a notebook that was sitting on his desk. He flipped past some notes he had taken in his thermal-fluids engineering class and found the first blank page. After grabbing a pen, he wrote down some of the key words he had learned.

ᗞI (KI) = to compel by force
ᒍK (IK) = to request politely

ᗞ/ᘓ (HAVA) = to explain in a manner that can be comprehended
ᔑᓭ (NAS) = to cause to depart or drive away
ᘓR (SER) = to obscure a form so it can't be seen
ᗹI (RIM) = to protect a person or thing
ᗞR (OR) = to adjust so as to leave a space, allowing access
ᘓU (CU) = to move a person or object in a particular direction
ᗞ/ᘓ (ONA) = to discover the exact position of an individual or object
ᒍN (INUNI) = to brighten with light
ᗹO (RO) = to put in a particular position in order to obstruct an entrance
ᗠM (TIMO) = to view past events that relate to a person or object
ᘓU (VU) = to move a body upward from the ground and often forward
ᗞI (OHIV) = to cause to rise or float in the air
ᗣV (AVA) = to separate the soul from the body
ᗣR (ARI) = to correct or improve bad effects
ᗣW (AWA) = to appeal to the emotions or senses by stimulating interest
ᗹE (RES) = to become aware of the presence of a person or thing

ᗞM (OM) = an entrance to a room or building
ᗣM (AME) = a rodent that resembles a large mouse
ᗣN (AN) = a cord or strand
ᔑI (SI) = a young woman

ᏩᎬ (CEM) = a hard, solid, nonmetallic mineral matter of which rock is made

ᏩᏟ (CA) = a single sheet of paper that is part of a collection of pages

There were so many words and definitions that his hand grew tired from writing. He put his pen down and glanced at the clock. To his surprise, it was already past six in the evening. His mind felt exhausted, so he decided to lie down for a quick nap. Within a few minutes, he was fast asleep.

*

The next day and for the days that followed, Ash continued his training. Elysium taught him many things. He learned to master the words of the ancient tongue, and though his vocabulary was limited, he spoke the words he knew as if it were second nature. He also learned how to empty his mind and use the clear gemstone from the wooden box to focus his energies. His training was far from complete, but he had progressed to the point that he was ready to cast his first spell.

Ash cleared a spot on a floor a few feet from his bed. Earlier in the morning, while strolling outside, he had picked up a small pile of pebbles from the ground. He placed the rocks on the floor.

He sat on the edge of his bed with the pile of stones between him and the window. As he looked around the room, he realized his window was still shut. Since he was going to attempt to push the rocks through the window, this obviously wasn't going to work. He walked over to the window, unlocked it, and lifted the pane from the bottom until the window was wide open. The window was facing the Charles River, but being extra cautious, Ash poked his head outside to double-check that no one was standing below. Seeing that the coast was clear, he returned to his seated position on the bed.

With nervousness and excitement, he gripped his clear gem tightly in the palm of his right hand. He could barely believe what he was about to do. He looked down at the piles of stones then at the window, doing this several times until he felt he had a clear picture of what he intended to do. Then he closed his eyes and began to calm his mind, trying his best to suppress his heightened emotions. He re-created the scene in his head, but this time he imagined the stones slowly floating into the air, flying out of the window, and landing safely in the river.

Ash opened his eyes and chanted the mantra "ᗰᐁ ᓯS ᑕᕮ (MA-NAS-CEM)."

His eyes took on a bluish glow as azure wisps of energy poured out their sides. At first it seemed as if the floor were shaking, causing the stones to vibrate up and down. Then suddenly the rocks flew into the air and shot straight through the opening in the window. Ash raced over to watch them splash into the river; however, they didn't. The stones flew fast and long, heading over the Charles River from Cambridge straight into Boston. They soon disappeared from his sight.

Somewhere in an insurance building far away, the pebbles burst through a window. It shattered it into a hundred pieces, and the rocks embedded themselves in the wall behind it.

With wide eyes and an open mouth, Ash slowly ducked his head out of sight. He had cast his first spell and, though it wasn't the exact effect he had intended, it was powerful indeed.

CHAPTER 3

MISS SARAH BLAKE

The girl's name was Sarah Blake. She had found shelter from the cold and rain in an abandoned barn off one of the main roads. The entire building swelled and leaked. Water dripped from the ceiling and splashed into puddles on the hay-covered dirt ground.

She had been walking in the rain for several hours and was soaking wet. Her long blond hair clung to the sides of her damp face, and her drenched clothing—a white blouse and pink skirt—hugged her thin frame. She was in her midteens, far too young to be out here on her own. Her harlequin-green eyes welled with tears.

It hadn't always been like this for her, homeless and on the run. Once, she had lived in a warm home with a loving family, but that all was over now. She never could go back. Thoughts of what she had done sped through her head then bubbled to the surface.

"I killed Billy!" she screamed. "God forgive me!"

She collapsed on the ground, crying.

*

31

Sarah was the daughter of two schoolteachers, Elizabeth and Tom. Before finding out about Elizabeth's pregnancy, they lived in Charlotte, North Carolina. They'd been dating for slightly more than two years and had just moved into a one-bedroom apartment. Both were planners by nature, and this was the next logical step. It was all part of a plan they'd set in their minds, a series of small but well-calculated steps in their relationship and their lives.

Though they both loved kids dearly, neither had plans for having children any time soon. They had just started their careers and were busy enjoying each other's company and the company of friends. Though they didn't have a lot of money, it was enough. The two frequently ate out at restaurants, watched movies, drank at bars, and enjoyed many other activities their city had to offer.

Finding out about Elizabeth's pregnancy changed all this as well as their well-laid plans. They quickly decided to arrange a wedding ceremony. Their parents and many of their friends often had questioned their relationship, and the rushed wedding just raised more questions. That was unavoidable, but the way they saw it, with all this questioning and judging, at the very least they could have unquestioning, unjudging wedding photos before Elizabeth began to show too much. Despite the hurry, the wedding turned out to be lovely.

There was no honeymoon after the wedding. Instead the couple hopped straight into the daunting task of trying to find a suitable home to raise their child. Neither Elizabeth nor Tom had been raised in a city, and they wanted the same experience for their child. So they searched for the best place they could afford in the suburbs. Eventually they found and closed on a modest home in Concord only a few weeks before Sarah was born. The neighborhood they moved into was quiet and quaint. Their old lives were officially over.

Shortly after Sarah's birth, Elizabeth quit her job and became a full-time caregiver. At first she was hesitant about giving up her career, but all that changed the first time she held Sarah in her arms. She loved that child more than anything in the world.

*

"I love you, Mommy," said a six-year-old Sarah as she leaned over to blow out the candles that decorated her birthday cake.

With a huge grin on her face, she closed her eyes, made a wish, then blew. As the candles went out, all the children and their parents clapped and cheered.

Elizabeth had spent the past few weeks planning and organizing the birthday party down to every last detail. She stood proudly, staring at her daughter with a smile, one that only a loving mother could wear. Everything had turned out exactly as she'd imagined, and Sarah was jubilant. This was the kind of day that made everything worthwhile.

Sarah looked over at her mother with a cake-smeared grin. Elizabeth smiled back and mouthed, "Presents?" The girl's plentiful smile grew even larger. Elizabeth and a few other parents left the room to collect the gifts.

Sarah watched as her mother walked out, then glanced across the table at her friend, Billy Windsworth. He was slightly older than her and had light-blond hair and deep-blue eyes. He was busily trying to scrub off some icing from a horrible polka-dot tie his mother had made him wear. Eventually he gave up, looked over at Sarah, and shrugged. They both broke into laughter.

When Elizabeth and the other parents returned, they were carrying what, from Sarah's perspective, seemed to be a hundred or more gifts. All the children jumped up and rushed over to find a good spot behind the birthday girl. Each one wanted the best place possible to watch the presents as they were unwrapped. Billy wanted to be the closest to Sarah, so he opted for a less-scenic route. He crawled under the table then pushed his way through until he was right beside her.

Before long, the entire table was filled with piles upon piles of wrapping paper, and Sarah was on her last present. It was the largest of all the boxes and was from her mom and dad. She searched the room to find her parents. Finally she spotted them standing directly across from her, smiling broadly. In Tom's hand was a camera. As Sarah opened the box, he took a picture. The flash was almost blinding.

*

Lightning illuminated the sky outside as thunder crackled. The weather wasn't getting any better, and the old shutters and doors on the barn whipped back and forth. They made a horrible rattling sound followed by a loud bang. Wet and shaking, Sarah curled up in a ball. She opened her eyes and watched the water drip down the cracked wooden slats of the walls.

Outside, along the road, a lone figure walked toward the building. As it grew nearer, Sarah sensed something wasn't quite right. She pulled herself up and, standing there, holding herself and shaking, awaited the entry of the visitor.

As the door swung open, Sarah had every intention of screaming but instead stood frozen. Standing before her, obscured by the shadows and the rain, was a dark figure.

"Greetings, Sarah Blake. I've been looking for you," said the figure in a low-pitched, ominous voice.

"Are you Death?" she muttered with a hint of fear.

"Some may have called me that in the past, but my name is Nihalus, and I mean you no harm," he replied. "I know you've been running, not only from your home but also from yourself. I'm here to help."

"I don't need your help! I don't need anyone's help!" she yelled. "Stay back. I don't want to hurt you."

She thought of Billy as she said this. She hadn't meant to hurt him.

*

Billy and his parents lived in an upscale home a few blocks from Sarah's house. His parents were busy, successful professionals driven by their careers, spending more time at work than at home. Often they relied on Elizabeth to take care of some of their parental duties. This wasn't without its benefits. They paid her extremely well, and Sarah's parents could use all the extra income they could get. Neither had fully anticipated how expensive it was to raise a child.

By the time they were in kindergarten, Billy and Sarah had become the best of friends, and their friendship would carry them well into their teenage years. Sarah often called Billy her brother, and he cared for as if she were his sister.

One summer Billy's dad had a giant tree house built for him in their backyard. It wasn't only massive but also extremely well constructed—the best tree house money could buy. Sarah thought it was one of the most beautiful things she'd ever seen. It was a maze of ropes and ladders, with a full room located at the top, and featured electricity, lights, and an integrated heater for chilly nights.

Billy's parents sent him to a private school, while Sarah's parents could only afford a public education for their child. But every day after school, without fail, the two children raced home and met up at the tree house, where they spent hours playing and talking. It was in this tree house that Sarah first told Billy about her imaginary friends.

Her mother had insisted that she quit talking to them, and this was the first time she had told anyone else. Billy was fascinated.

"There were three of them. They spoke in a language I could only hear inside my head, like faint whispers. They told me their real names, but I never could pronounce them. So I called them Jinx, Kynx, and Lynx.

"They looked like gargoyles of different sizes and colors. Jinx was the smallest. He wasn't more than a foot tall and had dark-blue skin. His sister, Kynx, was only a few inches taller and changed colors from a brownish orange to a rusty yellow. Their leader, Lynx, was almost two feet tall and was dark red, with a slight fiery glow about him. They all walked hunched over, with their wings curled up on their backs."

"Didn't they scare you?" asked Billy.

Sarah paused for a second to consider the question then continued. "Well, at first I was scared. I used to scream at the top of my lungs when they crept around the corner. My mother would have to rush in and calm me down, but over time I realized they weren't there to hurt me. They were just there to watch me."

"Watch you? Now that's pretty creepy!" exclaimed Billy.

"Maybe a little," replied Sarah, "but they became my friends. One day I held back my screams and let them get closer. They were so curious about me. They walked forward slowly then crawled all over me. It was as if I had some quality they couldn't quite figure out.

"I was very upset the day my mother told me they weren't real and not to talk to them anymore, but I wasn't as angry as they were. They snarled and hissed as I turned away from them."

"Do you think they were real?" asked Billy inquisitively.

"I don't know…They felt real to me, but they probably weren't. Guess it doesn't really matter anymore. After I started ignoring them, they started showing up less and less, and then one day they were gone."

*

"I know you didn't mean to hurt your friend," said Nihalus. "I sent my minions to help you learn to control your gifts before something like this would come to pass, but once you turned away from them, they turned away from you."

"Jinx, Kynx, and Lynx?" asked Sarah in a crackly voice.

"If that's what you called them. I'm sorry, Sarah, but this will all be easier when you understand what you are."

"What am I?" Sarah yelled, her eyes wide. "Am I a monster?"

Nihalus stepped forth from the shadows that had covered most of his face and body and walked toward Sarah. He wore a long dark cloak drenched in water. His face was obscured by a hood that covered the upper portion of his face. A mostly human-looking mouth with a black goatee was visible at the bottom. As he looked down at her, she saw that his eyes weren't human at all. They were of pure darkness, and behind them danced a smoky crimson fire.

He stretched out an arm, and his cloak fell to reveal his hand. His fingernails were short but sharp dark claws. He glanced down at his hand, and as Sarah watched, the nail on his pinky finger grew until it was several inches long. As she stood in horror, he thrust his finger through her blouse and into her shoulder then quickly pulled it out. The pain was sharp but quick. He then lifted his hand to his face and licked the blood from it.

"A monster, no—your blood tells me a different story entirely," he said. "Within you dwells an ancient power. You asked me what you are. You are one of the Touched. You are the drainer of men's souls. You are the succubus!"

*

Billy and Sarah were teenagers and entering high school. Together they had grown from children into young adults. Through the years they had remained best friends.

Because of Billy's poor grades, the prestigious private high school in the area had rejected his application. It wasn't that he was a dumb kid; he just didn't find school very interesting and preferred playing sports over studying. So, with no desire to relocate, his parents reluctantly sent him to public school. Billy didn't mind at all, and for the first time since they'd known each other, he and Sarah would attend the same school.

They walked to high school together each morning, often laughing and giggling along the way. At school they took many of the same classes and more than once were sent to the principal's office for what their teachers called "having too much fun in class." They were the closest of friends and had deep feelings for each other; however, the nature of their feelings was very different.

Over time Sarah's platonic feelings had changed to fascination and love. She often imagined her and Billy together, getting married one day and having children of their own. These daydreams always brought a smile to her face.

Billy was, for the most part, oblivious to Sarah's romantic feelings for him. To him she was still like a sister. He had an interest in other girls and a particular interest in a girl named Natasha. Although she was older and a grade ahead of him, that didn't stop him from pursuing her. While this filled Sarah with jealousy, she still wanted to be close to Billy. If all she could ever be was his friend, she would be sad, but she would accept it.

One day, when Billy's parents were out of town to attend a business conference in Atlanta, he invited Sarah and a few other friends over to his house for a party. Sarah was happy to find out that Natasha had once again declined Billy's invitation to hang out, telling him she was going to the movies with a friend. It wasn't that Sarah hated Natasha; she just didn't like the way Billy acted when he was around her. One of Billy's friends from the lacrosse team brought some beer over. Everyone laughed and danced as they listened to loud rock music and drank their beverages. Eventually they found themselves in the backyard.

They sat and looked up at the sky as the sun began to give way to the night. As they gazed upward, something in the tree house caught Sarah's attention from the corner of her eye. The door at the top was slightly ajar, and three tiny dark figures appeared to be peering at her. Slowly she got up and moved toward the tree house, never taking her eyes off the top.

Billy noticed and asked, "Where are you going?"

As Sarah turned around to look over at him, he saw that her eyes had taken on a slight hint of red. He thought perhaps it was just a reflection of the sunset, but whatever it was mesmerized him. He kept looking into her eyes and she into his. Something had changed. She always had wanted Billy, and now he felt an uncontrollable desire for her as well. His fixation on Sarah was so single-minded that all sound around him except the beating of his heart faded into silence. The other kids quickly quieted down and stared at the two of them staring at each other.

Sarah gestured with her head up toward the tree house as she gripped a rung of the ladder then started to climb. Billy wandered over slowly, as if in a daze. The other kids giggled as the two made their way to the top. As they ascended, and well before the door to the tree house closed, everyone else decided it was time to leave. They gathered their belongings and headed down the street. Silence set in within the confines of the tree house as the kids' voices faded in the distance. Sarah and Billy were alone.

Sarah pulled him toward her, and he fell into her uncontrollably. Slowly she tilted his head back, embraced him, and kissed him deeply. Her eyes never closed but instead stared at the six glowing eyes across the room.

With each kiss, Sarah felt more and more alive. She felt Billy's very life essence pour into her soul. Her senses heightened. She saw all the finer details of the wood grain of the tree house. She heard the tiniest sounds—from the creaking of the floor to the kids chatting down the street. The pumping of her heart grew deeper, and a newfound strength coursed through her veins. Her insecurities and self-doubts vanished, replaced with a profound feeling that she could do and accomplish anything. All the emptiness and rejection she had felt in the past gave way to a replenished, fulfilled passion. Even as she felt Billy weaken, she couldn't stop. The feeling was uncontrollable. It was everything to her.

Eventually Billy's body grew limp in her arms, and he sank to the wood floor, his body twitching. She pressed the back of her hand against her lips, as if wiping her mouth after eating a delicious meal. A smile came across her face as she looked at Billy's convulsing body.

Then suddenly the horror of what happened set in. Sarah's smile transformed into a look of panic. She fell to the floor and shook Billy, whose body finally had stopped moving.

"Wake up! Wake up!" she pleaded.

Slowly the door to the tree house swung open, and the sound of thunder entered from outside. The three tiny gargoyles huddled next to the base of the doorway. The largest one, Lynx, extended his gnarled finger and motioned for Sarah to follow. It started to rain outside. It was going to rain for a long time.

*

Nihalus opened his arms widely and gestured his hands gently, extending an invitation to Sarah to embrace him. She wrapped her arms around herself to keep herself warm and to comfort herself. Her feet stepped forward slowly, one by one, toward the man in the dark cloak. She closed her eyes and fell into his arms. He wrapped his arms around her and rested his right hand upon her head.

"There, child. You are with me now. Everything will be okay. I'll take care of you," he whispered in her ear.

In his arms, Sarah felt a deep sense of darkness mixed with comfort and understanding. Somehow she knew there was no other place she belonged. No one else would be able to understand her. No one else would be able to help her. No one else would be able to forgive her. No one else would be able to love her. She gave up the last of her will and surrendered to him.

The rain continued to pound the outside of the barn. Lightning lit up the skies. Inside, Nihalus and Sarah were gone.

CHAPTER 4

THE MAP

In Egypt, deep beneath the Pyramid of Khafre, there lay a secret, one that had remained hidden, unknown, and undiscovered by the mortal world for thousands of years. It was a series of chambers that formed the home for a group of mages who came together to protect this world from the relentless and ever-present darkness. This place was called Archmedea.

In the city of Giza was a small coffee and pastry shop, the Greeno Café. On the bottom floor of this establishment was a bookcase. With the proper incantations, the bookcase moved to reveal a long, winding staircase that led down into the depths. At the bottom of the staircase lay a mile-long tunnel that housed a shallow river. Traveling down this river was the only known method for entering Archmedea.

In the center of Archmedea was a circular room called the Great Chamber. This room had walls as high as a cathedral, with giant bookshelves and tapestries that ran its length. At its top was a stained-glass dome. Though it was well beneath the surface, it appeared as if sunlight were pouring through the glass, illuminating the room. On the floor below, arcane symbols were carved into the stone blocks. A circular table made of dark oak rested in the center. Ten chairs, each carved out of a single piece of wood, surrounded the table.

Sebastian, the leader of the mages, sat in the chair farthest from a pair of giant wooden doors. He was an elderly man dressed in a dark-gray cloak that was decorated with white stitched magical symbols that ran down its sides. The bangs of his long silver hair were pulled back and braided, while the rest hung below his shoulders.

Beside him were two similarly dressed men, Christopher and Robert. Christopher stood to Sebastian's left. He wore a long orange cloak and had scraggly brown hair. On Sebastian's other side stood Robert, who donned a dark-green cloak with a hooded top that covered his head.

Deeply engaged in conversation, the three were reviewing some parchments on the table in front of them.

"We can't just sit here and wait," said Christopher.

"We can and will wait," asserted Sebastian. "We already have two mages out there, and until such time as one of them reports back with some new information or they cease to exist, I'm not inclined to send anyone else. The last thing we need to do is rush out there and stumble around blindly."

Directly across from them, the pair of thick wooden doors swung open. A man with a dark cloak covering most of his body and face entered the room. The cloak floated behind him, dancing as if carried by a breeze. He approached the table and placed his hands along its edge. With his right hand he pulled down the hood from his head, revealing a man with short blond hair and a slightly darker blond goatee. His eyes had a swirling golden glow about them. Aleister had returned home.

*

It was late in the afternoon. Detectives Valle and Kent were at the police station. It had been a few days since they had started investigating the crime scene in the alley. To date, they had made little progress, though on this particular day they had a new clue to review. That morning forensics had delivered the pieced-together parchment from the scroll case the detectives had discovered.

Both were in Detective Valle's windowless, very messy office. It was rare for anyone in the precinct to have his or her own area, and this was more of a repurposed closet in the basement than anything else. Valle's sergeant had moved him down there a few years ago, when he no longer wanted to deal with the complaints from some of the other officers. They said he talked too much and was interrupting their work, but the truth was that they thought he was too damn weird. His cases always seemed to involve some tie to the occult, and his so-called witnesses gave them the creeps.

Detective Kent was seated in a chair on the opposite side of a desk facing a large blank sheet that was tacked to a corkboard. The desk was covered with papers, many of which bore circular coffee stains. Lying in the center of the desk was the rune-engraved ebony scroll case. Detective Valle paced in front of Kent before pausing for a moment, reaching into his pocket, and placing a cigar in his mouth.

"You know you can't smoke in here, right?" asked Detective Kent.

"It helps me think," replied Valle, as he started to light his cigar.

Within a few puffs, the cigar was lit, and Valle resumed his pacing. With each exhale, more and more smoke collected along the ceiling of the office.

Kent glanced up and spotted a smoke detector beneath the gray clouds above. "You know you might set off the fire alarm, right?" he said.

"I disabled that stupid thing years ago," said Valle. "Now focus, Kent! What do we know?"

"Well, we know we aren't missing any pieces of that thing," responded Kent, as he pointed at the large blank sheet of paper tacked to the board. "That's the good part. Unfortunately the bad part is that we also know the damn thing is completely blank!"

"Right," exclaimed Valle, as if the two of them had just now discovered this. "But what does it mean?"

"It doesn't mean anything! The damn thing is blank!" Kent repeated, throwing his hands into the air. After taking a moment to calm down, he rubbed his face with both hands, sighed, and continued. "Well, the damn thing appears to be blank anyway."

"You're absolutely right!" exclaimed Valle. "It *appears* to be blank—but perhaps there's something you and I can't see. Let's bring it down to forensics and have them use their gizmos on it. Maybe they can find something our naked eyes are missing."

*

Sebastian and his two companions immediately halted their conversation and focused their attention on Aleister, who had just barged into the room. The leader of the mages looked over at the doors and nodded slightly, signaling to Christopher and Robert that they should leave the room. After they gathered their parchments from the table, the two mages exited the chamber, closing the heavy doors behind them.

"Welcome back, Aleister," said Sebastian. "Judging by your expression, I'm guessing you didn't retrieve the map."

"They knew we were coming!" exclaimed Aleister.

"I need you to calm down," said Sebastian, placing his hands into a prayer position in front of him.

Aleister took a deep breath. "I'm sorry, Master."

"It's all right," said Sebastian. "Just tell me what happened."

Aleister continued, "I tracked down the map in New York City. It was in the hands of David Higgins, a trader in antiques. As he described it, he always had been able to find rare and unique items. It was if he could somehow sense them. I later determined that this ability was a latent magical talent. Unfortunately, as he was untrained, the use of this power drained the longevity from his body, and he had become quite frail and ill over the past few years.

"He acquired an ebony scroll case with Nordic runes on it during one of his trips to Augsburg, Germany. This case matched the last-known description of the map's container. My spells confirmed that the case was indeed in an area near his shop, but something was blocking my ability to sense its exact location. It was as if my vision were clouded."

"This is the spreading of the darkness," interrupted Sebastian. "My detection incantations are faltering as well, which will make it much more challenging to find the one we seek."

Aleister nodded. "Per your instructions, I was to obtain the map without harming any mortals. Using the opportunity that had been presented to me, I offered a cure for the man's illness in exchange for the map. He agreed, and we arranged a meeting. Shortly after I arrived, we were attacked by one of the Touched. This one was unlike any I had encountered before. He bore only the vaguest resemblance to a mortal being. He was also stronger and had command of a powerful energy similar to that wielded by ourselves.

"This creature knew my name, and though he didn't know I was there for the map, he did know we were looking for a boy. I managed to dispatch him, but I was injured and had to flee before I could retrieve the map. I'm not sure where it is." After finishing his story, Aleister asked, "How would they know about the child?"

"My dear boy," replied Sebastian, "though we reside on opposite sides, we and they are part of the same coin. Our stories are their stories; our legends are their legends—they're just told from a different vantage point. Now that their champion has risen, they know we will search for ours."

*

Detective Valle was sitting reclined in his office, drinking a cup of coffee. An ashtray with a lit cigar in it rested on his beer belly. The phone on his desk rang. Slowly he looked at it and let it ring a few more times before moving. After grabbing the ashtray with his free hand, he put his feet on the floor, placed his coffee mug on a pile of papers, and picked up the phone.

"Hello. Detective Valle here," he muttered.

"It's Kent," said the voice on the other end. "Forensics just called. They said they completed their examination."

"And?"

"You were right. They found something."

Hearing this news, Valle stood up so hastily that he accidently bumped his desk, knocking over his coffee. The spilled coffee quickly drenched the papers beneath it. Kent was still talking as Valle slowly let his phone arm fall to his side. He stared at the coffee, which was now dripping on the floor, with a look of annoyance. For a few moments, he did nothing else. Then he glanced over at his cigar, picked it up, placed it in his mouth, and inhaled deeply. After releasing a large puff of smoke into the air, he returned the phone to his ear.

"I missed that last part, Kent," interrupted Valle. "Can you repeat it?"

"Which part?" Kent asked.

"The part right after you said they found something."

Kent sighed. "So you're telling me you haven't listened to a word I've been saying."

"Yeah," Valle mumbled as he glanced back at the mess on his desk. "I had a work-related incident. Just tell me what they found."

"I'll just skip to the important part," said Kent. "When they applied a mild heat to the surface of the parchment, it revealed a map. You know, like when kids write hidden messages with lemon juice that can only be exposed using a candle."

"Lemon juice, right. So what's it a map of?"

"They said it was a highly detailed map of Pangea."

"Should I know what Pangea is?" Valle asked sarcastically.

"Seriously?" replied Kent in an equally sarcastic tone before pausing then continuing. "Before the world was as we know it today, there was one supercontinent. It slowly separated over hundreds of millions of years into seven continents. This supercontinent was known as Pangea."

"Why would someone have a hidden map of Pangea?"

"I have no idea—I was hoping you might. Do you want to see it?"

"Yeah, let's have a look at this thing," said Valle. "Bring it on over—and while you're at it, can you grab me a fresh cup of coffee and a stack of napkins?"

*

THE MAP

Aleister awoke in his bedroom within the halls of Archmedea. It was a simple room with stone blocks for walls and housed only a small bed and desk. On the ceiling was a moving image of clouds with sunlight creeping through. It reflected the state of the early-morning sky far above him. As Aleister stared upward, the image shifted and distorted until he saw the face of his master, Sebastian.

"Aleister," said the image. "I'm sorry to wake you so early. Your presence is needed in the Great Chamber."

"I'll be right there," replied Aleister.

Aleister quickly donned his cloak and made his way to the Great Chamber. When he opened the doors to the room, Sebastian was seated on the far opposite end, accompanied by Christopher and Robert at his sides. He was taken a bit by surprise to see the other mages there. They looked as if they'd been interrupted from an extended discussion.

"Have a seat," said Sebastian, motioning toward a chair along the left side of the circular table.

"Yes, Master," replied Aleister, as he walked over and sat down.

"We have new information," Sebastian said. "Our sources tell us the map is in police custody. It's being held in the seventh precinct on the Lower East Side of Manhattan. We also know Detective Nicholas Valle is involved."

Aleister knew who Detective Valle was; few mages who visited New York City didn't. This particular police officer had a knack for sniffing out and getting involved in the strange and unusual.

Sebastian continued, "As you know, the map would have allowed us to pinpoint the exact location of the Blessed One. Since it has slipped from our grasp, we have no choice but to shift our priorities to a less direct approach."

"You mean to use the Seer's Gate?" asked Aleister, with a slight look of shock.

"Absolutely not!" Sebastian exclaimed. "You of all people should know how dangerous that thing is. It has powers that aren't meant to be tampered with. The risk would be far too great."

"But we know it can—" said Aleister before being interrupted.

"Aleister, this isn't a discussion," Sebastian said sternly before calming his tone and continuing. "The council has decided to focus our attention on the girl. It is foretold that she will give rise to the Blessed One's full potential. We intend to track her down."

"What do you need me to do?" asked Aleister.

"You will remain here," stated Sebastian in a calm but assertive tone.

"What!" Aleister exclaimed, as he rose from his chair.

"Yes, Aleister!" said Sebastian, raising his voice as he stood as well. "We can't allow your personal feelings to get involved here. You'll remain in Archmedea. We'll dispatch another mage to find her when we're ready."

"You can't pull me out!" yelled Aleister. "You have no right! I'm part of this council too!"

"You gave up that right the first time you lost her," said Sebastian loudly. "Now sit down. We have other matters to discuss."

Aleister gripped the edge of the table tightly in protest and frustration. He wasn't at all pleased with this decision. Slowly and with the appearance of being calm, however, he took his seat. If this council wouldn't allow him to be involved, he would do it without their approval.

*

The parchment had returned to its tacked position on the wall of Detective Valle's smoke-filled office. This time, though, rather than staring at a blank sheet of paper, he and Detective Kent were looking at a highly detailed map of Pangea, the ancient supercontinent. They both rested against the desk with somewhat dumbfounded expressions.

"You know," said Kent, "if I cross my eyes, I can almost see the continents drifting apart."

"Staring at this thing is getting us nowhere," muttered Valle.

"Seriously, just cross your eyes," repeated Kent.

"Quit kidding around," Valle said in an annoyed tone.

"What do you want me to do? This weird stuff is your area of expertise, not mine. I just see a map of an ancient landmass with a weird compass in the corner."

"Compass?" asked Valle.

"Yeah, this thing." Kent got up and pointed to the bottom right-hand corner of the map.

Valle couldn't see anything near the edge of the map. He got up and walked over to have a closer look as he sucked on his cigar. Still unable to see anything, in an act of frustration, he blew out a large puff of smoke at the map. As the smoke rippled across its surface, something odd appeared in the corner. It wasn't a compass at all; it was a set of arcane symbols—"◓N"—in the center of a circle.

"Well, I'll be damned," said Valle.

"You see the compass?" asked Kent.

"That's no compass."

"Then what is it?"

"I've seen these symbols before," responded Valle as he put his hands on his hips. "I could be wrong, but I think it means 'blood.'"

Kent just stood there, unable to think of a reasonable way to respond.

"We might need some extra help on this one, Kent," continued Valle. "There's this guy Dorian I've used in the past on matters like this. He lives in Salem, Massachusetts. Grab your coat. We've got a long ride ahead of us."

CHAPTER 5

BLESSED ASHES

Ash was sitting on a bench in the Boston Commons. He had a bag of bread crumbs beside him and was slowly dispensing its contents to a small gathering of pigeons. So much had happened to him over the past few days, and he needed some time to get away from things. As he sprinkled a few more crumbs on the ground, he felt a presence behind him. As it grew stronger, Ash slowly reached his other hand under his jacket and gripped his gem.

"You won't need that," said a voice that surprisingly came from the seat right next to him.

Ash turned his head to see a man dressed in a dark-purple cloak sitting beside him. The man looked oddly relaxed and motionless, as if he'd been there a long time. From under the man's hood, Ash made out that he had a short white beard. He recognized this man from the pixelated image that had spoken to him on his computer. Not knowing his name, he would simply call him the Wizard. He slowly let the gem rest in his pocket and placed both hands on his knees.

"I'm sorry it took me so long to get here. I had to take many roads less traveled to lose their scent. I couldn't risk letting them get to you or detect your presence before you were ready," said the Wizard.

"Who's after me?" asked Ash, an uneasiness in his voice.

"They're known as the Touched, and at this moment, all you need to know is that they're very dangerous and will stop at nothing to get to you."

"But why are they after *me*?"

"They are simply after you because of what you are and your importance."

"Why am I so important?" asked Ash.

"For now let's just say I believe you have tremendous potential. It isn't wise to know too much too soon. Knowledge is required for you to understand your purpose, and by its nature, it must be acquired and can't be given."

"Great, more riddles," muttered Ash.

"Then perhaps I'll give you something more practical, but first I have a question."

"Okay, what's your question?"

"Why are you feeding these pigeons?" asked the Wizard.

"Because pigeons like bread, and I could use the company," answered Ash somewhat sarcastically.

"Why not just draw them to you without the bread?" The Wizard motioned his open palm over the flock of pigeons.

"Well, first of all, I actually like feeding the birds," said Ash, lifting a finger into the air to signal the number one. "Second, isn't it just plain wrong to control minds—even the minds of birds—by taking away their free will?" he said sternly, as he raised a second finger. He raised one more finger. "And third, I don't know how the hell to control minds, even if I wanted to!"

The Wizard shook his head. "My boy, I wasn't suggesting you control their minds. To do so would walk you down a dark path from which you might never return. There are lines that should never be crossed, because when you do, the lines slowly will disappear. Power can easily corrupt. What I suggested is entirely different. I suggested you *ask* the pigeons to join you. A request by whatever means is just a request, no different than a verbal invitation. It would be up to the pigeons to decide whether they wished to join you. Do you understand the difference?"

"Yeah, I understand. Okay, so how do I *ask* the pigeons?"

"Well, that would be kind of pointless. The pigeons are already here," said the Wizard, as if Ash weren't aware of the obvious.

"I think you know what I meant," Ash said with some frustration. "What if I wanted to attract something else?"

"The technique is no different from the other skills you've already developed. For this type of spell, since it isn't directed at something in particular, you could choose to use your wand or simply hold your gemstone in your hand. Casting with your wand will always have a greater effect, as your powers will be amplified as they pass through it into the gemstone. However, it should go without saying that whipping out a wand isn't always the wisest choice, as doing so could draw unwanted attention."

The choice to use a wand or not was a simple one for Ash, as he didn't have a wand. He reached back into the pocket of his jacket. Then, within his clenched fist, he pulled out his gem.

The Wizard waited then continued. "You already know the tongue that is used to focus your mind. Think of a word that means 'attract,' making sure to preface it with an invitation. Though it isn't necessary, many initiates are able to cause a greater effect by amplifying their voice. Again, always use your best judgment. Yelling in the ancient tongue can also draw unwanted attention. For now let's simply try something slightly louder than a whisper."

Ash nodded. "Got it. Now how do I decide what to attract? Can I attract a lion from the zoo?"

"Let's try to keep it to another city-dwelling creature. Extending your reach too far might cause something else to feel your presence, and we wouldn't want that."

"How about mice or rats?" Ash asked, pointing to a manhole at the edge of the park.

"Perfect," replied the Wizard. "Now you have two choices in focusing your power on these creatures. The first is the easiest. Simply include their names as part of your mantra in the ancient tongue. These words will act as a conduit to your higher mind, and it will know what you mean. The second is a bit harder but also, in many cases, more powerful. You can picture in your mind the events you wish to occur as you speak your desires in the ancient tongue. This is more difficult because the mind tends to drift, and random thoughts can cause effects that you don't want. Until you learn to completely quiet your mind, it can also be very dangerous." The Wizard waved a wrinkled hand in the air. "We were just talking about lions. You were just thinking about lions. In fact now that I've just mentioned them, you probably have an image of a lion in your head right now. Your higher mind can't tell the difference between these thoughts and what you're truly trying to focus on."

The Wizard chuckled for a moment to himself, as he too was picturing a scene in his head. In his imagination, he saw ten thousand lions pour into the park with their tongues hanging out the sides of their mouths, like in a silly cartoon. In his mind, the herd pounced forward, eventually tackling Ash to the ground and licking his face.

While still wearing a smile, the Wizard continued. "For now I suggest you be specific and use the ancient word for 'rodent.'"

Ash pondered for a few moments then stood up. He clenched both fists and held his gem tightly in his hand. As he whispered, his eyes took on a bright bluish glow. "ɈK ⌒ʊW ⌒ʊM (IK-AWA-AME)."

The manhole cover he was staring at slowly shook. Then he heard a rumbling farther down the street. Suddenly all the manhole covers in the area were shaking.

"Too strong. I suggest we leave—quickly," said the Wizard.

*

A group of students were sitting on a large couch in Bexley Hall in front of an old television. An open box of pizza lay on the table in front of them, with several pieces missing. They sipped on beer and snacked on pizza as the newscast started.

"It seems the Pied Piper paid a visit to Boston today," said a female anchor, "as thousands of rats invaded the Commons."

Ash, who was standing in the doorway behind most of the other students, smiled.

"At this time officials are still trying to determine the cause of the disturbance," said the anchor as the screen shifted to an aerial view of the Boston Commons.

Seas of rats were swarming everywhere. As the camera panned, the flashing of police cars could be seen around the entire perimeter of the park.

One of the students turned around and asked, "Ash, didn't you say you were going to the park today? Were you there when this happened?"

Ash, who was sipping a beer, coughed as he nearly swallowed it down the wrong tube. "Did I say that? Nope, I've been studying all day—big test tomorrow. In fact, I'd better get back to it," he said, making his way out of the room.

The guy shook his head as if to say "okay" then turned back toward the TV. After Ash had left, the guy, with a puzzled expression, turned to the girl sitting next to him and said, "Isn't tomorrow Sunday?"

*

The next day was bright and sunny. The Wizard and Ash strolled alongside the Charles River near Harvard University. They saw crew boats shuttling down the river, and many joggers passed by them as they walked. Despite the Wizard's odd attire, they went unnoticed. Not a single person glanced in their direction, and those who passed them from behind did so as if they were on autopilot, making their way around them.

"That was quite a performance yesterday in the park. You have the basics down and are clearly more gifted than I'd imagined," said the Wizard. "I warned you about some of the potential dangers and risks of using your abilities. What you did won't go unnoticed. I've done what I can to mask our presence here, but I fear that dark forces will soon be on the move."

"But for now I think we're safe," he continued. "Boston is a big city, and it'll take them a long time to track us down, as long as we don't use our abilities. So for today, I have a story to tell you. It'll be difficult to separate fact from fiction in this tale, but by now you should realize that the boundary between what is real and what is a dream is much fuzzier than most people believe. Reality and dreams often pass from one to the other then back again."

Ash looked at the Wizard and nodded in acknowledgment.

And so the Wizard began to tell his tale.

"As the story goes, humans are born of both light and dark. They have a spirit, and that spirit is good. The soul longs to bring the blessings of the spirit to all works that it creates. It is selfless, brave, caring, and kind. These are the forces that drive people to help others, protect the innocent, seek nature, and seek love.

"Humans also have flesh, and that flesh is evil. The flesh longs to bring chaos and destruction to everything it touches. It cares only about itself and quenching its own desires. These are the forces that drive humanity's quest for wealth, power, lust, and war.

"All people struggle with these forces. In the end, though they might think otherwise, the creator saw fit to leave the choice up to them for what type of people they eventually would become. They face these choices every day. This is what it means to be mortal.

"However, some of us are born different. When children are born of evil, they're said to be touched by darkness and are often referred to as 'the Touched.' Legend has it that the Touched are created when a demon and a mortal mate. I can't say whether this is true, but I can tell you they're definitely very real and very dangerous.

"When children are born of good, they're said to be blessed by the light. As with the Touched, they too have a nickname, 'the Blessed.' They also have an origin story. It's said the Blessed are the result of angels and mortals falling in love and having a child. I can definitely say that's simply not true. Both my parents were mortals, and I would guess yours were as well. Perhaps it's a legend that applies only to the first of us—or perhaps for each of us this life is simply one of our many lives. Again, I can't say.

"Both the Touched and the Blessed are born with extraordinary gifts and can do many things mortals can't. The Touched generally manifest this ability naturally, through a single, strong, supernatural power. Some have multiple gifts, but this is rare. Even rarer, some of the Touched can wield dark energies that allow them to do almost anything they desire. All of them possess physical strength and agility well beyond that of ordinary mortals. The Touched are extremely deadly, even more so when they're properly trained to use their abilities, and they'll usually kill you on sight, just for what you are.

"The Blessed typically don't manifest their abilities naturally. Instead, it's as if they all house incredible untapped power deep within themselves that will remain untouched without the proper discipline and training. Yes, there are also some rare exceptions with the Blessed as well. Some individuals are able to manifest magical powers without proper training, but it's almost always a minor ability and never results in anything beyond the ability to perform a few simple parlor tricks, like levitating coins, finding an unmarked card in a deck, or such other nonsense. But with the proper training, focus, and a wand at his or her side, one of the Blessed can accomplish almost anything.

"Since the dawn of what we perceive as time, the Touched and the Blessed have been at war. The Touched have always hunted us, and we in turn have always hunted them. It's a deadly game that has stretched many lifetimes, but the true threat to mortals came only a few thousand years ago. The Touched, unable to win the battle with the Blessed, began to recruit easily influenced mortals into their ranks. One would think these individuals were swayed by the use of deceptions and lies, but more so they were converted by the Touched playing to the greed and desires that already lived in their souls. Such acts were forbidden to the Blessed, as they believed in choice and freedom.

"Massive wars raged that engulfed the whole of the world. Through strategic strikes, the Blessed still managed to drive back the Touched time and time again, allowing for rays of light between the stretches of darkness. But now a new darkness is coming. I feel it growing stronger every day. It will stand against the Blessed, and it will be too strong for any or even all of us to face. It will soon have enough power to destroy us all.

"As the legend has foretold of the coming darkness, it also has predicted the light that will drive it back—a boy of immense power. He's referred to only as 'the Blessed One.' We've been searching for him."

After the Wizard finished, Ash asked his first question. "So our fates are bound by our birth, either for good or evil?"

The Wizard shook his head. "Not at all, Ash. Whether we're born as one of the Touched, one of the Blessed, or a mortal being, we all have a choice regarding what we'll do and who we'll become. We all have impulses and thoughts, probably hundreds or thousands per day. Granted, some of us have darker thoughts than others, but these thoughts don't determine who we are. Our *actions* determine who we are. Think about what I told you yesterday. You asked the rats to come visit you. You didn't force them to do so. And in the end, despite all the nonsense and commotion, the whole episode was harmless."

Ash stopped for a moment, then turned and wandered over to the railing and looked over the Charles River into the city of Boston. The Wizard followed and rested his arms beside Ash.

"I have another question," said Ash.

"I thought you might. Please, ask me what you will."

"In your story you mentioned a boy called the 'Blessed One,'" said Ash. "Am I him?"

The Wizard smirked slightly. "Ash, I have many abilities, but I'm not a seer. Though some of my peers might disagree, I feel we're all the creators of our own story, and we choose who we want to be. The future is an ever-fluctuating wave of possibilities. Are you the Blessed One? This I can't say, but I do know you have an important role to play in things to come."

The Wizard's answer puzzled Ash. He felt immense power within himself, power that was far greater and stronger than that of the man next to him. Why would the Wizard have sought him out if he wasn't the Blessed One?

"Come now," said the Wizard. "I have one more thing to show you today."

They walked quietly along the river for several more minutes, until the Wizard stopped in front of a small abandoned warehouse. He pointed to the building. "This is where we'll continue your training."

It didn't look like much, but any building along the Charles River must have been worth hundreds of thousands, if not millions, of dollars. Ash was also surprised that the Wizard already had a place in town. As far as he was aware, the Wizard had been here only for the past day.

"How did you find this place?" Ash asked curiously.

"The Blessed have many locations around the globe, and this is just one of them. We were very fortunate that we had one so close to your dorm. Do you want to have a look inside?"

"Absolutely," replied Ash.

*

Over the days that followed, the Wizard continued to instruct Ash. They either met up at the abandoned warehouse, or on some days when the Wizard felt so inclined, he would meet Ash at his dorm, and they'd walk over there together. Before each practice session, the Wizard would seal the area with a magical barrier to prevent detection from any outside entities that might be watching or listening.

Ash had more raw talent and ability than any other mage the Wizard had instructed. However, he lacked control, and his results often were chaotic and unfocused. For example, rather than bring up a small shield of protection, Ash's spell would erect a giant, immovable barrier that filled the length of the warehouse. Rather than summon a small ball of illumination, he would conjure a nearly blinding light.

The Wizard often joked, "One doesn't need to use a gun to kill a fly."

Ash also learned there was a great depth to the ancient tongue. Each word carried multiple interpretations that only a focused mind could decipher. The word "◯R," for example, could be used to open a door but could just as easily be used to open a person's mind and read his or her thoughts. There was also something mathematical about the language, as if it had been crafted by the engineers of a race that had a deep understanding of the inner workings of the universe.

Along the way, a sense of overconfidence and arrogance grew within him. He could sense his own power and what he was able to do. He often thought about how much longer he would need the Wizard's training before he could truly put his magical abilities to the test. Some of the Wizard's advice and riddles began to bore him. He felt as if he could accomplish anything, and the world no longer held any boundaries for him.

*

The Wizard arrived early in the morning at Ash's dorm. Ash was still in bed, but he quickly rose to his feet when he felt a presence approach. He hastily put on a pair of jeans that were lying on the floor and by the time the Wizard had reached the door to his room, Ash was already opening it.

"Did I miss the memo? Are we starting before the sun comes up today?" Ash asked as he moved aside to let the Wizard enter the room.

"I need to leave," said the Wizard abruptly.

"What?" Ash rubbed his eyes, trying to gain focus.

The Wizard paced the room, his hands behind his back. This was very uncharacteristic of him. He clearly was worried about something.

"I need to leave," repeated the Wizard. "Something dire has come up that requires my attention. I should be gone for only a few days...a week at most, less if I can manage it."

"Maybe I could come and help?" Ash asked eagerly.

The Wizard paused, as if momentarily contemplating the option, then said firmly, "No. I need you to stay here, and while I'm gone, I need two things from you."

Ash nodded. "Of course."

"First, I need you to promise that you won't use any of your abilities while I'm gone. This will be a dangerous time for you, and it'll be all too easy for the Touched to sense your location."

Ash nodded again. "Okay. What else?"

"Second, your abilities have progressed rapidly, and for the next steps of your training, you'll need a wand. It's time that you have one crafted for you. I need you to travel to Salem. I wanted to take you there myself, but that's no longer an option. Tucked away in an alley between New Derby Street and Front Street, you'll find an old bookstore called the Raven's Foot. There you'll find a man named Dorian. He'll help you through the process."

Ash's expression changed from one of worry to excitement. Images of himself casting more powerful spells filled his head as his eyes glowed a slight blue.

"Do you understand?" asked the Wizard in a slightly louder voice, waking Ash from his daydream.

"Yes. No magic. Get a wand. Raven's Foot. Dorian. Got it," replied Ash.

The Wizard walked over to the door and opened it. Before he left, he glanced back at Ash. "Take care of yourself. I'll be back as soon as I can."

He walked out of the room and quickly disappeared down the hall.

"I will," said Ash as he slowly reached into his pocket and gripped his gemstone. He whispered, "ᔑ/ᓚ ᘔ០ ◌ᗰ (MA-RO-OM)," and the door slammed shut.

CHAPTER 6
FAT JACK

Today you would know him as Smiling Jack, but back then his nickname was Fat Jack for very obvious reasons. He was a rather pudgy, short twelve-year-old with a round face. His weight was always on the rise, and he could only wear very baggy clothing that allowed for future expansion.

His chubby face was topped with a black mop. It hung down past the middle of his nose, completely covering the top part of his head. Though others may have wondered how the boy managed to see through his mane, it didn't seem to bother him at all.

The only exercise you'd ever catch him doing was chasing an ice cream truck down the street. His pants would jiggle all the way, full of coins to spend on frozen treats. The ice cream very rarely would make the return trip, and more often than not, at least some portion would wind up splattered on his face and clothing.

Jack lived with his parents in New Jersey. They loved him dearly, but he didn't have many friends. Most of the other kids made fun of him. However, he did have one close friend named Bruce. He was a skinny kid with freckles and short orange hair. The two were inseparable and made quite the pair.

It was the weekend, and Jack was still lying in bed, tired and groggy from a late night of playing video games. From his cracked window, a breeze blew in and made his curtains dance back and forth in a swaying motion. In the distance he heard the sound of children playing. He wondered what time it was. The sun was obviously up—perhaps it was late afternoon?

A pleasant sound crept in through the window. It was the jingle of the ice cream truck coming down the street. The shuffling noise of children soon followed as they broke from playing and ran to their homes to beg their parents for money. He now knew exactly what time it was—it was ice cream time!

Jack quickly pulled off his sheets and, to his pleasant surprise, was almost entirely dressed, save for his two bare feet. For some reason, no matter how tired he was, he never could sleep with his socks on and always managed to take them off before going to bed. His eyes were still only partway open as he rolled over and ran his hands along the floor, searching for his socks and shoes. With astonishing quickness for a half-awake child, he found both his socks and put them on. He continued to poke around for his shoes but couldn't find them. After sitting up and forcing his eyes fully open, he surmised that they definitely weren't in his room.

He glanced at his nightstand only to find that his coin jar was completely empty. The realization that he was going to lose valuable time asking his mom for money made him sigh loudly. However, determined not to miss this opportunity for delicious ice cream, he raced out of his room and down the stairs. As soon as he reached the bottom, his eyes scanned the area for his mother.

Unable to find her, he cried out, "Mom! Mom! Where are you?"

A soft motherly voice replied, "In the kitchen, Jack."

Jack raced around the corner to find his mother cooking in the kitchen. She had on her apron and was bent over, loading something into the oven. He stared impatiently at the back of her short silver hair, waiting for her to turn around. His mother was still quite young but had gone gray early in life and never had felt the need to fight her age. The kitchen smelled of peanut butter chocolate chip cookies. Jack loved cookies but not as much as he loved ice cream.

Hearing her son behind her, his mother turned around and said, "Well, you look to be in a hurry."

"Ice cream, Mom. Ice cream," was all he could utter.

She gave him a loving smile and said, "Well, I suppose" in a long, drawn-out manner.

Jack hung over the counter that separated him from his mother and stretched out his chubby hands. His mother reached under the counter. He heard the sounds of coins jingling as he waited in anticipation. She removed a large jar of coins and started to sort through them. As she did this, Jack motioned his own hands for her to hurry. She smiled, stopped counting, and filled his palms with coins until they spilled over onto the counter. He was going to get a lot of ice cream today.

Jack closed his hands, and before his mother could even say, "I love you" or "good-bye," he ran out of the kitchen. He still needed to find his shoes and wondered how far he could make it in his socks if it came down to it. Fortunately, as he was heading to the front door, he spotted his trusty old pair of sneakers next to the base of the stairs. In his haste to retrieve money from his mother, he must have missed them.

FAT JACK

He sat down on a step and looked at his shoes. Then he slowly looked at his coin-filled hands and back again at his shoes. It was as if he'd been presented with an unsolvable puzzle. He knew he needed to put on his shoes to get ice cream, and he knew he definitely needed money to buy the ice cream, but he also knew he needed his hands for both.

It took his brain a few seconds to offer up a viable solution to his dilemma. He slowly emptied his hands next to him, making as neat a pile of coins as he could. Since the laces on his shoes were always loosely tied, he quickly and easily slipped them on. With his hands free again, he plunged them down into the pile of coins, grabbing as many as he could. Ideally he would have liked to take all of them, but time was of the essence! Who knew how far down the street the ice cream truck already had gotten? He dashed out the door.

He spotted the ice cream truck only a few blocks away. Several children were sprawled out on the lawn across the street from the truck, already enjoying their newly acquired treats. A lone kid stood at the window of the ice cream truck and appeared to be paying. Jack knew the next stop was around the corner, past Bruce's house and several blocks down. He had to hurry.

It was then that things began to happen in slow motion. Jack started to run, picking up his pace with each step. He felt his feet pound the lawn beneath him. His pudge jiggled up and down, slightly exposing his belly at the bottom of his shirt. A sprinkler went off in the neighbor's yard. He jolted to the left, and his feet hit the pavement. The kids down the road turned their head toward him. He saw them starting to break into smiles. The boy at the window of the truck turned and began to cross the street. Jack heard the sound of the truck's engine as it started to rev up.

The truck picked up a bit of speed as it drove down the street. Jack panted as he tried to run faster. He saw the ice cream man lean out the window and wave at the kids as he made his way around the corner ahead. This was when Jack spotted his friend Bruce on a bicycle, coming down the street directly toward the ice cream truck. Bruce didn't have his eyes on the road but instead was looking toward Jack.

As the truck turned the corner, it was too late for anyone to do anything. It plowed straight into Bruce. A collision like this normally would have sent a child flying, but instead a far worse thing happened. The rim of the truck hooked onto the wheel of the bike and dragged Bruce underneath. The front of the truck rose as it continued forward and drove over him. Jack was still a few yards away but could see the blood from where he was.

Jack's hand slowly opened, and the coins fell to the ground. Bruce was dead.

*

Jack woke up quickly. The memory of what had happened was still vivid and fresh. He couldn't believe his best and only friend was dead. He wondered how long he'd been asleep or even how he'd managed to make it to his bed. He put his hands over his face, and his eyes filled with tears.

After a few moments of crying, he wiped his eyes and glanced at his nightstand. There was an empty jar sitting on it. Then he looked over at his window. The window was slightly cracked. A light breeze blew in, and his curtains swayed back and forth. Sunlight poured in from between the curtains.

He heard the sound of children playing outside, and then another sound followed it, as if played in slow motion. It was a familiar jingle that once had filled his heart with joy, but now only the memory of

FAT JACK

Bruce's accident remained. The ice cream truck was coming down the street, but why? How could the driver have the nerve to drive down this street ever again? He had killed Bruce! And that was only yesterday!

Jack was angry. He ripped off his sheets and quickly realized he still had most of his clothes on. He glanced down at his feet and saw they were bare. *The same as yesterday*, he thought. Looking near the base of his bed, he found two pairs of socks, but his shoes weren't there. *The same as yesterday*, he thought.

His heart was pounding as he hurried out of his room and down the stairs. Without stopping he ran into the kitchen. His mother was bent over the oven, baking something. The kitchen smelled of peanut butter chocolate chip cookies. *The same as yesterday*, he thought. And then something occurred to him. Perhaps it wasn't yesterday but today. Perhaps he was given a vision, like in the movies, and there was still time to save Bruce!

Without hesitation Jack ran out of the kitchen, and without stopping to put on his shoes, he was out the front door. His mother turned around, startled at the sound of the door opening and then slamming shut.

"Guess he really wants ice cream today," she said, smiling.

Jack dashed down the street. A few moments after running past the neighbors' lawn, he heard the sprinklers turn on behind him. *There's still time*, he thought. He glanced up and saw the truck driver hand a girl a cone dripping with chocolate ice cream. A boy eagerly waited behind her. The girl gave the truck driver a few coins then began to cross the street. The boy stepped forward. Jack was close enough to see his lips move.

One of the boys across the street chanted, "Run, fat boy! Run!"

"Fat Jack is going to get some ice cream!" yelled another.

But Jack wasn't stopping for ice cream. Not today. He ran right past the ice cream truck and continued down the street, running faster than he ever had before. All the kids looked on in astonishment.

As Jack ran past, one of them said, "That chubby dude was running so fast—I think he missed the truck."

Jack heard the truck's engine start as he rounded the corner. He spotted Bruce peddling his bike down the street and furiously waved his hands in the air as he continued to run. As soon as Bruce saw him, he slowed down and pulled over to the sidewalk. Then he braced himself for what was to come, an enormous flailing child was headed toward him, and there appeared to be no stopping him.

When Jack reached Bruce, despite almost being completely out of breath, he lifted him off his bike with a gigantic hug. Not knowing what to do, Bruce just hung limp as Jack shook him back and forth. Jack closed his eyes as he squeezed his best friend tightly. When he opened them again, he caught the rear of the ice cream truck driving by.

That was the first time Jack saw the future.

*

Several days passed before Jack worked up the nerve to tell his friend about his experience. They were hanging out in Bruce's room when he told his story. Bruce sat there speechless, with a puzzled look on his face. Even when the story was done, his expression didn't change. Jack was unable to determine whether it was a look of astonishment, fear, disbelief, or all three.

"So what do you think?" asked Jack.

One would imagine that, after such a tale, the reaction would be to get up slowly, walk away calmly, then inform someone of authority that their best friend had just cashed in his last sanity chip.

But these were boys, and they had wild imaginations—boys who spent much of their waking hours daydreaming about the impossible, hoping one day they would have a superpower of their own.

"This is…" Bruce began then looked down and paused for a second. He looked up with a smile and continued, "…totally awesome!"

By his expression, it was obvious that his mind was swirling with ideas.

"I didn't think you'd believe me," said Jack with a sigh of relief.

"Jack, I've known you for a long time. You're my best friend. I might not know much, but I know you'd never lie to me. Of course I believe you. But I have a question."

"I've been holding this in for so long. Ask me anything," Jack said with a grin.

"Do you think you can do it again?"

"What do you mean?"

"You know—maybe control it?" Bruce said, waving his hands by the side of his head, as if he were trying to simultaneously speak and communicate via telepathy.

"I haven't tried—I mean, it kind of freaked me out. I wouldn't even know how to start. Where would we begin?" responded Jack.

Bruce glanced over at the laptop on his desk. A screen saver filled with Japanese anime characters moved across a black background.

"That, my friend, is why they invented the Internet," he replied. He looked back at Jack somewhat mockingly and continued, "There's this thing called Google. Not sure if you've heard of it. We could start there."

"Wiseass," replied Jack with a smirk.

Bruce walked over to his desk, pulled out the chair, and sat down. Jack followed and hovered over his friend's shoulder as he typed in his password. The screen saver disappeared, and Bruce opened up his Internet browser. He looked back at Jack then back at his screen. Both wore puzzled expressions.

"Where do we begin?" Bruce whispered to himself. After a few seconds, he exclaimed, "Got it!" and typed "Time control."

*

Jack and Bruce spent the next few weeks researching everything from quantum mechanics, which neither of them understood, to metaphysics, which they also didn't understand. Eventually they stumbled upon a few articles about therapists using hypnosis on their patients to mentally alter events in their past, erasing bad memories and behaviors by changing their perceptions of what had happened. This turned out to be the key to unlocking Jack's latent abilities.

After several failed attempts, the two of them were in Bruce's room one night, ready to try again. The entire room was dark except for two black candles on the floor. Bruce and Jack sat across from each other on opposite sides of the candles. Their shadows swayed back and forth against the walls behind them.

Bruce looked at Jack and said, "So are you ready for try number forty-two?"

Jack looked back at Bruce and nodded.

"Remember what we talked about," Bruce continued. "Try to picture yourself in science class tomorrow—not thinking of it as the future but rather as if you were there—right now. Imagine the chemistry test being laid on your desk. See the paper in front of you. Read all the questions, and then come back," he instructed with a confidence that gave the perception that he actually knew what he was talking about.

Jack closed his eyes and inhaled and exhaled slowly, paying close attention to his breathing. He imagined the next day in great detail, and then his body shook slightly. Bruce leaned in to have a closer look at his friend when suddenly Jack's eyes flew open. They had a red glow to them, and wisps of crimson smoke issued from their sides.

*

Time-control attempt number forty-two had failed. With disappointment, Bruce got up, walked over to the wall, and switched on the light. Jack extinguished the two candles and also stood up. The two talked briefly about the experiment as Bruce carefully jotted down some notes in his binder. After a pat on the back from Bruce, Jack put on his coat and made his way home.

Jack's walk to his house seemed shorter than usual, but he was a little disoriented from the experiment, and his head still felt a little fuzzy. As he entered his home, he saw that his mother and father were on the couch, watching an old movie on television. Hearing him open the door, his mother leaned over the sofa and looked at him.

"Did you have a good time at Bruce's?" she asked.

Jack shrugged. "It was all right, but I'm really bushed. I'm going to go straight to bed."

"Okay, see you in the morning."

He scurried up the stairs. Both his parents said good night as they turned their heads back toward the television. Jack entered his room, closed the door, took off his clothes, and crawled into bed. He drifted off to sleep as he listened to the muffled ambient noise of the television downstairs.

He woke up several hours later to a knock at his door and his mother's voice.

"Get up, sleepyhead. You're going to be late for school. Breakfast is ready," she said.

Jack yawned loudly and stretched his arms in the air. Then he got up and walked over to his dresser. He pulled out a pair of jogging pants and put them on before heading downstairs. From the bottom of the stairs, he saw his dad sitting at the dining-room table just outside the kitchen, sipping a cup of coffee and clicking on a tablet in front of him.

His dad looked up. "Good morning, Jack. Are you ready for your big science test today?"

"I guess so," Jack said as he walked over to the table and took a seat.

A few moments later, his mother entered the dining room from the kitchen. She had a plate filled with eggs and bacon in one hand and a glass of milk in the other. She placed them in front of Jack as she looked at him and smiled. Without uttering a word, he quickly devoured his food. His mother's intuition told her that something wasn't quite right, and she patted his moppy head.

"Is everything okay, honey?" she asked.

"I'm sure he's just worried about his chemistry test today in Mrs. Templeton's class," Jack's dad answered for him. "Don't worry, son. You'll do fine. Tell you what—if you pass this thing, we'll head over to the store this weekend and see if we can find you that new gaming laptop you've been wanting."

Barely acknowledging the conversation, Jack kept his head down and continued to eat everything on his plate. After he was done, he gulped down his glass of fresh milk, leaving a white mustache on his upper lip. His mom walked over and wiped his face with a kitchen towel. Looking slightly annoyed, Jack lightly pushed her hand away.

With a full belly, he headed back upstairs to finish getting ready for school. With a quickness that only small children have, he was showered and dressed within a few minutes. He looked out the window and saw that many of the other kids already had gathered at the bus stop. After grabbing his backpack, he rushed downstairs. His mom was standing at the base of the stairs, holding a brown paper bag with his lunch. He quickly grabbed the bag, kissed his mom on the cheek, and headed out the door.

Jack made it to the bus stop just as the bus was pulling up. He sat down in an empty seat and placed his backpack next to him to save a spot for Bruce. This was probably a little unnecessary since Bruce's stop was the very next one, and he was almost always the very first person in line. The bus stopped, and Bruce got on, followed by a few other kids. Jack lifted his backpack as Bruce approached, and his friend took the seat next to him. On the ride to school, they whispered back and forth about last night's experiment. Their voices hinted of disappointment mixed with excitement about some new ideas they had about what to try next.

Most of the school day passed as usual. The only thing that struck Jack as a little odd was how exceptionally focused he seemed in his classes. On a typical day, he often found himself bored and was prone to drifting off into daydreams, but today everything seemed clearer and more fascinating. During his social studies class, his teacher's description of the adventures of Lewis and Clark on their expedition to the West Coast made him feel like he was watching a riveting movie. In math class, he was mesmerized by the simplicity and elegance of the Pythagorean Theorem and how it could actually be used to triangulate the location of a lost cell phone. It felt like he was reading a book for the second time and was now able to appreciate all the finer details.

After lunch, he had science class. His big test awaited him, but for some reason he felt less nervous than usual and for absolutely no good reason. He hadn't studied any harder than usual. In fact, because he and Bruce had been so focused on their experiments, he actually had studied less.

The walk over to the classroom was a bit hazy for him. He didn't remember passing any other children in the hallway, and by the time he reached the door to the classroom, he was beginning to wonder whether he was in the right place. As he slowly opened the door, he saw that the room was entirely empty except for Mrs. Templeton, who was sitting behind her desk, typing on her laptop.

Mrs. Templeton was in her early twenties, quite a bit younger than most of the other teachers in Jack's school, and always dressed more stylishly. Today she was wearing her gray cardigan over a white bow-top shirt with pink polka dots and a navy pencil skirt. Though his grades didn't reflect it, Jack thoroughly enjoyed her class and thought she was by far the friendliest and most energetic of his teachers. As she looked up from her laptop, she pushed up her maroon cat eyeglasses and smiled. She watched him as he walked over to his seat. After he had sat down, she returned her eyes to her laptop.

Soon the classroom began to fill with other students. Bruce arrived in the middle of the crowd and took his seat far away from Jack. Mrs. Templeton had separated them a few weeks earlier for talking too much in class. Bruce looked over at Jack and gave him two thumbs-up and smiled. Jack wasn't quite sure what to make of this, since he knew that neither of them had spent much time studying.

FAT JACK

Mrs. Templeton walked around the room, placing a test facedown on each student's desk. When she was finished, she looked up at the clock, as did all the pupils. Everyone watched with fixed eyes as the second hand slowly went past the top of the clock.

"All right, class, begin," instructed Mrs. Templeton.

Her announcement was followed by the rustle of pages as the students turned over their tests. As Jack reached down to pick up his test, he heard a faint voice in his head that sounded like Bruce's.

Read all the questions—and then come back, it whispered calmly.

These were the instructions he and Bruce had rehearsed. Jack read each of the questions before answering a single one. He didn't expect this to be of great assistance, but he figured what harm could it do? The questions were difficult; he definitely hadn't studied enough. Each one was more cryptic than the last. After completing a pass of the entire set of questions, he picked up his pencil. Wondering how much time he had left, he looked up at the clock and noticed something odd. The entire room had taken on a slight red glow, and the walls were pulsating.

His head hurt for a moment, and then he had a realization. He already had seen all these questions before. He already either had looked them up on the Internet or worked through each of them with Bruce. After putting his pencil down below the first question, he filled in the answer with ease. He quickly moved on to the second question and then the third. He was going to ace this test.

When Jack finished the first page of the exam, he flipped over the page. For a moment, his eyes had trouble focusing. He again wondered what time it was and looked up at the clock. This time the red in the room glowed brighter and brighter with each pulse. As he looked back down, he realized that his paper, his desk, his pencil, and even his hands had taken on the red pulsing of the room. The redness quickly engulfed him, and then there was darkness and silence.

*

All his senses had vanished, and he no longer had a perception of time. He felt as if he were drifting through empty space with only his own thoughts to comfort him. After what could have been seconds, minutes, or perhaps longer, he heard a faint voice in the distance. Then, suddenly and all at once, the voice was amplified to full volume.

Someone was yelling, "Jack! Jack! Wake up, Jack!"

Something gripped his shoulders and rocked him back and forth. With a jolt, he opened his eyes and saw it was Bruce, who wore a look of panic on his face. Jack reached up and placed his hands over Bruce's.

"I'm okay," said Jack.

"Oh, man. You scared the hell out of me. Your eyes were glowing red and smoke was coming out of them. It freaked the hell out of me! I didn't know what to do," replied Bruce.

Jack was beaming. "You aren't going to believe this."

"What? Did it work?" asked Bruce.

"Break out your notepad," Jack said. "We're going to own this test!"

CHAPTER 7
RAVEN'S ASHES

Ash leaned his head against the window of the train and looked outside. The train had just left North Station and was on its way to Salem. He was filled with a sense of adventure and excitement. Today he would meet Dorian and finally have his wand crafted. He daydreamed about all the things he could do once he was able to truly channel his powers.

After the second or third stop, Ash's mobile phone rang. He reached into his pocket and looked to see who was calling. It was someone with a Boston area code, but he didn't recognize the number.

"Hello?" he answered.

As soon as he heard the voice, he quickly realized it was his friend Mike.

"Hey, buddy!" said Mike.

Ash had known Mike for a little more than a year. Though they both went to MIT and had shared a few classes, it wasn't until they'd met at the Boston Comic Con that the two had bonded over discussions of comic books and *Dungeons and Dragons*. Mike was studying computer science and had moved to Boston from Austin, Texas. He was much more outgoing than Ash and was always trying to get him to be more social. Many times he was the catalyst that Ash needed to get out and do anything.

"Hey, Mike," responded Ash.

"It's been a while. How have you been?"

Ash paused for a moment. *How has it been?* he thought. *It's been absolutely freaking crazy! You wouldn't believe me if I told you. I met this wizard guy, and he taught me how to cast spells. Now I'm on my way to Salem to have a wand crafted and I—*

Stopping himself, he responded. "Fine. You know—same old, same old."

"Good to hear," Mike said. "You seemed kind of busy and distracted the last time I saw you. Anyway, some of us are headed out for drinks tonight, and I wanted to see if you were up for joining us. Are you in?"

Ash was unsure how long his trip to Salem would last, but one thing was for sure: he could use a little bit of normal. He needed a break from all the strangeness that had taken over his life. Also, he hadn't had a chance to hang out with Mike or any of his other friends in far too long.

"Sure, I'd love to," he said. "I'm running a few errands this afternoon, but maybe I could meet up with you guys later. Where are you going?"

"Awesome. We'll be at a bar called the Saloon. I heard about it from this chick I met last night. Supposedly it's modeled after an old-school speakeasy. It's totally up your alley. You'll love it," replied Mike.

"Interesting. Okay, so where do I find this Saloon?"

"It's right in Davis Square, just past the comedy club near the Burren."

"Great. See you there," said Ash.

"Looking forward to catching up. Later, Ash."

"Later, Mike." Ash hung up the phone and returned it to his pocket.

Ash had a smile on his face. Today was going to be a great day. First he would have his wand crafted, and then he would celebrate with his friends. He leaned his head against the window and watched the amber trees as they passed by. In a half hour, he would be in the heart of Salem.

*

Someone was poking at Ash's arm. He opened his eyes and looked up. It was the train conductor. Somehow he had managed to doze off during the last few minutes of his trip.

"Salem, Massachusetts, last stop. Everybody off," said the man.

Ash got up from his seat, gave himself a quick stretch, and made his way to the door. Stepping off the train, he felt a brisk wind. The summer finally was giving way to the fall. He zipped up his coat, put his hands in his pockets, and made his way out of the train station.

Right outside the station, he spotted a plaque with a map of the city on it. He originally had intended on using the GPS on his phone to find the Raven's Foot. But somehow he felt it would be more wizardly to use the primitive technology in front of him. He glanced over the map and quickly located both New Derby Street and Front Street. Front Street was the shorter of the two, and he figured he would look there for an alley that connected through to New Derby Street.

Front Street was very close by, and it took Ash only a few minutes to walk there. The streets were mildly crowded with tourists, but the real crowds wouldn't start until it got closer to Halloween. Most of the stores he passed seemed to cater to two sets of audiences: those interested in the history of the Salem witch trials and those with a fascination for the occult.

In one of Ash's elective American history classes, he had learned that the actual Salem witch trials hadn't taken place in this town at all. They occurred in a neighboring town called Danvers, which went by the name of Salem Village at the time. The name eventually was changed to avoid the association with the atrocities that had occurred during the trials. Subsequently the town of Danvers now missed out on the booming tourism industry in Salem.

Walking along Front Street, Ash had noticed only one path leading in the direction of New Derby Street. It wasn't a very long walkway that connected the two. However, after he had walked up and down the cobblestone path several times, he was unable to find the Raven's Foot. On his last pass, he paid closer attention to all the buildings and methodically read each sign in his head as he walked past them. Still unable to find the bookstore, he became a little frustrated and decided to ask someone for help. He walked into a store called the Broom Closet.

It was a small, quaint gift shop that sold various souvenir novelties as well as a selection of metaphysical and Wiccan items. The store managed to pack a lot into a tiny area, and there were sections for T-shirts, jewelry, cut stones, tarot decks, oils, herbs, candles, and even handmade broomsticks. As Ash entered, he was greeted by the pleasant smell of burning lavender incense. He immediately approached the counter near the front and addressed the person behind it.

"Excuse me," he said. "I'm looking for a bookstore called the Raven's Foot. I heard it was down this street but can't seem to find it. Could you help me out?"

An odd-looking old woman behind the counter, who was busy sorting through a pile of stones, looked up. She wore a dark-brown felt hat with a series of twigs wrapped around it and a few larger ones protruding. It looked as if she were wearing a winding tree upon her brow, with a few escaping branches. Her long white hair was a bit ratty and made her look as if she'd just gotten out of bed a few moments earlier. Her face bore soft wrinkles, except around her mouth, which had a few more, probably from too much smiling.

"The Raven's Foot," she repeated. "Why, it's right next door. I don't see how you could have missed it. Their sign is one of my favorites."

"Thank you very much," said Ash with a smile in return.

"Happy to help. Have a good day."

"You too," said Ash as he exited the store.

Once outside, Ash glanced at the stores next door, first to the right and then to the left. He still couldn't see any sign for the bookstore and wondered what the old woman was talking about. He decided to step across the street to get a better look at the area. When he looked up again, he noticed something he hadn't seen before. Above one of the doors on his left was a large brass claw holding a clear sphere. *Of course*, he thought.

Ash started to walk back across the street then paused when he saw two men exit the bookstore. One was slightly overweight and had a bushy mustache. The other was thinner, with auburn hair. Both were dressed in ill-fitting suits. They stopped after exiting the store, glanced at each other for a moment, then headed toward Front Street.

As they walked, the man with the mustache pulled out a cigar from his pocket.

Large puffs of smoke and the sharp smell of the cigar drifted down the alley. When the two made their way farther down the path, Ash continued toward the bookstore. When he got closer, he glanced up at the glass sphere. He made out the words THE RAVEN'S FOOT in faded letters.

*

The Raven's Foot was almost exactly like Ash had pictured it. Several ceiling-high bookshelves, filled to the brim, lined every wall of the entire room. Off in the distance, it appeared as if a door were cut in the middle of one of the bookshelves, creating a doorway that revealed even more books in the room behind it. A staircase with red carpets leading upstairs ran along the left side of the room. In the corner, just before the doorway, was a cushy-looking purple chair. Along the right side of the room stood two desks. Each was piled high with barely balanced books and two accompanying chairs beneath them. In sharp contrast to the rich, strong odor of the passing cigar outside, the faint and musty yet sweet vanilla scent of used books wafted through the air.

As he had entered, a small bell had chimed, triggered by the door opening. A head eventually poked around the corner of the bookshelf doorway. He was an older man with a purple newsboy hat, a thick black mustache, and a pair of spectacles resting on his pointy nose.

"Be right with you," he said, as he placed some books on the shelf next to him.

Ash let the door close behind him and waited patiently. Within a few moments, the man emerged and headed over while wiping his hands with a rag. He was wearing a half-buttoned maroon wool cardigan that partially covered his white dress shirt and gray-striped tie. As he approached, he looked Ash up and down, sometimes appearing to be looking at something behind him.

"Hello," Ash said. "My name's Ashley Drake. I'm looking for a man named Dorian. I was told he works here."

The man muttered to himself for a moment then said, "They say the eyes are truly the window to the soul. Already I can see the swirling blue energies behind yours coming in and out of focus."

"You can?" Ash asked with a gasp.

"Yes, Ashley, I can," he responded. "The one who sent you to me already should have told you these things."

"I take it you're Dorian then."

"Oh, we have a bright one here," the man said sarcastically. "Yes, I'm Dorian."

"Do you know why I'm here?"

"It's my business to know such things. Yes, I know why you're here, but before we get on to things, I need to ask you a favor."

Ash nodded. "Okay."

"When you leave here, go to the store next door. There's a nice old lady there. Buy yourself a pair of sunglasses from her. Any pair will do—just make sure they're dark. While the distortion in your eyes is only apparent to the trained eye right now, without your having some practice in shrouding these manifestations, soon others with less perceptive eyes will be able to see that something isn't quite right about you. Neither you nor I want any extra unwanted attention."

"Will do, sir," said Ash.

"Okay, then follow me upstairs," instructed Dorian.

Dorian walked over to the front door, locked it, and turned over a sign to let people know the shop was closed. He then made his way up the red staircase, with Ash following closely behind. Every step they took resulted in a long creak beneath them. At the top of the stairs was a wooden door barred across by several large metal straps and held in place by hefty metal hinges. Dorian pulled out a long old-looking brass key from his pocket and unlocked the door. He waited for Ash to enter the room then closed the door behind them.

It was a small room and bore the same decor as the downstairs area. Large bookshelves lined all the walls with the exception of the one directly across from them. This wall had a large oak door in the center, and two tapestries hung on opposite sides of it.

The tapestry on the left depicted a magician. He wore a long white robe with a black cloak draped over his shoulders. One of his hands pointed down, and the other held a wand raised toward the sky. A table was in front of him. On it rested a sword, a chalice, a pentagram, and a staff. An infinity symbol hovered above his head.

The tapestry on the right depicted a devil. He was bare chested and had the legs of a goat. Large gray wings extended from his back, and two curved horns protruded from his forehead. He too had one hand raised and one facing down. The hand facing down held a flaming branch, while the raised one was empty, palm forward. An inverted pentagram floated above his head.

Under each of the tapestries was a glass display case. From where Ash was standing, he was unable to see their contents but imagined they might contain ancient artifacts of incredible power or perhaps a few pages from an otherwise lost magical manuscript.

On one side of the room stood a large wooden desk bare of any contents. Dorian walked over to the chair closest to the wall then motioned for Ash to take the seat on the opposite side. Ash sat down as Dorian rummaged through the desk drawers. As he did this, he said, "Well, Mr. Drake, did you bring your gem with you?"

Ash reached into his pocket and placed the clear gem on the table. "Yes, here it is."

Dorian stopped what he was doing and glanced at the jewel. He picked it up with two fingers and held it up against the ceiling light. After turning and examining the stone a few times, he placed it back on the table.

"So how's it working for you?" he asked, as he looked down and continued to search through the drawers.

"Fine, I guess. I mean, I was able to summon a whole city's worth of rats," he answered, with a slight hint of bragging in his voice.

"Interesting," said Dorian, as he removed a large wooden box from the desk and placed it on the table. "Normally you don't see very dramatic effects with a clear practice gem."

With a slight look of disbelief, Ash asked, "A practice gem? Why would the Wizard give me a practice gem?"

"The who?" replied Dorian, before pausing for a moment then answering his own question. "Ah, yes, him."

Dorian clasped his hands together and looked directly at Ash, who was still staring at the clear gem on the table. "You see, Ashley, a mage needs a gem that's attuned to his personal being. Using a natural stone that isn't aligned with one's soul often results in the inability to bring the proper energies into the physical world. It varies from mage to mage. For the vast majority of casters, the correct gem is the one that corresponds to his or her birth sign. For others, it's the stone that corresponds to their dominant chakra. Yet for a few it's something else entirely. We won't know which one is right for you until we try."

He pointed at the clear gem on the table. "What you have in front of you is a clear quartz crystal. These types of gemstones are given to initiates before a properly attuned one has been determined. It usually works, at least to some degree, for all manner of aspiring mages. However, its effects are generally very limited. I'm surprised to know it worked so well for you. I heard about that incident on the news."

Ash smirked slightly and looked quite proud of himself.

Dorian flipped open the lid of the large wooden box and turned it toward Ash. Inside Ash saw a collection of gemstones separated into twelve sections. On the inside of the lid was a chart depicting zodiac symbols with dates below them. Underneath the dates were sketches of colored stones and their corresponding names written in the old tongue.

> *Capricorn (December 22–January 20) = turquoise/garnet*
> *Aquarius (January 21–February 19) = garnet/amethyst*
> *Pisces (February 20–March 20) = amethyst/bloodstone*
> *Aries (March 21–April 20) = bloodstone/diamond*
> *Taurus (April 21–May 21) = diamond/emerald*
> *Gemini (May 22–June 21) = emerald/agate*
> *Cancer (June 22–July 22) = agate/ruby*
> *Leo (July 23–August 22) = ruby/sardonyx*
> *Virgo (August 23–September 23) = sardonyx/sapphire*
> *Libra (September 24–October 23) = sapphire/opal*
> *Scorpio (October 24–November 22) = opal/topaz*
> *Sagittarius (November 23–December 21) = topaz/turquoise*

"I tend to have a feeling for such things, and my first intuition is right more often than it's wrong. Judging by the blue wisps I see dancing behind your eyes, I'd guess you likely were born in September. Given that, we should start with a blue sapphire," said Dorian, as he reached into the tenth container and removed a translucent-blue, shiny, cut gemstone.

Ash, in fact, wasn't born in September, but he wanted to see how this would play out, so he opened his hand to receive the gem.

Placing the gem in Ash's palm, Dorian asked, "So how does it feel?"

At first there was only a slight tingle in his hand as the gem made contact with his skin. Then a sensation like a crawling electrical current moved up his arm. He looked over as if he were able to see the energy flowing over him and watched it as it began to engulf his body. It moved to his other arm then down his chest, toward his feet. His muscles tensed slightly. When it reached his feet, he felt a strong grounding to the earth, as if his feet were slightly heavier and somehow tied to it. Then the energy traveled up his chest, toward his head. This movement was slower, and he felt it not only on the surface of his skin but also deeper within him. He opened his eyes wide as the energy reached the top of his crown. Ash's entire body was tingling and pulsing. A cleansing wave rippled down his body and covered him.

"I actually feel an energy moving through me, washing over me!" Ash said, gasping.

"I told you I was good at this," said Dorian, smiling. "Now let's try something. I assume you have some mastery of the ancient tongue?"

"I'm still learning, but I know the basics."

"That'll be good enough," said Dorian. "I've spent years shielding this room, so we don't need to worry about any energies escaping or being detected by watchful eyes. That being said, I care dearly for my collection of books and trinkets and don't wish to see any harm come to them. So we'll try something tame that won't cause harm to you, me, or any of my precious possessions."

Dorian closed the lid of the wooden box and placed it back in one of the drawers. He stood up, walked over to a bookcase, and scanned through the titles of the books while moving his finger across them in the air. He stopped at a rather sizable volume called *The Golden Dawn* by Israel Regardie. After removing it from the shelf, he walked back to the table, sat down, and placed it in the center.

"Now," he said, "as I'm sure you've already been instructed; magic is just a matter of focusing your energy. Simply calm your mind, direct your energy toward what you want to happen, and see it not as if it's going to happen but as if it already has. I want you to use a levitation mantra to float this book into the air. Your powers will be somewhat undirected without the use of a wand, so a few other items might move slightly. That's okay. We're just testing your level of attunement to the sapphire."

Ash didn't know the correct word for *levitation* in the ancient tongue, but he did recall the proper word for *fly*. He assumed this would be good enough. Remembering what the Wizard had taught him in the park, he knew he would need a word for *book*. He also didn't know the exact word for *book*, but as an engineering student, he thought that a book was just a collection of pages, and he did know the proper word for *paper*.

Ash stood up and pushed his chair back. He gripped the blue sapphire tightly and stared at the book for a few moments. Then he closed his eyes and pictured it floating and hovering in the air above the desk. He was ready.

He chanted, "ᗰ/Ƙ ᗴI Ƙ/Ƙ (MA-OHIV-CA)," as he slowly opened his eyes.

His eyes took on a deeper bluish glow as the gemstone trembled in his hand. All the books on all the shelves shook, slowly at first, but then it quickly turned into an audible, beating rumble. Dorian hopped up from his chair and stood back until his body was pressed against the bookshelf behind him. His expression was one of terror as his eyes darted around the room, then back at Ash, then at the book on the table in front of him.

The book was also moving, as if it were being shaken by an invisible entity. For just a moment, all the movement in the room subsided, and then suddenly the book shot straight up into the air at an incredible rate. It smacked hard against the ceiling above, causing the spine of the book to break and scattering hundreds of floating pages in all directions. The pages hovered and glided along the ceiling above Dorian and Ash, spreading out until they covered it. Then, in an instant, the rumbling stopped, and the pages slowly floated down like a calm paper rain.

Dorian and Ash watched as the pages fell to the floor and covered the room in a sea of print. One page landed right on Dorian's head, covering his eyes. He blew a few times, trying to remove it, but it only fluttered up and down. Finally he reached up, pulled it off, and looked at Ash.

"Well, my boy, I think it's safe to say two things," he said, brushing off a few remaining pages from his shoulders. "One, I think we've definitely found your gemstone, and two, we won't be practicing in here anymore."

They both smiled and giggled slightly. The truth, unknown to either of them, was that any of the birthstones would have worked for Ash.

"I'm so sorry," said Ash.

"Don't worry about it. The book wasn't of any significance. I have several copies, and honestly, if I ever needed another copy, I could just order it from Amazon."

"They have books on spell casting on Amazon?" said Ash, rather surprised.

"Didn't you know? You can find anything on Amazon," Dorian answered with a smirk. "They have quite a few, but it's hard to distinguish the good ones from most of the rubbish that's out there. Many so-called experts and masters have only glimpsed the surface of what a true mage can accomplish.

"Now let's clean up this place a bit, and then we'll see about crafting the rest of your wand. Lord knows you could use something to direct those energies!" he exclaimed, picking up some of the pages from the floor.

Ash placed the blue sapphire on the table and started to help Dorian clean up. This was going to take a while—there were pages everywhere.

*

All the pages of the book were stacked in a rather untidy manner at the corner of the desk. Ash was seated and fumbling with the blue sapphire in his hands. Dorian was searching through his desk drawers. Finally he pulled out a long wooden box and placed it on the table.

"A mage's wand allows him to direct his energies," Dorian stated, as he moved his hands across the box, "focusing them on a particular person or thing. Now, that's not to say that with a wand one can't affect an entire area or multiple individuals or objects. One most certainly can, but this will be a choice, rather than an inevitable outcome. Think of a wand as a channel that will both amplify and direct your powers."

"I think I understand," said Ash.

"Good. This will be your most precious item, and you must never be without it."

Dorian removed the lid of the box and placed it to the side, next to the stack of pages. Inside the box were four long compartments, each containing a foot-long rod. The first compartment held a twisted piece of wood that was slightly discolored, as if it had been exposed to a flame. At the top were several twisted branches that formed a gnarled hand. The second compartment held a shiny copper rod with a small cup shape near its top. The third housed a smooth cylinder made of some sort of grayish stone. The last rod appeared to be made of a glasslike clear material with a slight greenish tint to it.

"You see before you the primary materials that we'll use to construct the base of your wand." Dorian gestured over the box. "We have wood, metal, stone, and hardened sand, or earth. A mage's wand is almost always crafted out of one of these fundamental materials."

He picked up the wooden rod from the box and handed it to Ash, who reached forward to grab it with the hand containing his blue gem. As soon as Dorian spotted the glimmer in Ash's palm, he quickly pulled back the rod.

"Why don't you place that on the table for now?" He motioned his eyes toward the edge of the desk. "We wouldn't want any side effects occurring here."

"Side effects?" asked Ash, with a somewhat surprised expression. "I thought one always needed the proper words to cast a spell?"

"My boy," replied Dorian, "not to underplay their value, but one must always remember that the words and the wand are just tools. The energies lie within you."

Very intrigued by this statement, Ash asked, "So is it possible to cast spells without them?"

Dorian paused for a moment as if to gather his thoughts. "Think of it like this," he said. "Imagine that you have a nail before you that you wish to hammer into this desk. One could, in theory, beat on the head of the nail with one's bare hands. With enough time, effort, and most likely a great deal of pain, one could eventually drive the nail into the wood. Now imagine that I give you a wooden rod. Though it would still take a lot of time and effort, it would make it much easier to drive the nail into the table. To make things even easier, imagine if we attached a metal end to the wooden rod to create a hammer. Using a hammer, the proper tool, you'd be able to easily accomplish your goal. Do you understand so far?"

Ash nodded. "That makes sense."

"The hammer represents your wand," Dorian continued. "Fully assembled, it will give you the ability to direct your powers and call upon them at your command, but in pieces their effects are at best undefined. It's just like if I asked you to juggle the pieces of an unassembled hammer. One part could slip and act on its own, not directed at the nail at all."

Ash nodded again in understanding. "If the wand is represented by the hammer, what are the words?"

"Insightful, young Ashley," replied Dorian, "and an excellent question. In this example, it's best to think of the words as making the difference between an untrained man and a carpenter. It's one thing to ask an untrained man to hammer a nail and entirely another task if I asked that same man to build a desk for me. For that one needs not only to have the desire to build a desk and a hammer but also the proper training to bring it into existence."

Dorian paused for a few moments to allow Ash to digest these thoughts. The example made a lot of sense to Ash and seemed much clearer to him than the arcane descriptions Elysium and the Wizard had given him. He liked the way Dorian was able to simplify these concepts, albeit by also avoiding answering his original question entirely.

"Lest you think I've avoided it," continued Dorian, seemingly reading Ash's mind, "let me answer your original question, 'Is it possible to cast spells without words or a wand?' In theory, yes, but in practice I've never known this to be the case. There are stories, from long ago, in which the ancient masters were able to cast spells without the words but never without the wand. This is why you should never be separated from it. It would leave you vulnerable and unarmed—so much so that there are even some overly paranoid mages that attach their wand to their arm with a string or cord."

Satisfied with Dorian's answer, Ash placed his gem near the corner of the desk. He rested his elbow on the desktop and extended his now-empty hand. Dorian reached forward with the wooden rod and handed it to him. This time, as Ash gripped the wand, there were no odd sensations, and he simply felt the texture of the wood against his palm.

"I don't think it's working," he said.

"Without a gemstone at the head of the wand, the sensations will be very slight." Dorian removed the copper rod from the box. "Balance it between your palms," he continued, holding the rod between his open hands. "Like this. This will complete a circuit with your body, and you should feel some slight sensations flowing through you."

Ash followed Dorian's example and placed the wooden rod between his palms. He felt a faint tingling at the points where the rod made contact with his skin. Closing his eyes, he focused on this sensation. A slight but perceptible flow of energy moved up his right arm, across his chest, and down his left arm. The tingling and flow were akin to licking a nine-volt battery with very little power remaining.

"Can you feel it?" asked Dorian.

"Yes, I can feel something, but it's very slight."

"That's normal. The base of the wand by itself will usually only have very mild sensations. The important thing is that you have an energy connection, which is what you feel passing through you now. Most mages feel something with each of these four materials. In fact, the differences between each of the bases are often so slight that many mages believe that, unlike the gemstone at the head, the base is more of a personal preference than anything else. Why don't you try the others and tell me which one you feel the strongest attunement with?"

Ash began by first holding each of the four rods between his palms for a few moments with his eyes closed. Unfortunately, as Dorian had described, the sensations with each of them were very slight and very similar. Ash sorted through the four bases, repeatedly comparing one versus the other to see which felt stronger to him. He was determined to make the best choice possible, though he could barely tell the difference between them. He eventually settled on the copper rod and handed it to Dorian.

"This one feels the strongest to me," he said.

Dorian took the rod from him. "Then your attunement is to metal. The subtleties between the different types of metals are even harder to determine. And this is one area where it could take days or even months to get it one hundred percent right. Very few mages are willing to put that much time into this, and even fewer actually have the perceptive abilities to tell the difference. In this case, I suggest that we go for aesthetics."

Ash definitely had no desire to spend the next few months or even the next few days trying to distinguish between the various different types of metals for the base of his wand. Also, given how close each of the other four materials felt to him, he doubted he would be able to tell the difference anyway. He nodded in agreement.

"So which type of metal would you prefer?" asked Dorian.

Ash had studied various manufacturing compounds in one of his material engineering courses last year. He remembered reading about a metallic material called tungsten carbide. It was created by combining tungsten with carbon atoms and was one of the hardest materials known to man. If he could choose his own substance, then why not have the coolest wand ever made? He could clearly picture himself walking back to the train station with his cool, new, shiny white wand, topped with a brilliant blue sapphire, in his hand.

"Tungsten carbide," replied Ash, half expecting Dorian to deny his request.

"Well, that's a very unique choice. How very…geeky of you," Dorian said, stroking his chin. "It can be done. It'll take a few extra days, but it can be done."

"A few days?" gasped Ash, who had fully expected to have his wand in his hands by the time he had left the Raven's Foot later today.

"Yes, Ashley," replied Dorian. "Crafting a wand takes time, care, and precision. It isn't something one throws together idly in a few hours. I'd be more than happy to put you up at the Hawthorne Hotel until it's ready."

Thoughts of strolling home with his shiny new wand quickly faded, replaced with disappointment. Ash pondered the idea of staying in Salem for a few days, which wouldn't be so bad. He wouldn't mind ditching school for a few days, but then he remembered he was supposed to meet up with Mike and his buddies later tonight.

"I'll have to come back for it. When can I pick it up?" asked Ash.

"I should have it ready for you in no more than seven days."

"Okay, I'll see you then," replied Ash, as he reached over to pick up the blue sapphire from the table.

"You'll have to leave that here," Dorian told him. "It'll be too dangerous to use without being embedded in a wand. You may, of course, take your practice gem with you."

Ash frowned a bit then picked up the clear quartz practice gem. He placed the gemstone in his pocket and made his way to the door. As he put his hand on the doorknob, he heard Dorian putting the rods back in their container.

"Don't forget what I told you about stopping next door to pick up a pair of sunglasses before you head home," Dorian said.

*

The woman at the Broom Closet was still sorting through stones when Ash entered. She stopped and peered up. From under her brown branch-covered hat, a slightly annoyed look appeared on her face.

"You and that Dorian fellow—were you starting a damn earthquake over there?" she asked. "Rumbling, walls shaking, scaring an old lady!"

"I'm so sorry. Dorian asked if I could help rearrange some of his books. I didn't realize we were being so loud," replied Ash.

"It's okay," she said. "Things startle me a bit more these days, and my hearing isn't what it used to be. Can I help you with something?"

"Dorian said you sold sunglasses here. It's getting kind of bright outside, and I wanted to buy a pair."

The woman turned around to look outside. It was neither bright nor sunny. In fact, it looked like it might start to rain sometime soon. She looked back at Ash with a puzzled expression. Meanwhile, Ash was glancing at the stones on the counter in front of him.

"We only have a few. They're in the back," said the woman, as she pointed her finger down the aisle.

"Also, I was wondering," said Ash as he looked up at her, "do you have any sapphires?"

CHAPTER 8

FOR SAFEKEEPING

The man known as the Wizard arrived late in the evening in Washington, DC. The council had informed him that there was an odd energy surge in the area, but they were unable to determine its exact location. It had the signature of a portal opening.

The Wizard knew of only one relic that could cause this, and he wanted to make sure it was safe. Most of these items were relatively harmless in the hands of mortals, but in the hands of someone or something with ill intent, the story was entirely different.

The relic had been on display in one of the Smithsonian National Museums for several years, so he had every reason to suspect its use. It was a relatively nondescript item and didn't garner much attention from viewers or researchers. They had no idea of the power that dwelled within it.

The Wizard knew one of the curators there, Professor Ian Keller, and had consulted with him in the past. There was always a careful dance when having conversations with Ian. Though the Wizard could never reveal his true identity or his real depth of knowledge of items of arcane origin, he considered him a friend and someone who could be trusted. He hoped he'd be working tomorrow.

The museum wouldn't be open again until the next day, so the Wizard found a nearby hotel and retired to bed.

The next morning, he stood in front of the mirror, pinning a small upside-down silver emblem of a shield bearing the symbols "ᘱU" onto his cloak. Once it was attached, he twisted it until it was facing upright. When he did this, his cloak and other attire morphed into a gray English-cut wool suit with a slim darker-gray tie. Looking satisfied, he headed over to the museum.

He arrived early at the Smithsonian's Information Center well before it was open to the public. It wasn't out of eagerness; he was just hoping to catch Professor Keller before the museum opened and he became distracted with his other duties.

Across the street from the museum was a small doughnut and coffee shop. He stopped there to pick up two cups of coffee and a selection of doughnuts. These would serve him well in a few minutes, or at least he hoped.

He walked back across the street then around the museum to the rear entrance. There he spotted a security station, where a small flow of museum workers were filing in. He didn't see Professor Keller; perhaps he was already inside.

The Wizard approached the security station. The guard seated inside was a heavyset man with a shaved head and wearing a white short-sleeved shirt. Over his left chest was a dull silver badge, and an ID tag with his picture on it hung from a pocket on his right. The Wizard knocked on the window to get the guard's attention. It seemed as if the man vaguely recognized him. He raised the bag of doughnuts and cups of coffee in the air. The guard smiled.

"Thanks, man," said the guard, as he accepted the coffee and doughnuts.

"You're welcome," replied the Wizard. "Say, do you know if Professor Keller is working today?"

"Yeah, I just let him in a few minutes ago, but don't think I'm going let you in just because you brought me coffee and doughnuts."

"I'd never dream of it. I just remembered that you liked them."

The Wizard was taking a gamble. The truth was he didn't know if he'd ever seen this guard before. But the man appeared to have recognized him, and besides, he always brought coffee and doughnuts when he came here, so there was a good chance this would work.

"Can't believe you remembered, Mr. Zauberer," the guard said with a smile. "So many people just walk on by, never paying attention to me. Tell you what, I'll give Professor Keller's office a call and see what I can do."

"That would be much appreciated," said the Wizard.

"Okay, just give me a minute."

The guard slid the glass window closed and picked up an old telephone hanging on the wall. Although the Wizard could see he was talking to someone, he couldn't make out his words. A few moments later, the guard opened the window and leaned out slightly.

"Professor Keller said he'll be right down," he said. "You can wait over there."

"Thanks again," said the Wizard.

"No, thank *you* for the coffee and doughnuts," the guard said, as he opened the bag and removed a glazed doughnut.

A few minutes later, Professor Keller arrived at the rear door. He was an older gentleman, in his late fifties. His silver hair was slightly thinning, but he looked to be in good shape for a man of his age. He wore a simple blue suit with a thin beige tie. The tie bore the marks of splattered coffee and perhaps some of his breakfast. The Wizard recalled that he was always a bit clumsy.

"Good to see you," said the Wizard.

"What a pleasant surprise. Good to see you as well," replied the professor. "It's been a long time."

The professor looked at the guard and said, "Can you please put Mr. Eric Zauberer down as a guest for the day?"

"Already done," said the guard with a smile.

"Shall we go inside?" the professor asked the Wizard as he stood to the side and motioned him into the building.

The two engaged in a brief but pleasant conversation on their way to Professor Keller's office. Their interactions had become increasingly sparse over the years, but despite the passing of time, they still considered each other friends.

The Wizard recalled the first time they had met, but the more interesting and more relevant story was the first time the Wizard had to ask the professor for a favor.

*

It was many years ago. The Wizard was sitting outside Professor Keller's office, waiting for him to return from lunch. In the large briefcase next to his feet was a relic of immense power. He had just recovered it during his travels to Peru.

The professor almost walked past him before the Wizard said, "Professor Keller!"

"Oh, I'm sorry. I didn't see you sitting there," replied the professor.

The Wizard smirked. "That happens to me more often than you know."

"Please come in." The professor fumbled with his keys, dropping them on the floor. He shook his head as he picked them up then unlocked the door and motioned the Wizard in.

Professor Keller's office was far from modest. It didn't suit his quiet demeanor or humble nature at all. Sunlight poured in through the floor-to-ceiling windows. A large bookshelf with an almost uncountable number of historical books lined an entire wall. Numerous ancient sculptures and trinkets sat in glass stands, almost as if they were part of a mini museum on their own.

"Thank you for seeing me on such short notice," said the Wizard, as he took a seat in one of the plush chairs arranged in a comfortable seating area near the windows.

"You said it was important," responded the professor, who sat behind a vast oak desk.

"It is, and I need to ask you for a favor."

Professor Keller smiled. "I'll do it if I can."

"I need you to hold something for me," said the Wizard, "to hide it in plain sight."

Intrigued, the professor asked, "What is it?"

"I have it right here." The Wizard opened the briefcase, pulled out the relic, and faced it toward the professor.

Professor Keller got up from his chair and wandered over to the seating area to have a better look. The disc-shaped artifact was slightly larger than two feet in diameter and close to a half foot in thickness. It was made of a lightweight petrified wood and was decorated with a multitude of faded overlapping crude paintings, including a large one in the center of a sun. By the way the Wizard handled it, the professor could tell it was quite heavy.

"It's exquisite!" exclaimed Professor Keller. "It's Incan, yes?"

FOR SAFEKEEPING

The Wizard knew the relic wasn't of Incan origin, but he also knew it had been in the Incans' possession for some time, and they had added their own drawings and paintings on top of it. He also knew the item of real value was encased within the relic before them.

"I believe so," replied the Wizard.

"I'd love to have this piece! What are you asking for it?"

"As I said, I just need you to hold on to it and promise me that it'll never leave this facility."

Professor Keller raised a bushy eyebrow. "So you're donating it?"

"Something like that," replied the Wizard.

"Then I'll fetch the paperwork."

"That's where part of the favor comes in," said the Wizard. "You can put the relic on display, but I want no paper trail, and I also need your word that it won't be examined or tampered with. Can you do that?"

"Um…I think we can do that. We'll simply say the donor wishes to remain anonymous and has certain conditions. It's a little unusual, but we've made some similar arrangements in the past with some of our more eccentric donors."

"Great. Much appreciated," replied the Wizard. "Then I'll leave it in your care."

Professor Keller looked at the Wizard in anticipation, and the Wizard knew exactly what he wanted. In previous encounters, the Wizard always had shared with him an interesting story about the item. The professor had a wide breadth of historical knowledge and didn't always believe the stories, but he still loved to hear them. The Wizard was always careful not to give away too much detail and tended to set his tales in certain civilizations, though many of the items in his possession dated much further back. And so the Wizard indulged Professor Keller.

The Wizard started his tale. "In ancient Incan mythology, the universe was created by a supreme deity called Viracocha. He divided the universe into three realms called *pachas*. His children were gods in their own right and occupied these realms.

"The upper realm was called Hanan Pacha. It was home to the benevolent deities, led by Inti, the sun god. Inti's right-hand soldier and best friend was Apu, the god of the mountains.

"The middle realm was called Kay Pacha. It was home to the mortals and represented the world we live in.

"The lower realm was called Uku Pacha. It was known as the underworld and was home to the malevolent deities. The most powerful of these and the ruler of the realm was Supay, the god of death.

"It's important to note that the Incans hadn't originally conceived the gods from either of the other realms to be truly good or evil. This didn't occur until European settlers enforced their own religious beliefs upon them. However, the deities from Hanan Pacha were worshiped, and those from Uku Pacha were feared.

"The realms were connected not only on a spiritual level but also on a physical one. The Incans believed Kay Pacha was the gateway between the other two realms. Hanan Pacha could be reached by ascending a rainbow, and Uku Pacha could be reached by traveling down into deep and dark forbidden caves.

"The Incans also believed that while Hanan Pacha and Uku Pacha were eternal, the world that we know, Kay Pacha, had been destroyed and re-created several times. In the world's previous incarnation before this one, the deities from the other realms visited our world quite often.

"The deities from both realms instigated many wars, and the mortals suffered, which deeply saddened Viracocha. So one day, when most of the gods from the other realms were on Kay Pacha, Viracocha severed the ties between the worlds. The rainbows disappeared, and the deep caves collapsed in on themselves.

"The deities on both sides knew that while they were cut off from Hanan Pacha and Uku Pacha, if their physical forms died, their spirits would be unable to return home and therefore would be utterly destroyed. While this made them fearful, it also presented them with a unique opportunity. If they could kill the deities from the other realm during this time, they would be rid of them forever.

"Colossal battles took place that shook heaven and earth. As the conflict raged over the course of years, many mortals were slain. Unable to enter Hanan Pacha or Uku Pacha, their spirits remained trapped in this world. Supay, the god of death, learned to absorb these souls to strengthen his power. With each death in every battle, he grew stronger, and Inti knew that soon he would become so powerful that he would be unstoppable.

"It was then that Inti asked his best friend, Apu, to accept a dangerous task. Inti wielded a great sun disc that had the ability to tear through space and time, creating violent portals to the other realms that sucked in anything in its path. If they got close enough to Supay, they could use it to send him back to the underworld, freeing all the spirits he had absorbed. Without hesitation Apu accepted.

"The deities engaged in one final massive battle. In the center of the battlefield was Supay. His power had grown so enormous that he was wiping out hundreds of mortals at a time, and no deity dared approach him—except for Apu.

"When the opportunity presented itself, Apu leaped in front of Supay with Inti's sun disc in hand. He gripped the disc with both hands, pointed it at Supay, and started to speak the command word that Inti had taught him, but Supay reacted too quickly. He knocked

Apu to the ground with a nearly fatal blow. Then he walked over to Apu's body and placed one foot on his back as a sign of victory.

"As all deities like to do, this was when Supay gloated. He was so consumed in his braggadocio that he didn't realize Apu was very much still alive and slowly reaching for the sun disc. When Apu's fingertips touched the disc, he spoke the command word.

"An immense portal of red energy shot into the heavens. At first its force knocked back all the combatants in the area, but then it changed direction and started to suck in everything around it. Supay flew uncontrollably through the air and was nearly sucked in but managed to grab Apu's legs. Apu was the god of the mountains, and the earth was his to command. He dug his fingers deep into the dirt and told it to hold onto him. The ground obeyed, soil and root wrapped tightly around his hands, but it wasn't enough. The portal continued to pull them in.

"Just as Apu was about to be sucked in, Inti emerged on the scene. He fell to the ground and reached toward Apu, who quickly accepted his friend's hand. As Inti pulled to save Apu, he noticed he was also saving Supay, for Supay was still holding on to Apu's legs.

"It was then that Inti did the unthinkable. He released Apu's hand. Apu and Supay were sucked into the portal to dwell in the underworld forever."

While the Wizard finished his story, Professor Keller was resting his chin on his hand, listening intensely. Though some of the elements in the story seemed accurate, he didn't believe most of the tale. Even so, he smiled broadly.

"My friend," said the professor, "that might be one of the best Incan legends I've ever heard. I'd be happy to help you out and even happier to have the relic as part of the museum's collection."

*

FOR SAFEKEEPING

Professor Keller led the Wizard into his office. It was exactly the same as the Wizard had remembered, far from modest and not suited at all for the professor. As he looked around, he noticed that some of the sculptures and other relics on display had changed, but otherwise it was the same. They walked over to the seating area and sat down.

"Ian, I need to ask you about that artifact I asked you to store for me a few years ago," said the Wizard.

Professor Keller nodded. "Ah, yes, the Incan sun disc."

"Is it still here, under your care?"

"Of course. I gave you my word. It's still part of our Incan exhibit, safely behind a glass display case."

"Are you absolutely certain?" asked the Wizard.

"I haven't been down to examine it personally in quite some time, but I have no reason to believe otherwise. We can go check on it if you wish."

"Do you know if anyone has examined it or tampered with it?" asked the Wizard.

Professor Keller leaned forward in his seat, his interest clearly piqued. "Not that I'm aware of, but if it puts your mind at ease, I can check the log files."

"Would you please check for me?"

"Of course."

Professor Keller got up and headed to his desk, slightly stumbling over a small raised area of the floor on his way. He sat down and typed away on his computer. Rubbing his chin, he read through the entries related to the Incan exhibit. After a few moments, his eyes widened. He leaned over and looked at the Wizard.

"Um, Eric, there does appear to be an entry here from a few days ago."

"What does it say?" the Wizard asked with a slight look of panic.

"According to this entry, there was a Professor Markus Albrecht from New York University here a few days ago. He was doing some research on the sun god Inti and was given private access to the Incan exhibit. It says he was there for a few hours, but there's no record of his leaving with anything."

"Do you know this Professor Albrecht?" asked the Wizard.

Professor Keller shook his head. "No, I've never heard of him before. However, I do know the dean who runs the Institute for the Study of the Ancient World at New York University. I could give him a call and see if he's heard of him if you like."

"Perhaps later. Right now I'd like to take you up on your offer to check on the sun disc."

"We'll head right over," said the professor.

The Smithsonian National Museums encompassed several buildings spread along more than a mile. The Incan exhibit was on display at the National Museum of the American Indian, located down the road from the Smithsonian Information Center. On a nice day, it would be a pleasant walk. But Professor Keller could tell the Wizard was worried, and he wanted to put his mind at ease as quickly as possible. So he offered to drive them.

The National Museum of the American Indian had a design befitting its name and contents. The building was made of curved yellow stone and had a cave-like appearance. The windows intermingled with the surface of the building as if they'd been added later and now enclosed once-open areas. The roof of the structure extended out past its base, providing shade beneath and adding to the Native American ambiance.

The museum was still closed when they arrived, and the large glass front doors were locked. Professor Keller rapped on the window until a security guard appeared. Upon recognizing the professor, he opened the door and let the two of them in.

The Incan exhibit was located on the fourth floor. The Wizard and Professor Keller made their way to the elevator but soon realized it wasn't turned on yet, so they had to use the stairs. Though the Wizard was eager to reach the exhibit as soon as possible, the professor was a mortal man no longer in his youth, so he kept his pace reasonable. When they eventually reached the top, Professor Keller directed them to the main Incan exhibit area.

The gallery was a winding maze of displays filled with artifacts from the many ancient cultures that once had inhabited the South American continent. Those related to Peru and Incans were located near the back. They weaved through the gallery until they arrived at the glass display case where the sun disc was housed.

The professor was still catching his breath when he said, "See, Eric? There it is."

The Wizard stepped toward the glass case, trying to examine the sun disc closer. He couldn't sense any magical forces around the disc. Something was wrong.

"Would you mind if I had a few minutes alone with it?" asked the Wizard.

"Of course not. Would you like me to get one of the security guards to open the display case for you?" asked the professor.

The Wizard shook his head. "That won't be necessary."

"Okay, I'll leave you to it then. The museum won't be open for another hour or so. I'll meet you downstairs when you're done."

"Much appreciated, Ian. I won't be long."

Every object carries with it a history of all those who have interacted with it. It carries their signature like a fingerprint. In the arcane arts, the ability to perceive this history is known as psychometric reading.

Once Professor Keller had left the room and the Wizard heard his footsteps descend the stairs, he dropped his illusionary facade by twisting the shield emblem on his jacket. Standing there in his cloak, he removed his wand. The wand was a short gnarled branch, etched by flames and tipped with a faceted amethyst. He stood back several feet and pointed the wand at the display case. Then he chanted, "ᚹᚸᚷᛉᛗ (MA-TIMO)."

The purple gemstone on top of the Wizard's wand glowed. He lifted his free hand into the air and motioned it toward himself, as if pulling the space backward. Before him he saw a ghostly image of himself walking toward the display case. When the image reached the case, a ghostly image of Professor Keller appeared, walking backward into the room. The Wizard was replaying time.

He pulled his hand back farther, and the ghostly images of the many visitors to the exhibit came in and out of view at an increasingly faster pace. He saw groups of children on a field trip, a family on vacation, a man in a seersucker suit, a security guard on break, and many other individuals. The Wizard's hunch was that something must have transpired during Professor Albrecht's visit a few days ago. Suddenly a blur of red appeared in the area around the disc. The Wizard stayed his hand then slowly pushed it in the direction of the display case, which made the images before him move forward in time.

When he reached the point of the red blur, he rewound and fast-forwarded time over and over, but something was wrong. The images were like a cloud of red dust floating in the area around the disc. Either something was moving incredibly fast, or something was purposefully obscuring his vision for that period of time.

He refined his search, trying to look for any clues as to what was going on. Eventually he stumbled across a very brief moment where the disc disappeared then reappeared. Someone or something had tampered with it. Whether or not the disc before him right now was a copy didn't matter; what did matter is that the contents of the sun disc were likely missing.

The Wizard ceased his spell and tucked his wand back into his cloak. As he twisted the emblem on his cloak, his form shifted and again took on the appearance of a gray wool suit. He made his way to the staircase and headed downstairs. He would have to inform the council about this.

When he reached the bottom of the stairs, he saw Professor Keller talking to a security guard. As he was walking over, the professor spotted him and politely ended his conversation with the guard.

"Did you find what you were looking for?" Professor Keller asked.

The Wizard nodded. "Unfortunately, yes. My suspicions were correct. Someone has tampered with the disc."

"You have my sincerest apologies," said the professor. "I'll correct this in any way I can. What would you like me to do?"

"I assume the relic was properly photographed and cataloged before it was put on display?" asked the Wizard.

"Of course. All items in our museums are."

"Then I'll need you to pull those files and have someone examine the sun disc to see if there are any discrepancies," said the Wizard.

"I'll have someone on it as soon as we get back to the office. May I ask what you're looking for?"

"I think what you have on display is a very convincing copy, but I can't be sure."

"Do you think this Professor Albrecht might have had anything to do with it?" asked the professor.

"I can't be certain, but it's quite likely," the Wizard said. "I think I'll take you up on that offer to contact your friend at New York University. Please find out what you can about this Professor Albrecht."

"Of course. I'll give him a call right away. Anything else?"

"That's it for now," said the Wizard. "Thanks for your help. I'll need to be on my way. There are some people I need to inform about this. Please contact me as soon as you know anything."

"I will," replied the professor.

*

The Wizard delayed his return back to Boston and to Ash. Over the next few days, he continued his investigation of the stolen relic and reported his findings back to the council.

A further examination of the sun disc revealed that while it wasn't a copy, someone had in fact tampered with it. A seam was visible along its circumference that didn't appear in any of the original photographs. Also, upon weighing it, Professor Keller found it to be several pounds lighter than when it was first cataloged.

Professor Keller's contact at New York University revealed that Professor Albrecht was in fact on their staff but had recently taken an extended leave of absence. When his records were examined further, they were found to be incomplete, and he had no known address or other method of contact listed. Those he associated with had only a vague memory of him and were almost unable to describe him at all. Something was definitely amiss.

CHAPTER 9
JACK OF ALL TRADES

Jack had lost a great deal of weight over the years, and while he was still far from thin, by the time he graduated from high school he had a medium-size build, and the nickname "Fat Jack" had long been forgotten. It would still be a few more years before he would become known under the alias "Smiling Jack," and for now he was simply known as Jack. Over the years, he had remained close friends with Bruce, who was still thin as a rail.

Jack's powers had grown immensely. He was now able to trigger his ability to see into the future at any time, by his will alone, and no longer required any aids. He also realized that when he used his powers too often, his eyes would maintain a red glow for an extended period of time. For this reason, he used his power sparingly in public and carried with him a pair of dark sunglasses at all times.

After graduating from high school, Jack landed a job in New York City at a brokerage firm. Using his ability, he was able to see trades days in advance and quickly rose from an office assistant to the firm's most promising young trader. Within a few months, he was able to afford a large loft condo right in the heart of the city. Bruce moved in with Jack shortly after and attended New York University, where he was pursuing a degree in veterinary science.

One afternoon, Jack and Bruce were sitting on their couch with their legs resting on the coffee table. An enormous curved television was mounted on the wall in front of them. They were furiously competing in an epic video game battle. Ever since Bruce was a kid, he had had the oddest habit of jolting his controller up and down and left and right, as if trying to control his on-screen character with these motions. This always brought a smile to Jack's face.

"You're cheating again, aren't you?" exclaimed Bruce.

"I don't need to see the future to tell you how this is going to end!" responded Jack.

At that moment, the flailing of Bruce's hands got the better of him. As he jerked his hands sharply to the right, he smacked a glass of soda on the table next to him. The drink went flying off the table and sprayed the beverage over the side. As Bruce looked over to see the mess that he should have made, he noticed someone already had placed a towel in the exact location that his drink would have spilled its contents. He looked over at Jack, who was laughing loudly.

"You know I hate you, right?" said Bruce.

"Then you're really going to hate this part," said Jack, as his on-screen character dealt a fatal gunshot to the back of Bruce's character's head. "And that, my friend, is game!"

Bruce tossed his controller to the side and got up from the couch. Even though the towel had caught most of his soda, there was still a small mess to clean up. After soaking up the rest of his drink, he rolled up the towel and headed for the kitchen. On his way, there was a knock at the door.

"While you're up, can you get that?" Jack asked, as he clicked the button to start a new game.

"Sure," Bruce muttered. He placed the towel in the sink and headed to the door.

Before Bruce could reach the entrance, there was another knock. This time it was harder and louder. He peered through the peephole before opening the door and saw it was Stevie, his cousin. Stevie was a little more than five years older than Bruce. He and his parents had moved to the city while Bruce was still in middle school. Before Bruce had left home, his parents had warned him to avoid Stevie. They said he rolled with a bad crowd and was nothing but trouble. Until now Bruce had taken their advice. He wondered how Stevie even had found him. He opened the door.

Stevie was a few inches shorter than Bruce but had several other characteristics that clearly identified them as kin. He had a shaggy orange mane that hung like a furry bowl around the top of his head, stopping at his eyebrows. His freckles were more pronounced than Bruce's, especially around his cheeks. A pair of rimless glasses rested on his nose, and he was dressed in a blue workout suit.

"Bruce! Good to see you. It's been a long time. How are you? Can I come in?" he said in a hurried voice.

Before Bruce could even open his mouth, Stevie had made his way past him and was headed inside.

"Sure, come right in," Bruce whispered to himself as he stared out into the hallway and slowly closed the door.

Stevie raised his arms in the air, as if he were giving a long-distance hug, and yelled, "Jack!"

"Stevie!" responded Jack in a loud, somewhat sarcastic tone, never taking his eyes off the video game in front of him.

"I bet you're both wondering what I'm doing here. Am I right?" asked Stevie.

Bruce and Jack began to open their mouths to respond, but Stevie had started talking again.

"Well, you see, I'm opening up a new club called the Venue tonight, and look what I have right here." He unzipped the top of his jogging suit and pulled out an envelope. "Two VIP tickets, baby! You two are going to be my special guests!"

The warning from Bruce's parents echoed through his head as he said, "You know, Stevie—"

"VIP! Awesome! What time do you want us there?" interrupted Jack.

"Show up anytime you want. The place will be open early, but it won't really get going until ten."

"Then we'll be there at eleven," said Jack.

"Sweet. I'll leave your tickets right here," said Stevie, as he placed the envelope on a table next to the couch. "Well, boys, I gotta run. I'll catch you later. I'll let myself out."

As quickly as Stevie had entered, he was out the door and gone. Bruce strolled over to the couch and retook his seat next to Jack. He picked up his controller then tilted his head as he stared directly at Jack with a disapproving look.

Without looking at Bruce, Jack said, "Oh, wipe that frown off your face. This is going be fun. Wait a second—I changed my mind. Keep the frown. It'll make your defeat more bearable."

Jack smiled and started a new game. Bruce quietly tilted his head back toward the screen. He knew there was no way he would win this next game, let alone an argument about going to the club.

*

JACK OF ALL TRADES

It was that night that everything changed for Jack. Growing up in a small, sheltered suburb, he'd never been exposed to the many vices that the night could offer. The Venue was a large over-the-top nightclub with two sprawling dance floors, several bars, and seating areas for invited guests or those willing to pay top dollar. The DJs played a mash-up of hip-hop, house, and pop music, creating a vibrant, energetic atmosphere. The drinks flowed freely; there were women; there were drugs—and Jack loved all of it. While Bruce was fascinated as well and had a good time that first evening, the thickness and pushing of the crowds weren't his thing, and he often retreated to the comfort of the seating area that Stevie had set up for them. After their first visit to the Venue, Jack returned many times, often without Bruce.

The drugs, in particular, had some odd effects on Jack's abilities. When he took stimulants like cocaine or ecstasy, he often slipped in and out of reality, hopping into the future at erratic and unexpected times. These episodes were also filled with a detachment from reality. Alcohol, cannabis, and other depressants had the opposite effect; they limited his ability to see future events. Being conscious of this, he carefully monitored his intake of stimulants and was careful never to take too much. He probably should have stayed off them entirely, but he had grown to like the feeling of disassociation they provided.

Jack's work soon began to suffer, as his ability to predict the future had become erratic at best, and he often showed up to work late or not at all. Yet when he was on his game, he was unstoppable, and overall he made more good trades than bad. It seemed as if no matter how badly people perceived him, as long as he made significantly more money at the end of the day for the firm than he lost, they would tolerate anything.

In an altered state, one night Jack revealed his secret to Stevie. At first Stevie didn't believe him, but he soon came to realize there were truths to Jack's words, and there was indeed something very special about him. Stevie would coax him into doing stimulants then ask him questions about the outcomes of upcoming sporting events. Jack couldn't help but comply. Though his predictions often were intermingled with dreams, he was right most of the time, and he made Stevie a lot of money. This behavior continued for months, but one night Stevie took things too far.

It was late at night. Bruce was fast asleep on the couch at the condo. He had passed out watching a movie, and the flicker of the credits on the screen provided the only lights in the room. The volume on the television was turned down to a whisper.

With a loud bang, the door to the condo burst open. Jack was barely holding himself up between the door and the wall next to it. Red flames oozed from behind his sunglasses. He pulled them off, and the room filled with a bright red light, shooting in all directions. He screamed as if he were in a tremendous amount of pain.

Thoroughly startled, Bruce jumped off the couch. In an instant, he went from lying down and sleeping to standing and being completely awake. He looked at the doorway, where Jack was on his knees, covering his eyes with his hands. Red light leaked brightly from between his fingers. Bruce ran over to see what was going on.

"He's here! He can see me!" yelled Jack.

*

It was late at the Venue. Jack and Stevie had gone upstairs to Stevie's office. The room was gigantic and covered the same area as one of the dance floors directly below it. At one end of the room was a large glass desk with a leather chair behind it and two in front of it. It was here that Stevie handled the ins and outs of his business. Along one of the edges was a long bar with a fully stocked liquor selection behind it. At the other end of the room was the entertainment area. It had a curved sofa that faced a large flat-screen TV and was framed by floor-to-ceiling windows that looked out toward the city.

Jack had been in this room many times. A bit exhausted and a little drunk, he made his way to the sofa and took a seat. Though he could barely hear it, he could feel the rhythm of the music from below pulsing through his feet. Stevie walked over to the bar and pulled various bottles from the shelves.

As Jack sat there, he drifted away.

*

It was dark. Then an image began to come into focus, at first blurry and then with more and more clarity. Jack could see he was in an extensive study. A magnificent fireplace burned along the wall. He was seated in the corner of an enormous couch. His hands were on his lap. They looked wrinkled and older, and he felt heavier than he remembered.

A beautiful woman lay across from him on another couch, staring at the ceiling with one hand over her forehead. She wore an elegant black dress that hugged her form. Long blond hair draped down the sides of her face. Her full, deep-red lips were moving, but Jack heard no sounds.

Three forms emerged from the top of the woman's couch. Unlike the rest of his vision, they were still blurry and had a smoky aura swirling around them. Jack was only able to roughly make out their shapes. They looked like little gargoyles. Two of them appeared to be no more than a foot in height and sat crouched at the center of the couch. A larger one, perhaps two feet tall, sat closer to the woman's head and appeared to be peering at him.

Slowly sounds began to fill his ears. At first there was only static. Then he clearly heard every crackle of the wood burning in the fireplace as though the sounds were being amplified. Soon the other noises in the room followed. Eventually they faded to a normal volume, and he was able to hear the woman speaking.

"We know where he is. Why don't we just go there and get him?" she asked.

For a moment Jack assumed she was speaking to him. He had no idea what this lady was talking about. While he pondered the best possible way to respond to her, he heard another voice. This one sounded very deep and dark.

"If only it were so simple, Sarah. This boy is protected. The Blessed have taken him into their care."

When Jack looked over toward where the voice was coming from, he saw a lone figure in a long black cloak. The mantle covered his entire body, and a cowl covered the top part of his face. His arms were crossed in front of him, and his pale hands were tipped with sharp black claws. As his lips moved above his black goatee, Jack saw that his teeth were sharp as well.

"All right," said the woman, "then can't Jack just use his ability to look into the future and tell us when the best opportunity would be to grab him?"

"Jack already has played his part in helping us locate the boy," replied the figure. "Looking too deeply into events yet to pass isn't wise, as Jack well knows."

Jack had no idea what this man was talking about.

The woman slowly sat up and stared straight into Jack's eyes. He noticed that her eyes were like his. They swirled with smoky red flames.

"Come on, Jack," she said. "You can do it. I'll be your special friend."

Her lips put on a flirtatious smile, and Jack couldn't help smile back. This woman was absolutely stunning. Everything about her was flawless and beautiful. Never in his life had a woman like this shown him the slightest bit of interest.

Thinking this must be a dream, Jack responded, "Of course I'll do it."

*

Jack snapped back to reality. He was still sitting on the couch in Stevie's office. His exhaustion must have gotten the better of him. He looked over at Stevie, who was still busy mixing drinks behind the bar.

"You know, Stevie," said Jack. "I'm exhausted. It might be best if I went home."

"Hold on, buddy," said Stevie, as he continued to work on the drinks. "Just give me a few more seconds. It'll be worth the wait."

With hesitation, Jack replied, "Okay…maybe just one more."

Stevie walked over and handed Jack a drink.

"What is this?" asked Jack.

"It's a surprise. You'll like it. I made it especially for you."

Jack took a small sip. The drink tasted fruity, with only a slight hint of alcohol. He already had slipped into a daydream and didn't want to risk having some sort of episode tonight. The drink was delicious, however, and before he knew it, he had consumed most of it.

"This is great," said Jack. "What's in it?"

"Passion fruit puree, lime, soda, dark rum, a pinch of sugar, and a little pick-me-up," replied Stevie.

"A pick-me-up!" exclaimed Jack as he spat some of the drink back into his glass.

"Yeah," Stevie said with a smirk. "You seemed a little tired and down. I wanted to keep partying with you."

"What did you put in this?" Jack asked, panic in his voice.

"Oh, calm down. It's just a tiny bit of cocaine," Stevie said, then paused. "Well, okay, you got me. It was more than a tiny bit."

"You don't know what you've done!" exclaimed Jack.

Steve grinned broadly. "Oh, yes, I do."

*

A soft wind blew against Jack's face. He was standing at the edge of a cliff. Waves crashed against the side of a rock face several hundred feet below. His feet were bare and hung halfway off the edge. His hands were stretched out to his sides. A dark voice echoed behind him.

"It's a shame it had to come to this," said the voice.

Jack tried to turn his head but couldn't. It was as if he were being controlled by something, a puppet master without the need for strings. He was terrified; his body was frozen and faced forward. Then he felt his feet slowly inch toward the edge.

"You should have reconsidered before helping him," continued the dark voice. "He isn't one of us. He's one of them. And betrayal can't be tolerated."

Jack went over the edge. He felt the air rush up against his face and body. The water and rocks below were quickly approaching. He wanted to close his eyes but couldn't. He wanted to scream but couldn't. It was all going to be over soon.

"Good-bye, Jack," whispered the voice.

*

Jack's heart started to race. The cocaine was in his system, and there was nothing he could do about it now. He closed his eyes and tried to recall one of the many mind-calming techniques he had learned as a kid. If he could hold on until the drug cleared his system, he might be okay.

"You see, Jack," said Stevie, "I have this problem—a problem only you can help me with."

Jack was trying to ignore Stevie and focused his attention within himself.

I see you, whispered a dark, deep voice in his head.

Someone else is in here with us, Jack thought, his heart pounding harder and harder.

Vague, blurry images of different times and places flashed before him. For a moment, he was in one place and then another. He was seated in a loud club; a man dressed in a blue hooded robe was talking to him. Then it was late at night, and he was in a train station. He stood there waving as he watched a passenger train leaving. And then the sun was hovering in the sky above a large clock tower, and the crowd around him was speaking in a language he couldn't understand. These were potential futures intermingled with things that might never come to pass. His mind screamed as it tried to hold on to the here and now.

"I don't think I ever told you what I studied in college," said Stevie, as he stood and began to pace in front of the TV. "Philosophy—I know what you're thinking: totally useless degree, right? I used to think so too, but I pulled out an old book the other day and stumbled upon this thing called a paradox. Do you know what that is?"

The voice in Jack's head said, *You've been hiding from me.*

Jack collapsed sidewise on the couch then rolled onto the floor. His body was shaking, and a pressure was building behind his eyes. Stevie paused for a moment to look down at him before continuing to pace in front of him.

"You'll be all right," said Stevie. "And I'll tell you what. After we're done, I'll give you a nice, big, fat roofie. You won't remember a thing."

But I can see you now, said the voice in Jack's head as an image of a dark, cloaked figure emerged in his mind.

"Now where was I?" continued Stevie. "Oh, yeah, a paradox. That's basically when something contradicts itself. One of the most famous paradoxes is about time travel. It's called the grandfather paradox. In this story, a man invents a time machine and travels back in time and murders his grandfather before his father is born. Now, you see, if he killed his grandfather, then he never would have existed. Hence, he never could have traveled back in time. Hence, he never could have killed his grandfather. You get the idea."

On the floor, Jack continued to convulse and shake. He felt as if he were fighting an oncoming sleep with all his might, knowing that a nightmare was on the horizon. Red wisps seeped from the sides of his shut eyes.

"This kind of stuff blows the minds of normal people," Stevie said, taking a seat on the couch. "But you aren't exactly normal, are you, Jack? Now we get to the part that relates to your current predicament. You see, someone stole something very important from me, and you're going to tell me exactly where this thief is. How am I going to do this? Well, I'll tell you how: a paradox. You're going to look into the future and see us driving up to the house of this thief. Then you're going to see us causing him a lot of bodily harm. Do you know why you're going to see this future? Because right after you tell me where this guy is, that's exactly what we're going to do! This might be beyond your normal abilities, but with the amount of cocaine I mixed into that drink, I'm thinking your abilities should shoot through the damn roof."

I can feel your power, whispered the voice in Jack's head. *I'm coming for you.*

*

Jack, unable to move, lay at the bottom of a deep grave. Steep walls of dirt surrounded him, and light seeped in from a rectangular hole in the distance. Far above, people were shuffling back and forth. Their long shadows passed over him. He heard many voices but couldn't make out any words. Then, as if the other voices were being filtered out, one by one he heard a few clearly.

"I'm so sorry," said a voice he didn't recognize.

"I miss him so much," said his mother, sobbing.

"Going to miss you, buddy," said Bruce's voice, though he sounded older.

He wanted to scream, "I'm not dead! I'm down here!" but he had no voice to bring.

A dark, cloaked figure slowly emerged at the top of the hole, casting its shadow deep down into the grave. It blotted out almost all the light, leaving only its silhouette. Jack saw the swirling of red fire around the places where the figure's eyes should have been.

"I told you I'd find you," said the figure in a raspy voice.

*

"He can see me!" Jack yelled, as Bruce held him in his arms and rocked him back and forth.

Jack held his eyes shut tightly, as tears ran down his face and red light seeped out of their corners. In all their years of friendship, Bruce never had seen Jack like this. His powers were out of control, and something needed to be done.

Ever since Jack had started hanging out with Stevie, Bruce feared this day might come. With this in mind, he'd been smuggling sedatives from the vet labs at school and storing them in the condo. The strongest of these was ketamine, a sedative that required an injection.

Bruce laid Jack's head on the floor and headed to the bathroom. He lifted the mirror from the wall; behind it was a safe. Then he scrambled to open the combination lock. In his haste, he fumbled and failed several times. He heard Jack crying and yelling in the other room. Taking a deep breath, he focused and slowly turned the dial. The safe opened, and he grabbed a small vial of ketamine and a syringe wrapped in plastic.

As Bruce rushed out of the bathroom, Jack lay writhing on the floor. Red beams from his eyes created waves of intense illumination that flickered against the walls.

"Make it stop!" cried Jack.

"I'm here, buddy," Bruce said, as he knelt next to him.

He tore open the plastic bag containing the syringe and tossed it aside. After thrusting the needle into the top of the vial of ketamine, he slowly extracted the drug. While he did this, he glanced down at Jack several times. His friend was in a great deal of pain, both physically and mentally. When the syringe was full, Bruce pulled it out and tapped it a few times to make sure the liquid was flowing out of the top. He had done this before a few times on animals but never on a friend.

"I know you hate needles, but this is going to help," Bruce said, as he held Jack down and slowly pushed the needle into his arm.

Bruce held Jack tightly as the drug took effect. Within a few moments, the red faded from the room then from Jack's eyes. Jack soon fell into a deep slumber then lay motionless. A few last tears streamed down his face.

*

When Jack groggily awoke the next morning, he couldn't recall any of the events that had transpired after he had borne witness to his own demise. He didn't know who or what the ominous figure was, but he was damn sure he never wanted to see him again. His brief life in this city and what it meant for him had come to an end.

Bruce helped Jack pack his belongings and drove him back to New Jersey. Jack stayed with his parents for a few days then moved into a small apartment in a crowded housing complex. The money he had tucked away during his time as a stockbroker would go a long way here. Bruce returned to the city and moved into a one-bedroom loft close to New York University. He tried to visit Jack as often as he could, but the commute was long, and his veterinary studies had become very demanding of his time.

Jack knew he never wanted to have another episode like he'd had that night, nor would anyone else who had witnessed what he had seen. For this reason, and driven by fear, he turned to anything that would dull his senses, mostly in the form of alcohol and marijuana.

Being medicated almost all the time, in one form or another, drastically hindered Jack's ability to see the future. He became limited to only being able to see a few seconds—or in rare cases, minutes—of what was to come. Honestly, after what he had experienced, he never wanted to see any further than that ever again.

Jack became a hermit and rarely socialized aside from the occasional visit from his parents or Bruce. The window shades in his apartment were always drawn, as he wanted to shut out the light of the world. He spent most of his days in the dark, sitting on the couch, drinking, smoking weed, eating junk food, and watching television. Steadily he began to put on weight, until one day he saw that pudgy kid from his youth staring back at him in the mirror. Over time depression sunk in, and Jack was no longer the vibrant, successful young man he once was.

Months passed this way, but then one morning, when Bruce stopped by, he found the window shades open and the sun pouring into the apartment. The front door was wide open, and he walked in to look around. He soon found Jack in his bedroom, busily packing. When Jack looked up, there was something on his face that Bruce hadn't seen in a very long time. It was a smile.

"So," said Bruce, "are you going somewhere?"

"Get back to your place and pack your things, buddy," said Jack. "You're coming with me."

"Jack, I've got school, bills, responsibilities. I can't just leave."

"Bruce, the place I have in mind, you won't need to worry about any of that anymore."

"Okay," Bruce replied, raising an eyebrow. "So where exactly are we going?"

"When I woke up this morning, I had an epiphany. I still have power. I don't need to be able to see that far into the future to be somebody. What I need is to be in a place where a few seconds of foresight can make me somebody."

He placed a hand on Bruce's shoulder, pointed out the window, and said, "We're going to Vegas, baby!"

CHAPTER 10

FALLEN ASHES

Ash took a late train from Salem back into Boston. By the time he arrived in Davis Square, it was a little past ten in the evening. The walk from the T Station to the Burren pub was quick, which was good, for there was a slight chill in the air. Once there, he looked around for the Saloon, where he was going to meet up with Mike and a few of their friends.

Unable to find it, he took out his mobile phone and searched for the address of the bar. According to the GPS, it was just a few feet down the street. He walked toward it with his phone out before him, glancing up every so often to look for the bar. Then the GPS told him he had passed it. He turned back around and carefully walked till the GPS told him he was right on top of it. Still he couldn't find it.

Then he spotted something, a small lamplight with SALOON written on it. Below the sign was a relatively nondescript door that looked more like the entrance to an apartment building than a bar.

Odd, he thought. This was the second time today that he was going into a new place whose sign was a simple glass globe.

The doors opened to a steep staircase that led down. At the bottom stood a hefty bouncer dressed in a well-fitting suit and a bow tie. Behind the man was an empty reception desk with a large, ornate, brass-framed mirror hanging on the wall behind it. As Ash approached, he heard the noise of patrons in a room off to the left.

"Password, sir?" said the bouncer.

Ash stood there with a befuddled expression. He had heard that speakeasies often required secret words to get in, but Mike hadn't mentioned anything about one.

"Just kidding," said the bouncer as he smiled. "I will, however, have to see an ID."

A look of relief came over Ash's face. He reached into his jacket pocket. His hand searched for his wallet but instead found a pair of sunglasses and a blue sapphire, both of which he had purchased earlier in the day in Salem. The blue sapphire wasn't of good quality and had cost him a fair amount more than he'd wanted to spend, but he was still excited to have it. Perhaps he would even have the opportunity to try it tonight.

Determining that his wallet must be in his other pocket, he searched that one as well. He quickly found it, removed his ID, and handed it to the bouncer. The bouncer inspected the ID and glanced up at Ash several times.

"Have a good time, sir," he said, as he handed the ID back to Ash.

The Saloon was definitely a unique establishment, much like a speakeasy, as Mike had described it. As Ash entered, he spotted a large U-shaped bar to his right with several patrons sitting around it. The two bartenders behind the bar looked like they'd just stepped straight out of an old black-and-white movie. Each wore a white dress shirt, suspenders, and a tie. They were in constant motion, mixing exotic drinks and taking orders. To the left stood a long, high table. A small group of young people sat around it, talking and laughing. The rest of the bar was comprised of small booths and tables. All were filled with people, enjoying their company and their drinks.

Ash glanced around to see if he could spot Mike or any of his other friends. As he did, a blond waitress, in a dark dress and with tattoos running up her left arm, brushed past him and almost dropped her tray of drinks. She spun around and glared at Ash with a slightly annoyed expression. Unsure what else to do, he shrugged apologetically. She could tell he looked lost, but she simply turned around and kept walking. Ash resumed his search for his friends but couldn't find them anywhere.

He decided to walk farther into the room and soon noticed that over to his right, across from the main bar, was another room. He wandered over to find an open area filled with a series of dining tables. This area was probably used to serve food during the bar's daytime hours but was now being used for excess seating capacity. Over in one of the corners, he spotted Mike, who was standing as he held a martini glass high in the air.

Mike wasn't what one would call a very attractive man, but he made up for it in style and attitude. He wore a decorative cowboy hat, and his long black hair was pulled into a ponytail beneath it. He was mostly clean-shaven, save for a small soul patch under his lip. Both his ears were pierced; he had a large silver loop in one ear and a dark onyx triangle in the other.

His attire varied considerably, depending on the occasion and his mood—but mostly his mood. This evening he wore a black gothic

Victorian coat. It was military in style and featured large copper buttons that were buttoned all the way to the top. He looked more like he was going to a Renaissance faire than a night out on the town, but it worked for him.

Mike spotted his friend and yelled, "Ash!" in a fairly intoxicated voice. "Get over here and give your old buddy a hug!"

As Ash headed to the table, Mike stumbled over his other friends to make his way to him. He gave Ash a very firm hug, slightly spilling some of his martini down Ash's back in the process. Ash wasn't bothered by this; rather, he was happy to see Mike, happy to be away from all the craziness of the past few weeks. He could use a bit of normalness and drunkenness.

"Have a seat. I'll get you a drink," said Mike, motioning Ash to the table and scanning the room for a waitress. When he spotted one, he yelled, "Sophie!"

A redheaded waitress, dressed in a black pantsuit, turned around. By the look on her face, Ash could tell she recognized Mike. This wasn't unusual; Mike was boisterous, loud, and social. He either made friends or enemies wherever he went, sometimes both. The waitress paused and, with a slightly impatient expression, waited to take his order.

"I need a Maker's Mark and Coke for my friend here," hollered Mike, as he pointed at Ash. But before the waitress could even respond, he proceeded to quaff down the entire remainder of his martini then said, "Better make that two."

The waitress smiled. "Okay, two Maker's Mark and Cokes coming right up."

This is going to be one of those nights, thought Ash.

Several hours and several drinks later, Mike and Ash were the only two still left from their group at the Saloon. Sophie was on her way over to their table to deliver them a new round of drinks when Ash spotted two girls taking a seat at the table directly across from them. As he watched the girls, he realized he recognized one of them from school. It was April, the girl he'd asked out a couple of times.

April was a cute girl, in her early twenties, just old enough to make it into the bar. She had shoulder-length blond hair and wore a stylish pair of glasses. Her bare legs and brown boots protruded from beneath a knee-length coat. When she removed her jacket, Ash saw she had on a pinkish-beige low-cut blouse and a brown skirt. Her attention-grabbing attire was far too skimpy for tonight's cold weather, and she rubbed her hands along her arms to warm herself.

Her friend had short hair that was dyed pink and hung just below her eyes. She wore a black silk shirt and a tight pair of gray jeans. She was slightly heavier than April, and skintight jeans probably weren't the best choice for her. She had several piercings in her ears and also a small ring in her nose looping around her left nostril.

Mike caught Ash looking at the girls. "Hey, man," he said, "isn't that the chick you like from your study group? April, right?"

"Yeah," replied Ash in a low, hesitant voice. "I think that's her."

Although Ash knew full well that it was April, he was trying to play it cool, as if he barely recognized her. When Sophie reached them and placed their drinks on the table, her body blocked the view of the girls' table. Ash leaned his head over slightly to continue watching them. Mike, of course, saw this.

"Will there be anything else?" asked Sophie.

"Actually, yes," said Mike. "We'd like to buy those two ladies a round of drinks!"

"No, we wouldn't," interrupted Ash before the waitress could respond.

"So do you or don't you want to buy them drinks?" asked Sophie, trying to decide who to listen to.

Simultaneously Mike said yes, and Ash said no.

"Well," said Sophie, looking at Mike, "when your friend decides to put on his big-girl panties, you let me know."

Mike laughed so hard that he hugged his sides and almost fell over. Ash just sat there, a bit shocked from being insulted by the waitress and a bit embarrassed by the loud laughter emanating from his friend. He was also a bit thankful, as April and her friend hadn't seemed to notice the commotion. Sophie smirked as she collected a few empty glasses and walked over to April's table.

Barely catching his breath, Mike said, "Now that was hilarious! I think I almost pissed myself."

"Yeah, thanks for that. Hysterical," said Ash.

"No, seriously," Mike continued. "I totally have to take a pee now. I'll be right back. Let me know if you discover your nerve."

Ash watched Mike walk to the restroom. Then he looked over at April's table, and the two accidentally and briefly exchanged glances. Ash still felt embarrassed, and when he realized they were looking at each other, he quickly lowered his head and stuck his hands in his pockets. In one of his pockets, he felt the sunglasses and the blue sapphire.

A thought grew in his mind, like a spark turning into a flame. At first it was small, and then it became all consuming. If he was the Blessed One and had all this power, why not use it for his own benefit? Why should he follow the advice of an old man who was obviously less powerful than him? The Wizard was holding him back. If Ash had controlled the minds of an army of rats, perhaps he could influence the thoughts of one girl. What could it hurt?

With his head still down, he pulled the sunglasses from his pocket and placed them over his eyes. Then he returned his hand to his pocket and gripped the blue sapphire in his fist. With his eyes closed and a clear picture of him and April together in his mind, he quietly chanted, "ᘯ| /ᘺW ᔈ| (KI-AWA-SI)."

Behind his sunglasses, a soft blue flame ignited in his eyes. He slowly raised his head and looked at April. She was smiling and heavily engaged in conversation with her friend when she stopped in midsentence and turned her head toward Ash. With a fierce look of desire in her eyes, she slowly licked her lips.

As Mike was making his way back from the restroom, he saw that the two girls were sitting around Ash. April had one arm around him and one of her bare legs wrapped around his. All three were smiling and laughing as if they'd been doing so all night. April toyed with one of her fingers in her mouth as she continued to stare at Ash. Mike was in complete shock. His jaw hung open as he stood motionless, watching them.

Looking up, Ash spotted Mike standing there. With a newfound confidence, he raised his arm and waved him over. Mike wondered what had happened while he was in the restroom. He was unsure which was stranger: the fact that Ash had managed to attract two girls during his brief exit to take a leak or that he was sitting there with a pair of sunglasses on in a very poorly lit area of the bar. He pondered for a moment, deciding what to do, but the answer was obvious—the same thing he had done in all similar situations in his life: roll with it!

"Rock on!" yelled Mike, as he raised his hands in the air and made a pair of horn signs.

As he walked over, Ash tilted his head, suggesting that April's friend, Jennifer, scoot closer to him to make room for Mike. As if upon command, she did so. Mike sat next to her and, grinning wildly, grabbed his drink and took a huge sip. Within a few minutes, their voices resounded throughout the room as they celebrated. They continued to drink and laugh for what seemed like hours.

"Sophie!" Mike yelled as he spotted the waitress. "Another round!"

"Sorry, Mike," replied Sophie. "I told you the last one was last call."

Mike briefly put on a fake frown before turning back to the group with a smirk and a look of mischief.

"I know this great after-hours place," he whispered. "They stay open till the sun comes up. Who's in?"

April leaned in close to Ash and pressed her body against his. She softly blew away some of the hair hanging over his ear and whispered, "I have another idea. Why don't you walk me home instead?"

Ash never had been this close to a woman before, and she was definitely pushing all his right buttons. His spell had worked better than he could have imagined. He had gone from being a loser, whom April wouldn't even have a cup of coffee with, to potentially having sex with her tonight.

With a slightly nervous stutter, he said, "April's tired. I'm going to walk her home."

Mike smiled and winked at Ash. "All right, buddy." He turned toward Jennifer and asked, "How about you? You ready to pass out like these losers or you want to keep this party going?"

"I don't know," she said with some hesitation. "April, are you sure you'll be okay?"

"Oh, I'm going to be just fine," April said, before turning back toward Ash and licking his ear.

"Okay," said Jennifer. "I guess I'm in. You two have a good night."

"I'm sure they will," Mike said with another smirk before turning toward Sophie and yelling, "Check, please!"

*

Ash wasn't exactly using mind control on April. Her will was still her own. However, his spell of attraction had removed her normal social inhibitions and made her perceive him not as he was but rather as the most attractive, interesting man she'd ever laid eyes on. He was no longer that geeky kid in her class—to her he had become the embodiment of everything she'd ever wanted in a man.

That night, after walking April back to her apartment, she invited him in. After hours of making out on the couch, Ash finally worked up the nerve to make his move. He picked up April and carried her into the bedroom. They continued to kiss as Ash moved his hands down her body to remove her skirt.

April reached down to stop him. She took a deep breath, pressed her forehead against his then said, "This is moving a little too fast for me."

His response did not match what was going through his mind as he replied, "Okay, April."

He felt as if she had rejected him yet again and his ego turned to other thoughts. If she would not accept his advances, than perhaps there would be other women that would.

When April awoke the next morning, Ash was gone, but the memory of how she felt about him remained. She tried calling him several times, but he never returned any of her phone calls and avoided seeing her in class, leaving her feeling used and manipulated. He wasn't who she thought he was.

Ash had crossed a line that evening and as the Wizard had cautioned that line became easier and easier to cross until eventually it disappeared entirely. With his abilities, no woman was out of his reach. He went out several nights a week, always to different places and always ending up with a different woman. None of them could resist him. With a few simple words spoken in a whisper, they were his.

He was having the best time of his life. Each evening an increasing sense of power and confidence filled him. Ash had fallen prey to his own desires; there was nothing or no one beyond his abilities. Over the days that followed, he quickly forgot about the lessons and warnings the Wizard had given him. This was something Ash would soon come to regret, for he was only an initiate, and his powers were calling out like a beacon of light in the darkness. A darkness that had a mind of its own and now knew about his presence.

CHAPTER 11
THE GATE

Sebastian had given Aleister strict orders to leave the matters of the map, the Blessed One, and the girl to the other mages. He did his best to obey this decision, but after weeks of trying to resist, he no longer could stand idly by. One night, when the other mages were fast asleep, he slipped out of his room and made his way to the storage chamber at the bottom level of Archmedea. The chamber housed powerful artifacts and relics that had been collected by the mages over hundreds of years. Aleister was looking for one item in particular, something he had helped retrieve many years ago on his first mission for the council. He feared it as much as he needed it.

The chamber was protected by a magical seal that could only be opened with the blood of a council member. Though he'd never been in the chamber before, he was a member of the council and had his blood sampled during his initiation ceremony long ago. There was, however, a slight worry in his head that, based on recent events, his master might have revoked his privileges, but he thought this unlikely. The council had trust in him. A trust he was about to betray.

After descending a staircase, he reached the entrance to the storage chamber. It was a room made entirely of dark black stones. Etched on the ground in the center of the room was a circle surrounded by arcane symbols. Standing before the circle was a pedestal crafted out of white marble. Attached to the top of the stand was a bowl made of copper. As Aleister entered the chamber, the torches along the walls ignited themselves.

Approaching the pedestal, he removed a small dagger from his pocket. He held his hand a few inches above the copper bowl and made a minor incision on the tip of his finger. Blood dripped into the container below. By the time the seventh drop fell, the blood was slowly swirling clockwise around the inside of the bowl. Aleister pulled his hand back. The blood spun faster and faster, until it became a red blur, forming a ring in the bowl. The ring slowly rose upward until it reached the very edge of the bowl's top.

As the blood rose, he heard and saw a rumbling centered around the arcane circle on the ground. In the pattern of a spiral, pieces of the floor within the circle slowly sank. When the stones had finished moving, the blood in the bowl stopped spinning and vanished into the air. A spiral staircase leading down to the storage chamber was revealed.

Aleister walked over to the stairs. The torchlight from the room didn't reach down past the first few steps. He took out his wand, extended it, and raised it above his head. As he chanted "ᛗᚲᛚᛃᚾ (MA-INUNI)," the golden tip of his wand glowed a brighter and brighter white until it illuminated the entire room.

THE GATE

As he cautiously made his way down the steps, a deep feeling of dread crept into his mind. He hadn't fared so well the last time he had encountered the artifact.

*

A much younger Aleister and the man known as the Wizard stood on top of a building in London. It was getting late in the day, and the sun was shedding its last few gasps of light. Cars drove by on the busy street below. Aleister watched the doorway of a building across the street, while the Wizard sat a few feet away in a meditative posture with his eyes closed.

"Tell me again—why are we here?" asked Aleister.

"Just keep watching," replied the Wizard, "and let me know when they've left."

"I don't understand. I mean, they're just mortals. Shouldn't we be doing more important things? You know, like hunting down the Touched?"

"We *are* doing important things," said the Wizard, as he opened his eyes and looked at Aleister. "These mortals possess a powerful artifact, one that could turn the tide of this war even further."

"Okay, but I thought we were always told to let the mortals be."

"Sometimes the rules need to be bent. That's why we're waiting for them to leave," replied the Wizard. "If we do our part correctly, no harm will come to them and they'll never be aware of our involvement. When they return, they'll simply assume someone broke in and stole it…probably blame it on a rival cult."

"Explain to me again what this thing is," said Aleister.

The Wizard sighed. "The mortals are in possession of an ancient relic known as a Seer's Gate. Only two are known to exist. The other remains undetected and undisturbed at the Smithsonian in Washington, DC. In the physical world, a Seer's Gate appears as a large copper torus etched with arcane symbols. With the proper incantations, however, it can be used to open a gateway to another location on this world or even to the realms beyond this one."

"But how would the mortals know the proper incantations or, even if they did, be able to speak them?" asked Aleister.

"You're correct. It's unlikely they'd be able to speak the words of the ancient tongue. However, it isn't impossible. It wasn't so long ago that you couldn't speak the words yourself. In any case, my sources tell me they're also in possession of a book of incantations, and we can't afford to take the risk."

"Do we know what they're trying to do with it?" asked Aleister.

"A Seer's Gate serves two purposes," the Wizard explained. "First, it can be used to view the happenings of faraway locations. Second, it can actually be used as a doorway to travel between these locations. Only a pure-blooded creature or an entire group of highly skilled mages would be able to do the latter. It's beyond the capabilities of a single mage and definitely beyond the capabilities of a coven of mortals."

"Then what's the danger?" said Aleister. "So worse comes to worst, they get to peer at some woman in the shower in London. Big deal."

"The danger," said the Wizard, whose voice had turned very serious, "is that the gateway works in both directions once it's opened. While the mortals may only be able to peer into the realm beyond, something more powerful could step through. The information we have tells us that this cult worships demons and, they're attempting to contact the Nether itself!"

"The realm of the Touched!" exclaimed Aleister.

"Close. It's the realm where those of pure demon blood reside. A place so hellish that it can't be described in words."

"I guess we'd better get that damn disc then!" stated Aleister with a newfound purpose and resolve.

"Have they left yet?" asked the Wizard again, as he closed his eyes and resumed his meditative pose.

"I think the last one just got into his car," said Aleister. "I'll double-check."

Aleister held his wand a few inches in front of his eyes and chanted, "ᐣᐸᗝ ᗩE (MA-RES)" repeatedly. As he did, his vision changed, and the walls of the building in front of him appeared as if they had transformed into a blurry but transparent glass. Though it was difficult to see clearly, he knew the heat signatures of living creatures, and none were present.

"The coast is clear," Aleister said, dropping his arm to his side and turning toward the Wizard.

The Wizard rose slowly. "Then let's get this done."

The two mages walked to the other side of the roof before turning back around.

"Aleister," said the Wizard, placing his hand on the young man's shoulder. "Before we go, there's one thing I must tell you. It's very important that we don't cast any spells while we're in there. The Seer's Gate is a powerful artifact and responds to magic. Even by accident we could trigger it, and it's best that we're overcautious in its presence."

Aleister nodded.

Both mages held their wands in front of them as they sprinted toward the other side of the building. They chanted, "ᐣᐸᗝ ᗝu (MA-VU)" as they ran. When they reached the edge of the building, they jumped off. The two buildings were probably thirty or more feet apart, farther than any normal person could jump, but Aleister and the Wizard weren't exactly normal, and their spells allowed them to leap vast distances. They easily leaped across the street and landed safely on the roof of the other building. Once there, they made their way to a skylight a few feet away.

*

The storage chamber was a vast room filled with boxes stacked upon boxes, each containing ancient items and secrets meant to be sealed away. The room was completely covered in dust. It would take Aleister hours to sort through these and find the Seer's Gate.

He soon found that each box was labeled with what appeared to be the date on which each relic was obtained. Unfortunately for him, the dates weren't from the standard Gregorian calendar with which he was familiar. He thought perhaps they were from the Mayan calendar or perhaps some other ancient culture. It didn't really matter, though, as he didn't know any of these systems in any detail anyway. However, he did know there was a distinct pattern to the numbers, which gave him an idea.

He looked up at his glowing wand and chanted, "ᔕᡝ ⊙ᖺᒎ (MA-OHIV-INUNI)." The white light from the tip of his wand floated into the air. It hovered a few feet above his head, illuminating the room. As he walked a few steps forward then back, it followed his motions. He held his wand close to one of the boxes and chanted, "ᔕᡝ ᒷᡝ (MA-HAVA)." The numbers on the label on the box he was looking at blurred then shifted into a date he could understand. This box was from November 1605.

While Aleister was now able to read all the dates on the boxes, unfortunately they weren't organized in any reasonable order. It took him more than an hour to find the box he was looking for. He would never forget that date. It was burned into his memory, like a brand he'd never be able to remove. His heart pounding, he took a deep breath and opened the container.

THE GATE

*

Aleister and the Wizard dropped through the skylight and into the top floor of the building. Though the cult occupied the entire structure, their activity seemed to be concentrated on the top two floors. This is where they would begin their search.

Much to Aleister's surprise, given the very formal attire of the people leaving the building, the rooms were filthy. The room they'd entered contained old couches covered in blankets. Well-worn sleeping bags lined the floors, and overflowing ashtrays and drug paraphernalia rested on many of the tables. The Wizard told Aleister this was likely a room that was used for drugs and orgies. He explained that such practices weren't uncommon for mortals with an inadequate understanding and gross misinterpretation of magical doctrines.

They decided to split up to cover more ground, for they had no idea how long they had before one of the cult members returned. The Wizard quickly found a staircase leading down. He instructed Aleister to continue to search the top floor while he made his way to the next level. Despite the Wizard's warning about casting spells, this was Aleister's first time in the field, and he held his wand at the ready, prepared for anything that might come at him.

Most of the rooms Aleister searched were as dirty and disorganized as the first, and some were in even worse shape. The doors to all the rooms he encountered were either open or unlocked until he reached one far in the back. This door also seemed to be slightly out of place. It appeared much older than the others and was made of solid wood and had been left unpainted; this was likely a private room reserved for the leader of the cult. The lock and handle of the door were made of tarnished dark iron. He tried to open it, but it was locked.

Usually, in a situation like this, Aleister would just cast an unlocking spell to gain access to the room, but this wasn't an option. If any room on this floor contained the Seer's Gate, this would be the one, and the Wizard had warned him not to use any magic in its vicinity. Unable to think of another way to open the door, he decided to continue searching the other rooms, hoping to find a key to this room.

As luck or fate might have it, in a room nearby, hidden in the pages of a dusty leather-bound book, he found an old iron key. He wondered whether he should wait for the Wizard to return so they could open the door and explore the cult master's room together, but he decided to move forward on his own. Both the key and the lock were old and required a bit of finagling before they clicked and unlocked the door.

The windows of the cult master's room were painted black, and there were no apparent light sources. However, the light from the hallway was sufficient for Aleister to make out most of the room's contents. Directly across from him was a large desk upon which rested many books. Some were stacked on top of one another, while others lay open. The walls were painted dark red. Along one of them was a sparsely populated bookshelf. The entire floor was littered with pieces of paper. Some of the pages contain printed text, while others had handwritten notes and scribbles on them.

Looking closer, Aleister noticed the pages in the center of the floor were stacked higher than the rest of the room, perhaps obscuring something beneath it. He lifted and shuffled the pages around with the tip of his wand, eventually revealing a large copper torus. He jumped back when he realized he had found the Seer's Gate.

THE GATE

His first instinct was to immediately go find the Wizard, but his curiosity got the better of him. He knew that interacting with the Seer's Gate could be dangerous, but what could it hurt to look around the rest of the room a bit? After carefully walking around the torus, he made his way to the desk.

Sifting through the papers on top, he uncovered an old, large, open tome. As he glanced over the pages, he realized they were in the ancient tongue. He recognized most of the words from his training, but there were a few he'd never seen before. Perhaps the mages were keeping things from him.

Unconsciously and in a whisper, Aleister accidentally read one of the words out loud: "ᔑR (NER)."

Suddenly a large column of blood-red energy shot up from the Seer's Gate, bellowing out along the ceiling. At first it was bright, causing Aleister to shield his eyes with his arm, but then it slowly turned into a red reflective column that appeared to be flowing as a liquid. Undaunted by what had just happened, he walked over for a closer look.

As Aleister was approaching the Seer's Gate, something from within suddenly reached out. A pale white hand with clawed fingers gripped his throat. The powerful hand easily pulled him forward. His face was within inches of the red column when a face emerged next to his. It was male but very pale and inhuman and had coal-black eyes that swirled with a red fire about them. A black goatee surrounded the creature's mouth, and it had long black hair pulled back in a ponytail.

"You're mine now," it snarled, pulling Aleister closer.

Aleister wanted to scream for help, but the grip on his throat was too tight. As he gasped for air, he felt the energy being drained from his body as if his soul were being sucked into the red gate before him.

Another hand emerged from the Seer's Gate. The nail on its pinky finger started to grow and extend. There was nothing Aleister could do but watch. The creature thrust its long, dark fingernail deep into Aleister's arm then licked the blood from it.

"Wretched Blessed," said the creature, "your time has come, for I am Nihalus, the bringer of the end of days. While your soul rots in the Nether, I shall rule this world."

Aleister had little fight left in him. He grew weaker and weaker by the second. His body was going limp, and his vision was blurring. The creature slowly pulled itself back into the red column, and it was taking Aleister with it.

As Aleister's face dipped into the Seer's Gate, the Wizard appeared at the doorway. He quickly pointed his wand at Aleister and chanted, "ᕹᛁ ᚱᑎ (KI-AN)." A beam of purple energy shot forth from the tip of his wand and wrapped around Aleister. The Wizard raised the wand into the air as if pulling back a wrangled bull. As he tugged, Aleister was pulled back a little, but a stronger force was fighting to pull him back in. This was a game of tug-of-war that the Wizard was going to lose if he didn't do something fast.

He arched his arm farther back as he repeatedly chanted, "ᕹᛁ ᚱᑌ (KI-CU)." The rope of purple energy grew in strength as new energy pulsated around it. The Wizard's eyes ignited in purple flames. He wasn't going to lose Aleister!

As Aleister's body fully emerged from the column, two demonic hands clutched at him with all their might. The Wizard mustered his last bit of energy, and with a final tug, the creature's hands slipped off Aleister and were sucked back into the gate. Aleister flew across the room, hitting the wall next to the Wizard and tumbling to the floor, unconscious.

The Wizard glanced at Aleister then back at the gate. It was still open. He pointed his wand at it and chanted, "ᑢᒪᑕ ᕐᗝ (MA-RO)." A flash of bright-red light filled the room as the Seer's Gate sealed. The gate was closed, but it had left something behind.

Standing in the room before the Wizard was Nihalus. He appeared severely weakened by his recent struggle and his abrupt passage from the Nether into this reality. The Wizard stepped in front of Aleister and pointed his wand toward the creature, ready to face him with what little energy he had left in him.

Though Nihalus and the Wizard were too weak to engage in battle, they stared at each other with determination in their eyes. Nihalus slowly turned his gaze toward the black-painted windows then back at the Wizard. He crossed his arms in front of his chest as an enormous pair of bat-like wings emerged from his back.

"The day is yours," snarled Nihalus before he burst through the glass windows and flew off into the distance.

*

The council was too fearful to use the Seer's Gate themselves, but Aleister believed they stood little or no chance of finding the Blessed One without it. The girl was also on his mind. If he could determine the boy's location fast enough, perhaps they would keep her out of it. She undoubtedly still bore the scars from their last encounter, and he only wished that she had found happiness wherever she might be.

While Aleister unpacked the container, he recalled the Wizard's warning about tampering with the Seer's Gate. Sweat gathered on his brow, and his heart beat faster and faster, for he recalled all too well what had happened the last time. Few people had ever stared into the abyss, and as far as he knew, no one else had lived to tell the tale.

Inside the box was the large tome that Aleister and the Wizard had recovered from the cult in London many years ago. Below it, wrapped in brown silk, he saw the outline of a torus. He removed the tome and placed it on the floor next to him. Then he slowly and hesitantly lifted the Seer's Gate out of the box. He walked over to an open area on the floor and cautiously placed it down.

He sat in front of the wrapped device for several minutes before working up the courage to remove it from its silk wrapper. Once revealed, the shiny copper of the Seer's Gate reflected a distorted image of himself as he stared at it. His face stretched around its curves, widening his dark-blond goatee along the bottom and stretching his forehead and light-blond hair across the bend at the top. As he looked into his own gold-speckled eyes, again the Wizard's warning echoed in his head.

Aleister walked back over to the container and picked up the large tome. Before opening it, he placed his wand in his mouth and clenched his teeth upon it. He had once said a stray word near the Seer's Gate and wasn't prepared to have another mishap. He spent the next few hours reading through the book's contents until he felt he had a good enough understanding of how to properly use the device.

The book told him that the Seer's Gate acted as if it had a mind of its own when interpreting the words that were spoken to it. It also seemed to have a memory from all its previous uses and used this information when deciphering locations. Given how it had reacted last time to the whisper of a single word, Aleister surmised that it probably had spent much of its existence being used by the Touched.

He also read that, though the device required the ancient tongue to be activated, the location one wanted to view could be spoken in any common language. Specificity was the key, since the device acted on its own accord and didn't have the guided mental clarity of a mage. It would always open a gate to somewhere, and if the location were unclear, it would piece together one from the fragments and memories of its previous uses. Fortunately for Aleister, he knew exactly where he wanted to gaze and had been there before.

Being as prepared as he could be, Aleister took a few steps back from the Seer's Gate and pointed his wand at it. He then said, "I desire to see the office of Detective Nicholas Valle in the seventh precinct of the New York City Police Department on the Lower East Side of Manhattan," then chanted, "⊘R (OR)."

A silvery glowing energy shot up from the torus and fanned out against the high ceilings of the storage chamber. The swell of energy then subsided as it solidified into a column of flowing liquid. The mercury-like surface was highly reflective, and Aleister stood there staring at his reflection. As he fought his fears and past memories, he inched forward then dipped his head into the Seer's Gate.

Moments later, Aleister's head was violently thrust back, and his limp body fell to the floor. As he lay there unconscious, the silvery column of liquid collapsed to the floor and spread out before dissipating into the air. His floating light source gave one last twinkle, and then the room went dark.

CHAPTER 12
MISS MURDER

Industrial metal music echoed throughout the Ceremony nightclub. The beat was pulsating like a tribal drum. It was the type of sound one felt deep in the core of his or her being, shaking the person but at the same time drawing them in. Outside an early snowfall had covered Boston in a light blanket of white, and it was bitterly cold, but inside, the heat generated by the warmth of a hundred or more dancing bodies made it feel like a sweaty summer day.

As Ash stepped in through the doorway, small gusts of snow followed him. The door closed, and he approached the bouncer. The man recognized him, nodded, and motioned him in. Ash removed his coat and handed it to a woman behind the counter next to the door. He smiled at her, and she smiled back at him. She handed him a torn slip of paper with his coat number on it. He'd been here many times before.

As if moving to the rhythm of the music, he waded through the crowd until he reached the farthest bar at the end of the dance floor.

He sat down. The place was surprisingly busy for a cold night, and the woman behind the bar didn't even seem to notice he had taken a seat. This was something he was about to correct.

He reached into his pocket, placed his blue gem in the palm of his hand, cupped it, then removed his closed fist. Resting his elbows on the table, he brought his hands together and placed them in front of his mouth. In a muffled voice, he whispered, "ᕐᒷᔑᓭᓭᔑ (KI-AWA-SI)." Then he lowered his hands until they rested, crossed, on the bar in front of him.

The bartender raised her head. She quickly finished handing off some drinks to a couple at the end of the bar then focused her attention on Ash. She was attractive, perhaps in her midtwenties, and her short red hair covered the left side of her face. Her one exposed blue eye was surrounded by black eye shadow. She spoke in an elevated Irish accent over the loud music.

"Hey, handsome. What can I do for you?" she said, leaning over the bar toward Ash.

"Do for me?" he replied. "I'll just have a Jack and Coke—for now."

"Sure thing, sugar," she responded.

She walked over and began to mix the drink for Ash, glancing back often and smiling. As she did this, Ash slowly returned his blue gem to his pants pocket. When she was done, she returned to Ash, placed the drink on the bar, and slowly pushed it toward him.

"Anything else I can…do for you?" she asked.

"That's all I need right now. I wouldn't want you to ignore the rest of your customers."

They smiled at each other briefly, and then she wandered off to tend to some of the other patrons at the bar. Ash swiveled his chair around so he could have a better view of the dance floor. He slowly sipped his drink as he surveyed the scene. The DJ had just turned on the smoke machine, and the floor was filling with a waist-high fog. Laser lights shot through and reflected off the smoke as it resonated to the beat of the music.

At first slowly, but then quickly, something caught Ash's eye. A female silhouette emerged from the clouds of the crowded dance floor. She moved slowly and gracefully, somehow out of sync with the rapid beat of the music, but at the same time obeying the rhythm underneath. When she finally broke through the veil of smoke, Ash saw the sexiest woman he'd ever seen in his life.

This woman was stunning. She was dressed in a black corset with a short black miniskirt. Her legs appeared to be wrapped in a continuous black lace that began under her skirt and ended at her knee-high boots. Her teased blond hair hung slightly below her shoulders and perfectly framed her face. She seemed to be looking directly at Ash, but at the same time, she was staring at something behind him, as if she were looking through him. There was something strange and beautiful about her eyes—they appeared to be red. A lace veil covered the lower portion of her face.

As she strutted confidently toward the bar, her gaze shifted from Ash to the bartender. She leaned over the seat next to Ash and spoke to the bartender. Intrigued and interested, Ash tried to eavesdrop in on their conversation, but the noise in the club was too loud for him to discern anything they were saying.

After the bartender handed the woman her drink, Ash turned to her and said, "Why don't you let me get that for you?" Not giving her time to turn down his offer, he looked at the bartender and said, "This one's on me."

The woman looked at Ash then slowly reached up and unsnapped the veil from a clasp under her left ear and then her right ear. As she removed the veil, a pouty smile came across her full, deep-red lips.

"How very old school of you—buying a lady a drink at the bar," she said, before slowly pressing her straw against her lips and taking a sip.

Her presence intoxicated Ash; everything about her was perfect.

He leaned in closer to her and replied, "It was the least I could do. I've been staring at you, unable to take my eyes off you, since I first saw you."

"Have you now?" she replied in a sultry voice as she leaned in closer.

Her perfume carried the smell of vanilla liqueur. He wanted to taste her neck right then and had to fight every urge he had not to do so.

"I'm Ash," he said with a slight stutter. "There's something about you that I can't quite place my finger on."

She flashed him a sexy grin. "My name's Sarah—and fingers are off limits…for now."

The two continued to talk and flirt for what, to Ash, seemed to be an indeterminable amount of time. He told her about being an MIT student and how he wasn't sure what to do with his life after college. He described his recent foray into the nightlife of the city, constantly weaving in comments about how beautiful he thought she was. Sarah told him about her upbringing in a small town in North Carolina and how she felt torn between the simplicities that it offered and the energies that pumped through the veins of a city. Ash was deeply immersed in everything she had to say and was so enthralled by her that he completely forgot whether this was true attraction or whether he had a cast a spell on her.

Throughout their conversation, he threw back one drink after another, and by the time last call rolled around, he was fairly intoxicated. Sarah had kept pace with him but seemed to be in the same semi-sober state she was in when their evening together had first started.

Ash looked deeply into her red eyes. He put his hand on top of hers and said, "I'd like to see more of you. Do you want to get out of here?"

As she leaned in close, he felt her breath on his ear. She whispered, "You know, I might not be good for you."

*

It was midday. Sarah was in the kitchen of her apartment, somewhat scantily clad. The radio was playing loudly as she danced around in a white T-shirt and pink panties. On the table in front of her were her three tiny demon friends: Jinx, Kynx, and Lynx. They were busily helping her prepare lunch.

Jinx was standing next to a jar, stirring its contents as if he were brewing a potion in a cauldron. Kynx was busy pulling pieces off a head of lettuce, and Lynx was wielding a large chef's knife, which for him appeared to be a giant sword straight out of a Japanese anime. He brought the blade down swiftly and sliced through the loaf of bread in front of him. As it slammed into the cutting board, it startled Sarah. She glanced over with a slight look of annoyance. Lynx shrugged as if to say, "Hey, lady, I'm a demon. What's a brother to do?" Her look quickly turned to a smile, and he continued to slice away.

Sarah started to sway to the music again and was just beginning to get back into her groove when she was startled again, this time by something much more sinister. As she spun around, standing before her was Nihalus. His presence was undeniably strong, yet it had been entirely absent just moments ago. His dark cloak covered most of his body, and his black hood covered most of his head. His only uncovered flesh was the lower area of his face, exposing his mouth and a black goatee. Fanged teeth protruded from his slightly open lips as he spoke.

"I'm sorry to have startled you, dear," he said in an ominous tone.

"Nihalus," she said in a somewhat shaken voice, "I wasn't expecting you."

"You're looking quite well—though a bit weak, I suspect."

He placed his right hand on the kitchen table and glanced at the three tiny demons. They quickly stopped what they were doing, gathered next to one another, and crouched in cowardly, submissive positions. They bowed their heads in respect and let out almost-silent, muffled growls.

"It's the hunger, sire," she admitted. "Though I hate myself for it, I grow weaker every day I go without feeding. Mortal food sustains my body but not my soul."

"There's no reason to hate yourself, my child." Nihalus turned his head toward her and placed his hand on her shoulder. "It's your nature. It's who and what you are. There's no fighting it. There's only acceptance and then doing the best you can with the gifts you've been given."

Feeling the comfort of his hand upon her, Sarah lowered her head toward him. She once again was reminded that he was the only one who could ever understand her. It had been years since she had seen or even spoken to her parents, and during that time, Nihalus had become like a father to her. While she missed her mom and dad, she knew that if they ever found out what she truly was, though they might try, they never would look at her the same again. She couldn't bear the thought. They never would be able to accept her like Nihalus had; he never would judge her. It was better that she was lost to them.

"You're one of the Touched," he continued. "You aren't like the rest of these…sleeping sheep."

She slowly nodded in understanding.

"Now I have need of you and your abilities, my sweet Sarah," he said.

"I don't know…I think I can last a bit longer before I have to do it again," she replied softly.

A single tear streamed down the left side of her face.

"Sarah, I need your help, and you need mine." Nihalus placed a claw-like hand under her chin and lifted her head. She could now see into the darkness of his ebony eyes. "This one is special. He'll sustain you for a very long time. He's also dangerous to people like us and will eventually hunt you down and kill you—we must treat him the same."

Sarah shook her head. "I'm too weak. I don't have the strength."

"Then, for the time being, take some of mine," he said, as he lifted her lips close to his.

A red energy passed between them, and she felt it filling her soul. He had only done this for her a few times, as it weakened him considerably and left him vulnerable. Sadly its effects also never lasted very long, and it was just enough to get her by. It was like eating a meal filled with only sugar and caffeine—it would give her energy and strength but wouldn't give her the nutrients she required; it wouldn't sustain her. Eventually she would need to feed.

*

Sarah's loft was located in the Back Bay of Boston. The walk there was mostly a blur for Ash. She often pulled him aside into an alley, pushed her body against his, and embraced him with long kisses. With each kiss, though it felt like something was being drained from within him, his attraction and desire for her only grew. It was like sipping from a refreshing drink that one somehow knew was laced with poison.

"You're so strong. I could feast on your lips all night," she whispered in his ear.

"I want you, Sarah," he whispered back.

"They all do," she replied, gazing into his eyes. Her fiery-red eyes pierced deep into his soul.

The stairs up to Sarah's apartment were narrow and winding. She slinked up them slowly, and with each few steps, she'd tilt her head back to glance at Ash and gradually slip off an article of clothing, leaving them on the steps below. As he admired her firm, toned body, he took each step equally as slow, pausing at each piece of her discarded attire, picking it up, and holding it close to his chest. Her smell was on everything; it was intoxicating.

By the time Sarah had reached the top of the stairs, only a few strategically placed pieces of clothing remained. She smiled flirtatiously as she slowly ran her fingers through her blond hair. With every ounce of his being, he wanted her. He looked down for a moment to pick up the skirt she had dropped on one of the steps. When he looked up again, Sarah was no longer standing there. It was as if she had vanished.

Ash picked up his pace and raced up the staircase. When he reached the top, he saw a long narrow hallway with a lone open door near its end. He walked toward it. As he got closer to the doorway, he saw inside the apartment, and just for a moment, he thought he saw three tiny dark figures recoil their heads behind the back of the door. From what he could see, there was a dark-red Victorian couch laid against the background of large black velvet drapes that covered the windows. The room seemed to flicker, as if lit by hundreds of candles from within.

As Ash entered the room, he peered over at the couch, where Sarah was waiting for him. She was lying on her back with her upper body lifted by her elbows and one knee slightly bent. He slowly moved his eyes over her body. Her long legs were still wrapped in winding black laces. A thin pair of black panties followed and then her slim stomach. Next his eyes hovered over her firm breasts, which were cupped in an elegant black lace bra. After he made his way over to her, he lowered his head over her puckered red lips and stared into her eyes. She stared back into his and lifted one of her fingers, motioning him to come even closer.

"You're mine now, Ash," she whispered in a sultry voice.

The flicker in the room intensified, and the shadows danced against the walls. He felt a slight gust of cold air from outside as the door shut. Something behind him had closed it. He wanted to look back but was unable to do so. He couldn't take his gaze off Sarah. He was drawn to her; he wanted only her.

He slowly let the articles of clothing he was holding fall from his hands. They rolled down his chest, stomach, and legs. Finally they hit the floor and lay at his feet. He climbed over the couch until he was above her. Sarah stared into his eyes as she wrapped her arms and legs around him. Her body pulled him closer to her. As she embraced him with another deep kiss, and just before he closed his eyes, he saw three tiny dark figures perched at the top of the couch, watching.

He wanted to open his eyes but couldn't. There was only Sarah. There was only her embrace. It was all that mattered.

*

The next day, when Ash awoke, he was so weak that he could barely move. He was lying naked on the red couch, covered only by a lightweight black blanket. The sun crept in through the edges of the velvet curtains. His eyes were blurry. He raised his hands to rub them, barely finding the strength to do so. When his vision finally began to focus, he saw three tiny dark beings crouched over him, watching him with their ruby-red eyes.

What happened? Where am I? he thought.

Slowly he tried to raise his body in an effort to get up. The three creatures scuttled about, hunched over, and stared at him ominously. He was unsure if it was his own frailty or whether these monsters were somehow using their powers to keep him down, but one thing was for certain: he wasn't going anywhere anytime soon. His body collapsed back onto the couch.

"I told you I might not be good for you," said a soft yet confident female voice as a figure entered the room.

Ash looked over and saw Sarah. She was dressed in a dark jogging suit and was walking in his direction, applying a crimson lipstick as she strolled. A few feet before reaching him, she stopped and looked down at him with glowing red eyes. Then she puckered her lips and blew a light kiss in his direction.

Ash wanted to say something, but he couldn't find the strength to do so. Instead he could only watch as Sarah turned around and made her way to the door.

She tilted her head, glanced over at her demonic pets, and said, "Come on, kids. Let the poor man rest."

Jinx, Kynx, and Lynx hopped down from the couch with a catlike grace before scurrying across the floor and gathering at her feet. Sarah opened the door slightly and held it ajar. The creatures hopped outside. From behind the door, they peered back at Ash for a moment before ducking their heads behind it and disappearing.

Ash somehow managed to roll off the couch. With an outstretched hand and pain evident on his face, he reached toward Sarah. His lips opened as he tried again to speak. He had only the strength to squeak out one word: "Why?"

"Probably best not to think about it too hard, sugar," Sarah told him. "Try to enjoy your last few moments. You have very little time left. Your life-force runs as thin as the wind and will soon flicker and fade out like a dying flame. We had fun though, right? I really have to thank you. He was right about you. You have strength like I've never tasted before. It's a shame it had to end like this. We could have made quite the pair, but it wasn't meant to be—for one day you would have come for me, but I got to you first."

Ash inched forward, trying to crawl toward her, but he knew she was right. He didn't have much time left. He had abused his powers and his gifts. Perhaps this was what he deserved, to be here, in this spot, right now, dying.

"Ta-ta, sweetie" were her last words as she gave Ash one last glance, slinked between the small gap of the entrance, and shut the door behind her.

With no energy left and in acceptance of not only his fate but also of his misdeeds, Ash collapsed to the floor and closed his eyes. All he saw was darkness, and as if the volume of a radio were slowly being turned down, all the sounds around him faded to silence. *This is the end. This is what I deserve*, he thought.

*

Ash's soul floated in a place between this world and the next. His mortal coil lay nearly silent on the floor. A brilliant light emerged above him, and he felt himself being drawn toward it as if being lifted by invisible hands. He didn't have the energy or will left to fight back, so he let the force take hold of him.

Images of his life passed over him like a rush of water, and in an instant, he relived every moment. He remembered his childhood: growing up, going to high school, falling in love with mechanical engineering, feeling the excitement of being accepted to MIT, meeting his friend Mike, studying for hours, playing too many video games. And then there was the Wizard, April, and all those women he had seduced. He had been given so many gifts, so many opportunities, and he had squandered and abused them all. It was fitting that it should end like this, for it was he who had abused his power to seduce women, and now a seductress had caused his demise. With great regret, he thought what a shame it was that only at this moment could he finally see the truth of it all. If only he had more time, to redeem himself, to make the wrong things right.

Then there was an odd feeling. At a great distance below him, he felt the head of his physical body being lifted. Something began to tug at him, drawing him back. Suddenly a shocking jolt coursed through him, and then he instantly found himself back in Sarah's apartment, lying on the floor. He gasped for air. He was breathing again. At first he could only a see a blur, and then the Wizard's face came into focus.

"Be still," said the Wizard. "I have you."

CHAPTER 13

OF MONSTERS AND MEN

Detective Valle sat in his office, smoking a cigar. The case of the murder in the alley had gone cold for a few weeks now, and his sergeant had assigned him and Kent to other less intriguing cases. The map of Pangea still hung pinned to the wall in front of him, and every now and then, he'd glance up and wonder about it. Soon he would have to box it up and retire it to the unsolved crimes storage unit in the basement of the seventh precinct. Though he hated admitting defeat, it wouldn't be the first time he had to do so in his line of work.

With the case creeping into his mind again, Valle got up, made his way to the map, and rested his palm on it. He scratched the back of his head with his other hand and muttered to himself. This case would remain a mystery, with many unanswered questions: Who killed David Higgins, the antique dealer? Why was he killed? Was it over this map of Pangea? And what was that strange shadow that was burned on the wall?

For a few minutes, Valle stood there and stared at the map. None of this made any sense, and it still bothered him. After a while, his mind drifted, recalling and playing back the events of his and Kent's visit to Dorian's bookshop in Salem.

*

Detectives Valle and Kent were seated in Dorian's office, upstairs above the Raven's Foot. They had laid out the map of Pangea on the desk in front of them and had explained to Dorian the odd circumstances by which they had acquired it. Dorian pushed up his purple newsboy hat and examined the map thoroughly with a magnifying glass, paying particular interest to the circle in the corner, which bore the arcane set of symbols "◑N."

"These are the symbols for the word *blood*," said Dorian as he slid his eyeglasses up the bridge of his pointy nose

"That's what I thought," replied Valle. "I saw them once on a talisman many years ago."

"What language is it?" asked Kent.

"An ancient tongue believed to be the language used by angels and those who have fallen from grace," answered Dorian.

Valle scratched the back of his salt-and-pepper hair. "Any idea what makes this map so special?" he asked.

"I might," said Dorian, as he got up and walked over to one of his many bookshelves.

As he scanned the books, he continued, "There's an old story about two ancient warring factions. One was born from light, and they were called angels. The other was born from darkness, and they were called demons. The demons sought to overtake the mortal realm and claim it for their own, but the angels fought to protect our world, driving back the demonic horde again and again.

"After ages of conflict, a leader emerged from the ranks of the demons with cunningness and power far greater than any had seen before. He began to corrupt the mortals with promises of wealth and power, turning more and more of them to the side of darkness. His armies grew vast in numbers, yet he still was unable to overcome the forces of the angels and their allies. Their faith gave them a resolve and strength that couldn't be matched. Then one day, seemingly overnight, the tide of the battles shifted."

Dorian stopped his search, removed a large, worn volume from a shelf, and said, "Here it is."

He walked back over to his desk, set the book in front of him, and fanned through the pages. As Detectives Valle and Kent watched, they noticed the text in the book seemed to be written in the same symbols that were on the map. They also saw numerous faded but highly detailed black-and-white illustrations on many of the pages.

"This is all very interesting, but is any of this, in any shape or form, related to this map?" asked Detective Valle, clearly frustrated.

"Patience," Dorian said, running his fingers over some of the text. "I'm getting there." He tapped his fingers over one of the drawings and continued. "You see, the leader of the demons uncovered an ancient relic: a map drawn from the blood of something that was even more ancient than them. At first he was unable to use the map, but then, in one fateful moment, its powers were revealed.

"During one of their many battles, a small group of angels managed to penetrate deep into the enemy's camp. There they confronted the leader of the demons in an attempt to end the war. However, they were no match for his strength and power. As he plunged his sword into the last of them, its blood spilled onto the map. Infused with angelic blood, it became activated. The angels had sealed their own fate.

"From that point forward, using the map, the demons were able to pinpoint the exact location of the angelic armies. At last they had within their means the power to defeat the angels. They knew exactly where they would be at all times, which allowed them to lead strategic and devastating strikes against them.

"Though its true name has been lost through the passing of the ages, in this story and in many others, it's known as the Sangrian Map. Over the course of history, it has exchanged hands many times and has been used by seers, kings, and conquerors.

"If this picture is correct, then I believe what you have before you could be the Sangrian Map."

Dorian turned the book toward the detectives and pointed at a drawing that depicted a large, hunched-over, gargoyle-like figure. The creature's clawed hands were clasping an unrolled parchment. Upon the parchment was a map—a map of the world as we know it today—and in its corner was a circle with arcane symbols within it.

"Let's assume for a moment that I'm going to suspend any disbelief I have about your story," said Detective Valle. "What makes you think this is our map? As far as I can tell, your picture shows the continents separated, and our map shows them all jammed together."

"Nothing slips by you, Detective," Dorian said somewhat sarcastically. "You are of course correct, but the Sangrian Map wasn't drawn with ordinary ink. As you may recall from my tale, it contains the blood of an ancient being—blood that still flows through it with its energies and life.

"What you see before you is the map in its inactivated, dormant state. When it's in this state, it represents the world in its most ancient form. However, when it's activated, the blood ink reflows to show the world as it exists today."

With a strong hint of disbelief, Detective Kent said, "Okay...well, I think we have all the information we're going to get out of here." He then turned toward Valle and rolled his eyes.

"One minute, Kent. I have one more question before we go," said Valle. "When we first found the map, it was torn into a thousand pieces. Is there anything about that in there?"

"According to the text, the angels eventually recovered the map, and when they did, they sought to destroy it so that its powers would never again fall into the wrong hands," Dorian explained. "However, it was ancient and powerful and couldn't be destroyed entirely, so they tore it apart and scattered its pieces across the known world."

*

A clanging at the door startled Detective Valle out of his daydream. He shook his head a few times then walked over and opened the door. Detective Kent was standing there with a cup of coffee in each of his hands.

"Still staring at that old map?" asked Kent as he handed Valle one of the cups.

"Yeah," muttered Valle as he accepted the coffee. "How did you know?"

"I'd like to tell you it was my keen intuition," replied Kent, as he pointed his thumb toward the door, "but the truth is that the door is made of frosted glass. I can't see everything in here, but I could see enough to make out your robust shape standing there."

Somewhat insulted, Valle replied, "Robust shape? What are you insinuating?"

Realizing he had stepped slightly over the line, Kent said, "I'm sorry. I didn't mean anything by it. Hey, are you okay? You seem a little more sensitive than usual."

"Yeah, I probably am. I'm just frustrated, I guess. I really hate to let this one go."

"I know, I feel the same way, but it's time. Every clue we found led to another dead end. Guess we'll never know what killed that man or anything more about that silly map. It's not like a new lead is going to fall into our laps."

At that exact moment, as if on cue, the desk phone rang. The two detectives turned toward it.

Valle walked over and picked it up. "Detective Valle here."

A female officer's voice on the other end replied, "Hey, I have a guy up here who says he has some information about your alley murder case."

"Take his statement and tell him we'll get back to him," Valle said unenthusiastically.

"Will do—hold on a second," she said, as Valle heard someone talking to her in the background. "He says it's urgent and that he once knew the owner of some map you have. What do you want me to do?"

Valle gulped then responded, "Tell him to stay right where he is! I'm sending Detective Kent over to get him."

"Get who?" asked Kent.

"Remember what you said about a clue falling into our laps?" replied Valle as he hung up the phone. "Well, one just did. There's a guy upstairs that not only knows about the map but says he knew the previous owner."

"Damn! Go, go, blind luck!" exclaimed Kent as he hurried out of the room to retrieve the man.

A few minutes later, Kent returned to the office escorting an elderly, frail-looking gentleman. The man walked hunched over, balancing himself with a cane. He wore a gray glen plaid suit with a light-green sweater underneath. His unkempt white hair was thinning on top, and his wrinkled face bore a short silver mustache. A pair of tortoiseshell spectacles rested midway down his thin nose.

Kent introduced the man to Detective Valle. "This is Professor Markus Albrecht."

"Please to meet you, Professor Albrecht," replied Valle. "I hear you have some information about one of our murder cases."

Albrecht didn't respond and, in fact, didn't even seem to acknowledge that he had been asked something. Instead he wobbled past the detectives until he stood directly in front of the map. He gripped one end of his glasses with his free hand and raised them until they were level with his eyes. His head moved back and forth as he examined the map.

"I was told you knew the map's previous owner," said Valle, once again trying to get a response out of the professor.

"That isn't exactly what I said," replied Albrecht in a thick German accent. "What I said was I once knew an owner of the map."

"Okay, so what exactly can you tell us about it?" asked Valle.

"I could tell you a great many things," replied Albrecht. "What is it that you would like to know?"

"Let's start with the basics," stated Valle. "Did you or did you not know the previous owner?"

"The antique dealer," responded Albrecht. "No, I had only recently become aware of his ownership of the map."

"Can you think of any reason why someone would commit murder over this thing?" Detective Valle continued.

Albrecht nodded. "I can think of many reasons someone would kill for it."

"And those would be?" interjected Kent in a leading tone.

Ignoring the question entirely, Albrecht looked at Kent and asked, "What do you see here?"

With more than a little frustration, Kent replied, "Professor, with all due respect, we're asking the questions here."

"Detective," Albrecht replied in an overly calm tone, "then you must learn to ask the right ones."

"All right," Kent said, with increasing frustration, "then what should we be asking you?"

"Well, for starters, you have yet to even ask me why I'm here."

At this point, steam was practically rising from Kent's face. He didn't have the patience for playing these sorts of games and enjoyed being jerked around even less. Detective Valle could tell his partner was about to lose his temper. He walked over and placed a hand on Kent's shoulder, signaling him to calm down and letting him know he was taking over the conversation.

"It was our understanding that you came here to help us with our case, Professor Albrecht," said Valle.

"I simply said I had information about your case and in particular about this map," Albrecht told him. "All of which is true, but I didn't come here to help you."

Detective Valle started to become agitated as well but held his cool. "Then why are you here, Professor?"

Albrecht turned his gaze back toward the map. "To claim what is rightfully mine."

"This map is evidence in a murder case, and it isn't going anywhere," stated Valle. "Thank you for your time, but we're going to have to ask you to leave."

Never taking his eyes off the map, Albrecht responded, "Dear detectives, to your kind the Sangrian Map is just another useless piece of paper hanging on a wall. But in my hands, it's so much more. We can do this with or without incident, but rest assured that when this conversation ends, I'll be taking the map with me."

Unable to bite his tongue any longer, Kent exclaimed, "The hell you will!"

"With incident then," replied Albrecht.

The old man's body shook as if several shivers of cold were rapidly and uncontrollably moving up his spine. He bent over as if in pain, and something moved under the back of his shirt. The detectives quickly stepped away from him and continued to walk backward as far as they could until they were stopped by the desk behind them.

Albrecht's shirt tore open as a set of massive black wings sprouted from his back. Still-moving flesh fell to the floor as a creature ripped its way out from within the professor's body. As the transformation completed, the room became quiet until all that could be heard was the deep, dark breathing of the monster. Its pale, white body glistened with fresh drops of blood as it stood to its full height and stretched out its wings.

The detectives quivered in fear for a moment, and then both made a dash for the door. Without turning around, the creature raised its right clawed hand into the air. A dark-red energy formed around it then wrapped around Valle and Kent. It lifted them into the air and hurled them against the wall.

"Please stay," said the creature in a raspy voice. "You're going to want to see this."

After struggling to stand, Valle said, "You're going to be disappointed."

"And why is that?" asked the creature.

"We were told the map only works for angels," replied Valle, "and while I try not to judge a book by its cover, I can tell you aren't one."

The creature turned its head toward the detectives, revealing its coal-black eyes. "Really? What makes you think I'm not?"

A single clawed fingernail on the creature's right hand extended. When its original length had more than doubled, the creature swung it toward its other hand and sliced open its palm. Blood dripped down its arm and onto the floor. Without a hint of pain and without looking away from the detectives, it placed its bloodied palm on the corner of the Sangrian Map.

The blood seeped into the parchment then moved across it, as if the parchment had veins pumping through it. The outline of the continents seemed to take on more of the blood and took on a deeper red tone. After they had their fill, the continents drifted apart as if replaying thousands and thousands of years of history within a few seconds. When they stopped moving, the map showed the world as we know it today.

The beast returned its gaze to the map and chanted, "⊘ᴸ ⊘ɴ (ONA-ON)."

With the utterance of these words from the ancient tongue, the true power of the map became activated. All the lines and drawings ignited, as if fueled by a fire beneath them. The flames flickered back and forth but didn't burn the parchment. The creature lifted its palm from the map and held both arms outstretched on its sides.

Then it bellowed, "Show me the location of the Blessed One!"

A blue flame emerged in the corner of the map, directly in the middle of the circle containing the arcane symbols. It gradually propagated around the map, slowing down in certain areas, trying to locate the boy. Soon his location would be revealed.

*

As Aleister dipped his head into the Seer's Gate, his vision was shuttled around, as if he were passing through the distance between Archmedea and Detective Valle's office at the speed of light. Then suddenly everything came to a rapid, jolting halt. He felt dizzy and nauseous but tried to focus on what was around him. What he saw wasn't good. With his back turned toward him was the form of Nihalus, standing in front of the activated map. Detective Valle stood a few feet away with his partner on the ground next to him. He had arrived too late.

"Aleister," snarled Nihalus as he turned around, "I can feel your presence."

Kent suddenly raised his pistol, pointed it at Nihalus, and said, "Can you feel this?"

The young detective knew his hands were unsteady, so he fired shot after shot until his clip was emptied. Although Nihalus's skin was inhumanly tough, it wasn't invulnerable. He also was still quite weakened from the energy he had given Sarah earlier. Several of the bullets pierced deep into his flesh, and he screamed out in pain and anger.

"You think you can kill me, mortal?" said Nihalus, raising a claw into the air in a gripping motion.

Nihalus's eyes ignited with crimson flames as his claw became engulfed in red energy. Kent felt a tightening around his throat as he slowly was lifted from the ground. The squeezing became tighter and tighter; Nihalus was choking the life out of him.

Though there was nothing Aleister could do, he yelled, "Stop!"

To his surprise, Nihalus and Detective Valle looked over in his direction. Somehow, though they couldn't see him, they could hear him. Perhaps there *was* something he could do. He reached his mind back and felt his body still in Archmedea, gripping his wand. With all the energy he could muster, he commanded his body to thrust the rod into the Seer's Gate.

As Aleister looked down, he saw a ghostly visage of his wand emerge. Without a second thought, he pointed it at Nihalus and chanted, "𐎺𐎡 𐎠𐎼 (KI-NAS)." A golden blast of energy materialized in the room and struck Nihalus. At the same time, Detective Valle drew his gun and shot at the creature.

Normally, even this combination of attacks would be of little threat to Nihalus, but his energies were weakened and they had caught him off guard. The spell and bullets propelled him against the wall. He quickly wrapped his wings in front of himself, forming a shield while he looked for a means of escape. There were no obvious exits from the room, except for the one door.

Nihalus reached up and tore the map from the wall. Then he charged forward and burst through the door into the hallway. Off in the distance, he spotted a small open window and ran toward it.

Detective Valle followed him out and continued to fire bullets at him as he fled. Despite his injuries and weakened state, Nihalus still moved faster than any mortal creature and dodged most of the bullets as he ran. When he got closer to the window, his form shifted into that of a large crow. The bird's claws caught the map as it fell, and then the creature flew out through the window. Nihalus had escaped with the map.

Detective Valle fired one last shot. Then he hurried back into the room to check on his partner. Kent was resting with his back against the desk and was taking several deep breaths, trying to make up for lost air. He nodded then raised his hand, signaling that he was okay.

Looking into the air, Detective Valle said, "Thanks, Aleister. Guess I owe you another one," but Aleister wasn't there to hear it.

The stress of casting a spell through the Seer's Gate was too much for him to take. His body lay limp in the storage chamber of Archmedea.

"So can we let this case go now?" asked Kent, clearly in pain and exhausted.

Valle walked over to the desk and slowly slid his back down it until he was seated next to his partner. He reached into his jacket pocket, pulled out a half-smoked cigar, and rolled it around between his lips as he puffed it to life with his lighter. Big clouds of smoke exited into the air as he exhaled.

"You know, Kent," said Valle, as he looked at his partner, "I'm still not inclined to let this one go."

CHAPTER 14

FROM THE ASHES

From a dreamless slumber, Ash awoke on his dorm-room bed. His head was throbbing and his body ached. Both felt as if they had been pressed to their limits. He saw the Wizard over at his computer, clicking and typing away.

"You know, I never pictured a wizard using a computer," said Ash.

The Wizard swiveled the chair around. "Yes, even us old wizards have a need to visit YouTube every now and then to catch up on celebrity gossip."

Ash broke into a smile and laughed. It hurt.

"Laughing—that's good," said the Wizard. "How are you feeling?"

"Pretty horrible actually."

"You'll start to feel better as your energy recovers," said the Wizard. "You're quite lucky to still be alive. Few people are strong enough to survive an encounter with Miss Murder."

"She said her name was Sarah." Ash tried to pull himself up but was too weak to do so.

The Wizard stood up and walked over to the bed. He placed two pillows under Ash's head and helped him move into an inclined position. Seeing that Ash was now more comfortable, he returned to the desk chair and sat back down.

"She goes by that name as well," said the Wizard. "I see she left you with a little gift."

Though Ash had no recollection of having sex with Sarah, the first thought that crossed his mind was that he had contracted some sort of venereal disease. Perhaps some sort of super-arcane kind that would plague him for the rest of his life, maybe even causing him to shoot fire out of his genitals when he peed. The thought was somewhat crazy, but given what he'd seen recently, it wasn't entirely out of the realm of possibility.

The Wizard raised a finger in the air then pointed it at the hair on the top of his head. Though impossible, Ash crossed his eyes and tried to look at his own head. The Wizard turned around to look for a mirror or perhaps some other reflective object on the desk. When he saw Ash's mobile phone, he picked it up and tossed it over to him. It landed softly on his lap. After unlocking his phone, Ash turned on the camera and used it as a mirror to look at himself. To his surprise, his dirty-blond hair now had two ebony streaks that ran down the sides of his head.

"I never should have left you," said the Wizard. "This is a dangerous time for all of us but especially for one who's just discovering his powers. They say power corrupts, and absolute power corrupts absolutely."

"This is entirely my own fault," replied Ash. "I'm so sorry. I should have listened to you. Can you forgive me?"

"Ash," said the Wizard, "I'm not a priest. I'm not here to absolve you of your sins. I'm your teacher, and it's my job to instruct you as best I can. The choice of what type of man you want to be is up to you. Will you use your powers for the greater good or for personal gain? The choice will always be yours, and if you need to seek forgiveness, you must always start with yourself."

"I've done such horrible things," whimpered Ash as tears welled in his eyes.

"Yes, you have," stated the Wizard. "Though this doesn't by any means justify what you've done, your actions were driven by your insecurities and fear of acceptance. You now see the consequence of being compelled by these emotions. Sometimes you have to fall before you can learn to stand. You've been given a second chance. There's still time for redemption. You can rise from this and be the man you know you were meant to be."

Ash sat for a moment in thought, letting the Wizard's words sink in. He had heard his words before but had never truly listened. Something resonated inside him, as if he were waking from a long dream and finally seeing the true world.

"I'll make the wrong things right," he said.

"Good," said the Wizard, smiling slightly. "Then let's get started."

"Now?" responded Ash with a look of surprise and mild frustration. "I can barely move!"

"You must find the strength. I can't do it for you."

Ash nodded then slowly pulled off his blankets and pushed them to the side. With a look of intense pain, he awkwardly moved into a seated position at the edge of his bed. He rested his feet on the floor, took a deep breath, and then, using his arms, struggled into a standing position. For a few moments, his body wavered slightly back and forth until he found his center.

"I'm ready," he said. "Let's go."

"You'll need this." The Wizard tossed a wooden box onto the bed.

"What is it?"

"Your wand. I picked it up for you from Dorian on my way back."

Ash looked over at the box. His visit to Salem seemed like it was a lifetime ago and he had all but forgotten about returning to the Raven's Foot to retrieve his wand. He had just managed to stand and was dreading the idea of bending over to pick up the box, but he was also filled with a sense of excitement. He slowly leaned over and took it into his hands. It slid open easily. Inside was a white metal wand with a clawed hand at the top, holding a brilliant blue sapphire. A smile spread across his face. The time had come for him to give up childish desires and truly become a wizard.

"Oh, and one more thing before we get started," said the Wizard in a serious tone.

"What?" asked Ash, ready to receive his next bit of wisdom.

"You might want to put on some pants," the Wizard said with a smirk.

Ash looked down to realize he'd been proudly standing there in his boxers.

"I'll be waiting for you outside." The Wizard opened the door, stepped outside, and closed it behind him.

*

That day and for the next few days that followed, Ash's training was tougher than it had ever been, but so were his determination and resolve. He always had been a brilliant kid and had coasted by in school on his intellectual gifts. This also had been true for his newfound magical abilities. Things always had come easy to him, and he never had really known what it was like to push himself, but now, for the first time in his life, things were different. He needed to try harder. He needed to become better than he was. The path to redemption was before him—he just needed to muster the strength to see it through.

The Wizard and Ash were back in the warehouse along the Charles River. Ash had just finished levitating a Lincoln Town Car and was holding it suspended in the air. With a clear and focused mind, he slowly and steadily began to lower it to the ground. Then suddenly he lost control, and the car fell, smashing to the concrete floor. He dropped his arms to his sides, took a deep breath, and turned toward the Wizard, prepared to receive a look of disapproval.

"Well, that was mostly well done," said the Wizard. "Your ability to direct your spells has greatly improved, but I can see from the look in your eyes that yet again some of your thoughts have drifted elsewhere."

"It's April again, Master," said Ash, as he lowered his head. "I still feel the regret of what I did to her. It claws and grips at me. I don't think it'll ever let me go."

The Wizard shrugged. "Then you should go to her."

"What would I say? I can't tell her I used a spell to manipulate her into liking me. Either she would hate me, think I was crazy, or most likely both!"

"Ash," said the Wizard, "you can't control her response or the outcome of all things. But that shouldn't stop you from trying to make amends and doing what you feel is right. This is the very thing that forms the foundation of courage."

Ash shook his head. "I don't know if I can face her."

"If we're going to go any further, you'll have to."

Ash knew the Wizard was right. He never would be able to fully control his abilities with this guilt hanging on his soul. It was time for him to see April. He walked over to the Wizard and handed him his wand.

"Please hold on to this for me," he said.

"It and I will be here when you return," replied the Wizard.

*

To Ash, April represented the sum of all the women he had manipulated into seeing him for more than what he was. She was also the only one who was once his friend and, to be quite frank, the only one whose address he remembered. If he could apologize to her, then perhaps he could forgive himself, though she never might. This would have to be good enough, since he knew it was the right thing to do.

Nervously he knocked at the front door of her apartment. He soon heard someone coming to the door. When it opened, it wasn't April standing there, but a young man, still dressed in his pajamas. He had a muscular build, curly light-brown hair, and a scruffy five-o'clock shadow. Ash recognized him as Matt, from their classes. April always had fancied him and often stared at him in class. Ash always had been jealous of him, but when he saw him this time, he actually felt a sense of relief and happiness. This was who April deserved to be with.

"Hey, you're April's friend, Ash, right?" asked Matt.

"Yeah, that's me. I'm sorry to bother you, but is April around?"

"Nah, man. She had a lot of work to do today and headed out early. I think she's in the mechanical engineering lab."

"Thanks. I'll go look for her there."

"Hey, when you find her," said Matt, "can you please remind her that I'm making dinner tonight? You know how forgetful she gets when she's really into her work."

Ash nodded. "Will do."

After Matt had closed the door, Ash headed to the mechanical engineering lab. When he got there, the lab was completely empty, save for one girl, who was busily working at one of the lab benches. As he walked through the entryway, his sneakers made a squeaking sound on the floor. April alertly raised her head, turned around, and looked over at Ash as she lifted up her lab goggles.

"Hey, April," Ash said as he walked over to her.

April put her goggles next to her on the bench and stood up, waiting for Ash to get closer. Though he couldn't quite decipher all the emotions on her face, he definitely saw a hint of surprise. When he reached her, he started to say, "I'm sorry," but well before he was able to finish his sentence, he was interrupted by a solid slap to the face.

"I deserved that," said Ash, as he turned back toward her and looked into her light-brown eyes.

"Damn right you did!" April snapped. "I thought I meant something to you, and then you just disappeared. You never even called!"

"April, I came here to apologize. What I did to you was unforgivable, and I don't expect you to forgive me. I just wanted to let you know I'm sorry."

April shook her head. "It's a little late. I'm with Matt now."

"I know," said Ash, before pausing and asking, "Are you happy?"

"Not that it's any of your business...but yes," responded April, as she nodded and brought a slight smile to her face.

"That's great," replied Ash.

April raised an eyebrow. "You mean you didn't come here to try to get back together?"

"No. I just came to say I'm sorry. We were friends once, and then I let you down. Like I said, I don't expect you to forgive me, but if you're open to it, I'd like the opportunity to try to be your friend again. I promise to treat you better this time, and I'll do anything I can to make it up to you."

April lowered her head in thought. She had heard his words but was still angry with him. He had hurt her, and she didn't know if she could forgive him. Then, for some reason, her thoughts drifted to Matt. As fate might have it, it was when she was at her lowest and needed someone the most that Matt finally had approached her and was there for her. He showed her such kindness and compassion, and she felt lucky and very happy to be with him. *The thread that weaves through the world can be strangely guided sometimes*, she thought. *One occurrence can lead to the next, and it's important not to look back but always forward.* While she wasn't quite ready to forgive Ash, she believed he was being sincere, and she missed their friendship.

"Well," she said, before pausing for a moment then lifting her head, "I could use some help with this assignment."

She smiled lightly as she looked up at Ash, who smiled back at her. While it wasn't completely gone, he felt some of the heaviness in his heart lift. He knew he had done the right thing, and he finally caught a small glimpse of what it felt like to be on the right path to becoming who he was meant to be.

"I'd love to," he said. "Now what are we working on?"

"It's this stupid robot for the next month's competition." April pointed at the workbench. "If you ever went to class anymore, you'd know. In this project, the robot needs to collect these foam blocks for points while your opponent tries to do the same. I had this idea that maybe I could build an anchor to shoot out, hook onto the foam cubes, and then reel them back in. But I can't seem to get enough force out of this contraption."

"Let me have a look." Ash walked over and examined the items on the workbench.

"And when we're done, I think someone owes me a cup of coffee," said April.

Ash and April were going to be friends for a long time. Everyone makes mistakes, but few have the courage to recognize them, learn from them, and correct them. Friends will stumble and fall, but they'll also always be there to forgive each other and pick them back up.

*

Later that day, when Ash returned to his dorm room, he felt proud of himself. Not only had he started to make amends with April, but he also had helped with her project. Things would be okay between them, and he was genuinely glad, without a hint of jealousy or an ounce of regret, that she had found happiness with Matt.

Ash sat down at his desk. He was still a bit wired from the coffee he and April had consumed and was pondering what to do next. Then suddenly a rush of inspiration rippled up in his mind. Perhaps he could use April's shooting-anchor idea for something else. He grabbed his notebook and feverishly sketched some design concepts. After a few hours, he looked up and smiled. He had the perfect schematics; now all he had to do was build it. He glanced at the clock—it was late but not past six yet. The hardware store was likely still open. He grabbed his coat and rushed out the door.

An hour later, after returning from the store, Ash went to work. He worked through the rest of the evening and straight into the next morning. As the sun started to rise and light poured in through the window, he leaned back in his chair and admired his completed masterpiece. He couldn't wait to show the Wizard. Exhausted, he crawled into bed and closed his eyes, hoping to get a few hours of sleep before his next training session started.

Several hours later, Ash arrived a bit groggy and a little late to the warehouse. As he quietly entered, he heard the Wizard talking to someone. This was very strange. As far as Ash was aware, the Wizard knew no one else in the area. He stealthily walked nearer and took a peek around the corner, only to find the Wizard standing by himself near the center of the room. However, as he looked closer and slightly unfocused his eyes, he made out the vague image of a ghostly, floating elderly mage. Nosily he strained to listen to what they were saying.

"We need you back at Archmedea immediately," said the floating mage. "We want you to send the boy."

"The boy?" replied the Wizard. "But he's barely recovered from his encounter with the Touched."

"This mission should be relatively safe. We only want him to retrieve the location of the girl and then report back to us," said the mage. "Is he ready for that?"

"The boy is…" the Wizard started before turning around and looking directly at Ash. "…right here."

The ghostly mage immediately vanished, and Ash stepped out from around the corner with a guilty expression.

"I'm sorry, Master," said Ash. "I didn't mean to intrude or listen in. My curiosity got the better of me."

"It's okay. No harm was done," said the Wizard.

"Can I ask what all that was about?"

"We'll talk about it later. Now I'd very much like to know how things went with April."

"Things actually went really well. I'm glad I went to her and apologized. It was definitely the right thing to do," replied Ash. "I also had this awesome idea, and I have something I really want to show you."

The Wizard gave Ash a wide smile, bringing out the crow's feet at the corners of his eyes. "Well, then, come over here. Let's see it."

"I'll need my wand back to show you," said Ash, as he walked over to the Wizard while removing his jacket.

With his coat removed, Ash revealed that he had something strapped to his right arm. It extended from his wrist to just below his elbow. It appeared to be made mostly of black leather but included a long metallic cylinder, along with some mechanical parts, strapped to the inside of the wrist. After the Wizard handed him his sapphire-tipped wand, he pushed it up into the metallic cylinder.

"Are you ready?" Ash asked excitedly.

"Can't wait," replied the Wizard.

Ash stepped back then flung his arm to his side while jerking his wrist back. As he completed this motion, the wand flew out of the metallic cylinder. As it soared forward, he moved his hand back just in time to catch it. He twirled the wand around a few times between his fingers before laying it to rest again in the palm of his hand. Then, using his middle finger, he pushed the wand toward the metallic cylinder. When the end of the wand was a little more than an inch inside, something grabbed hold of it and sucked it in the rest of the way.

"Pretty cool, huh?" asked Ash proudly.

The Wizard smiled broadly again. "You never cease to amaze me, my initiate."

"Well, should we get this day started?" Ash asked, as he shot his wand into his hand.

"Actually," said the Wizard, "I'm not sure how much you overheard from my conversation with Sebastian, but I have to spend the rest of the day making some preparations. You should take today off and get some rest. I'll come by to see you this evening."

While Ash was a little disappointed, he actually was exhausted. He'd gotten only a few hours of sleep and could use the extra rest. He left the Wizard in the warehouse and walked back to his dorm room. Within a few minutes, he was lying on his bed and quickly fell into a deep sleep.

*

The Wizard arrived at Ash's dorm room in the early evening. He dispensed with his usual pleasantries and got straight to the point. The time for training had ended, and Ash was going to be leaving on his first mission that night.

"I have something for you. You'll need it for where you're going," said the Wizard.

He reached into the right side of his robe and slowly pulled out a dark wooden box that was much larger than what could possibly have been stored beneath his cloak. It was as if it were materializing into existence as he drew it forward. When the complete box was revealed, the Wizard rotated it and caught the other end in his other hand. He bowed his head and handed the box to Ash.

Ash took the box from him. By its weight he could tell that it contained something light, perhaps a piece of clothing. After sitting on the edge of his bed, he laid the box on his lap and removed the cover. Inside was a dark, folded cloak. He placed the box to the side and stood up to reveal the full garment. It was a very deep black, with a royal-blue hood and trim that ran down the back and along each of the arms.

"This cloak will allow you to pass completely unnoticed by mortals," the Wizard explained. "While it won't make you invisible, you'll be able to walk through rivers of people, and they'll part before you, never paying you any mind. Technical machines created by mortals, like cameras, will find only blurred images or no images at all. To activate the cloak's powers, draw the hood down over your head."

Ash flipped the cloak over his head quickly, and as it came down, he slipped both arms into the sleeves. Somehow it was very familiar to him, as if he'd always known how to wear it. He put his hands behind his head and pulled the hood over his head and eyes. The end of the hood was hooked, like one might imagine the cowl of the Grim Reaper himself. Ash's eyes let out a vibrant blue glow beneath the hood, and light-azure smoke poured out of the sides.

The Wizard continued, "Be forewarned that the cloak won't hide your presence from any of our kind—or theirs. You've seen and felt the power of the Touched firsthand. You know what we're up against."

Ash nodded. "I'm ready. What do you need me to do?"

"There's a young woman of some importance. Though she doesn't know it yet, she needs our help, and I need you to find her whereabouts," said the Wizard. "Under no circumstance are you to try to retrieve her on your own. Once you have her location, report back to me."

"I understand," said Ash, as he fastened his wand to his wrist. "Where should I start looking?"

"Unfortunately even her rough location is being shrouded from us. But we're aware of someone we believe has the power to locate her. He might be the only one who can. His name is Jack, Smiling Jack. Getting his assistance, however, won't be an easy task. He's one of the Touched."

"One of the Touched—then why would he help us?" asked Ash.

"Like I said, he'll take some convincing, but he isn't like the other one you encountered. While he bears a soul tainted by darkness, he serves no one but himself. Use this to your advantage. We have little time, Ash."

"I won't fail you, Master," Ash said confidently.

The Wizard reached into his cloak again, this time pulling out an envelope and a stack of cash. He handed both of these to Ash, who peeked inside the envelope and saw a pair of airplane tickets, along with some other documents. As he read his travel destination, he thought, *Makes sense for a half demon to hide there*. He gave one last look and nod to the Wizard before he left the room. His first mission had just started, and once again his life never would be the same.

CHAPTER 15

SMILING JACK

Despite his odd attire and the fact that he had a strange contraption strapped to his arm, Ash had no problems getting through security at Logan Airport. As the Wizard had said, his cloak caused the mortals, by seeming coincidence, to accommodate him. In the security check line, a TSA agent conveniently pulled him aside for a pat down, allowing him to bypass the metal detector. Then, during the pat down, the agent conveniently forgot to search his right arm.

The Wizard had booked him in first class on the flight from Boston to Las Vegas. He had been on a plane only a few times and never had the opportunity or money to fly in first class. Taking his seat near the window in the front row, he leaned his head back and thought about how he would go about finding Smiling Jack. Vegas was a big city, and he had no clue where to start.

Shortly after takeoff, he removed the envelope from his pocket and looked through the other information it contained. Ash was so eager to start his first mission that he neglected to ask the Wizard more about it. Hopefully there would be some answers within. Inside he found a handwritten note from the Wizard, a typed memo containing information about Smiling Jack, and a photograph of the young woman he was supposed to locate.

He read the message from the Wizard first:

> *Ash,*
>
> > *As you read this letter, you'll have started your journey to find Smiling Jack. I'm truly sorry I can't join you on your first mission.*
> >
> > *The first time I left you, you weren't prepared for what was before you. Now I believe you are ready and will make me proud. You've always had great ability, but now you also have great direction and focus.*
> >
> > *By the word of the council, you're to convince Jack to help you by whatever means you deem necessary. Once he's revealed the location of the girl, you're to report back to me. I'll be a great distance away, and a telepathy spell likely won't be powerful enough to reach me. Thankfully the mortals have invented a device that will serve just as well. My cell number is 425-555-1409. Call me as soon as you have the girl's location.*
> >
> > *I have no additional words of wisdom for you, and all I can do now is wish you the best of luck.*
> *Your friend,*
> *—W*

Next he read the memo on Smiling Jack:

CONFIDENTIAL
NAME: Porter, Jack
ALIASES: "Smiling Jack" or "Fat Jack"

SMILING JACK

CLASSIFICATION: Touched
ABILITIES: precognition
HEIGHT: 5 ft. 8 in.
WEIGHT: 278 lbs.
HAIR COLOR: black
EYE COLOR: brown
SEX: male
LOCATION: Las Vegas, Nevada
REMARKS: Our sources tell us that Jack Porter has been living in Las Vegas for the past few years. He appears to be using his ability to predict the future to win at gambling. His favorite game is blackjack. Rarely alone, he travels with an entourage, including several bodyguards and a childhood friend named Bruce. He suffers from several drug addictions and is almost always at least mildly intoxicated. Though he rotates through many of the Las Vegas–area casinos, his recent favorite appears to be the Wynn. He often has a private area reserved for him in the upper level of a nightclub called XS.

In the top-right corner of the dossier was a slightly blurry picture of Jack. It was obviously out of date; given the weight listed on the memo, it looked like the man in the photo could be swallowed whole by the Jack of today. At least now Ash had a rough understanding of what Jack looked like and where he could start his search.

Finally he looked at the photograph of the girl. It was a little worse for wear, as the edges were torn and wrinkled. However, the image itself was reasonably intact. It was of a young woman, maybe in her late teens or early twenties. She had long dark-brown hair, fair skin, and mesmerizing blue eyes. Her face wore a smile, but there was a certain sadness to her.

BLOOD AND ASH

Ash flipped over the photograph to find some information written on the back. According to the date on the picture, it was taken eight years ago, and the girl's name was Sinthia Greyson. His best guess was that she would be in her midtwenties now. There were also some smaller notes near the bottom. They were severely smudged and nearly impossible to read, but Ash could tell they appeared to be in a different handwriting than the notes above. He was unable to discern anything from them, save for a signature that read, "Aleister."

Ash rested for the remainder of the flight until the captain announced that the plane was about to make its approach into Las Vegas. He looked out his window. It was nighttime over the desert, and all he could see was darkness. The plane slowly tilted its wing upward toward the moon as it started to turn. As the wing came back down, out of the blackness a glimmer of light appeared, and then suddenly a bright shiny city emerged. It was beautiful. Even from this distance, Ash felt its energy, its pulse, and he finally understood why people from all over the world flocked to it: to feel alive.

*

The Bellagio's high-roller lounge catered to Las Vegas's elite. You know those square chips that you only see in James Bond films that are worth tens of thousands of dollars? Well, this was where you'd see them for real. Jack was seated at a blackjack table with just the dealer. He had grown quite large over the years, and if it weren't for his tailor-made all-black Giorgio Armani suit, he would have garnered looks of disgust rather than ones of respect. As was customary for him these days, his eyes were covered with a pair of dark sunglasses.

SMILING JACK

On the table in front of Jack rested a mound of chips. He toyed with the top few as he sipped champagne from his glass. An open bottle of Roederer Cristal Rose was chilling in an ice bucket next to him.

"Sir," said the dealer, "would you like to hit?"

The dealer had an eight of diamonds showing. Jack looked down at his cards. He had a ten of clubs and a nine of diamonds: nineteen. No matter which book you read or how lucky you think you might be, this is a no-brainer; no reasonable person would hit on a nineteen with an eight showing.

Jack rubbed his chin for a moment then smiled. "Hit me."

*

After deplaning, Ash quickly made his way to the terminal exit. Though he had no idea exactly where Jack was, he knew time was of the essence, and the sooner he got out of the airport, the sooner he could get started. As he hurried past a gift shop, an idea struck him as to how to find Jack. He turned around and went inside to purchase a tourist map and a pen.

He walked over to an empty seat near one of the large airport windows, making sure it offered a good view of the city in the distance. After he had unfolded the map, he searched for and quickly found the airport. Judging by what he could see outside, he oriented the map as best he could and drew a small arrow towards the city.

Ash looked around and saw that a fair amount of people were still in the vicinity, and for the next part of his plan, he needed some privacy. He scanned the area until he spotted a sign for a men's restroom. It would have to do. He walked over and went in.

The restroom wasn't crowded but had a steady flow of people coming in and out. Ash thought it best to conduct his activities in one of the stalls and made his way to the one farthest from the entryway.

After closing the stall door, he lowered the toilet seat, sat down and laid the map on his lap, orienting it as best as he could.

He took out the dossier on Jack and stared at the picture. Then he closed and opened his eyes several times until he could clearly hold the image in his head. With this as the only thought in his mind, he flicked his wrist and shot his wand into his hand. As quietly as he could, he chanted, "ᏓᎶ ᎣᎶ (MA-ONA)."

Almost immediately, Ash felt his wand move in his hand, as if it were being pulled by a powerful magnet. The image in his head morphed and came alive. He saw Smiling Jack in a casino. He was seated alone at a table and playing blackjack. The visuals were vivid and clear. Unfortunately for Ash, he'd never been inside a single casino in Las Vegas and didn't recognize a damn thing.

He waited for the wand to quit moving then opened his eyes. The wand was pointing northwest. To the best of his ability, he drew a straight line from his current location, heading in the direction his wand was indicating to him. His future engineering degree was being put to work here. The line intersected the MGM Grand, the Cosmopolitan, the Bellagio, and the Rio. This would have to do for now. He retracted his wand, folded up the map, and made his way out of the stall.

As Ash was leaving the restroom, a young man with spiked green hair passed him and said, "Awesome contacts, bro!"

Ash froze in his tracks and slowly looked at the mirror. His eyes were swirling and dancing with blue energy. Frantically he searched his pockets for his sunglasses but realized he must have left them at home. With no other immediate solution, he pulled his hood over his head until it covered his eyes. With his head lowered, he continued on his way.

Once outside, he looked for a cab. He soon spotted a ridiculously long line that weaved back and forth like a giant snake of people and luggage. It would take forever to get a taxi this way. This simply wouldn't do. He looked around for a viable alternative and saw a sign for limousines. As he walked toward the sign, he thought, *Well, a hero's got to do what a hero's got to do.*

Ash quickly found the limo area; fortunately there wasn't a line here. He lowered the hood of his cloak to his shoulders and within a few moments was eagerly greeted by a tall, slim man dressed in an expensive suit with a pair of sunglasses tucked in his jacket pocket.

"Need a limousine, young man?" he said.

"Yes, I do," replied Ash. "How much is it?"

"Well, that depends on where you're going. Where are you headed?"

Honestly Ash didn't really know. He had four possible locations where Jack could be. Guessing was definitely an option, but perhaps he could narrow his search.

"Well, let's say I was a high roller and wanted access to an upscale private blackjack table," said Ash. "Where would you recommend?"

"Son," said the man, "that could be almost any casino in Las Vegas, but I guess I'd recommend the Aria, the Bellagio, or the Wynn."

"Then I'm headed to the Bellagio," said Ash, since the Bellagio was on his list of Jack's possible whereabouts.

"Okay, that would be one hundred dollars, not including tip. You good with that?"

"Tell you what, I'll give you two hundred if you throw in those sunglasses."

The man thought for a few seconds then exclaimed, "These are Maui Jims! Make it three hundred, and we have a deal."

Ash smiled. "Deal!"

*

Jack was pulling back a pile of chips from his last win when Bruce entered the high-roller room. Bruce was dressed in a tailored black Italian suit and a deep-red tie. His red hair was shaved very short, and he had an almost military look about him. He strutted confidently over to the table and placed a hand on Jack's shoulder.

"Hey, buddy," he said, "The boys are headed to the Wynn. You want to finish up here so we can join them?"

"Just a few more hands. I'm still feeling lucky," said Jack, as he looked up and winked at Bruce.

"All right," replied Bruce. "I'll go grab the car and meet you out front in a few minutes."

As Bruce walked out, Jack turned his attention back to the dealer. "You heard the man. I only have a few more hands. So make 'em good ones."

"I'll do my best, sir," said the dealer, as he grabbed the cards from the shuffle machine and started to deal.

This was the part where Jack would give some—or sometimes even all—of his winnings back to the casino. That was the first rule of Las Vegas: never let the house know you're winning. With his ability, he could have been the richest man in Vegas several times over. Of course this probably would have resulted in his being banned from the casinos for life or, worse yet, winding up as the deadest man in Vegas. He often shifted his wins and losses between casinos. One week he'd go to Caesars and win hundreds of thousands of dollars, and then he'd head over to the Mirage and lose hundreds of thousands of dollars. The next week, he'd do the reverse, or sometimes he'd spread the wins or losses out over a period of months. The key was to appear as random as possible, when in fact these weren't even games to Jack; he was the one who decided to win or lose with every flip of the cards, roll of the dice, or spin of the wheel.

After he felt he'd given enough money back, he took one last sip from his champagne. "Guess my luck ran out," he said. "Can you color me up?"

"Of course, sir," replied the dealer, as he started to stack and count Jack's chips. "I'm sure you'll have better luck next time."

When the dealer was done, he pushed a still-sizable stack of chips toward Jack. Jack grabbed one of the top chips, which was worth ten thousand dollars, and tossed it to the dealer. This was the second rule of Las Vegas: treat people well, and they'll treat you well. Everyone loved Jack, even when he was losing; he always had a smile on his face and never forgot to leave a big tip.

The dealer's eyes grew wide. "You're most gracious, sir, but this is more than I deserve. Are you sure?"

"Absolutely," said Jack, flashing an enormous smile. "They don't pay you guys nearly enough. This is my way of saying I appreciate what you do."

"Thank you so much. Have a good rest of your evening, sir."

Jack slowly got up—a man of his girth rarely moves quickly—and headed out of the high-roller room, carrying his stack of chips. He made a quick stop at the cashier's office on his way. The nice woman behind the counter handed him several clean, crisp thousand-dollar bills. By his count, he'd made approximately $42,000 tonight, not bad for a "hard" night's work.

As Jack approached the Bellagio's lobby, two well-built, well-dressed men stood up at a nearby piano bar and joined him. They were his personal bodyguards, and despite his size, he almost never traveled without them. The men escorted Jack out of the building, walking a few feet in front of him. It would be too bold to say they cleared a path for him, but with their build, attire, and demeanor, people just moved out of the way.

As soon as Jack got outside, he took a deep breath of the brisk evening desert air. A stretch limousine pulled up a few moments later. One of the men walked forward and opened the door for Jack. Bruce was seated in the back, sipping on a glass of Glenfarclas Scotch. He moved over to make room for Jack. Though not a single one of them would ever point it out, it took Jack several awkward motions to squeeze into the car. The two men got in afterward and closed the door behind them.

The driver's voice came over the speaker system in the limo. "Where to tonight?"

"To the Wynn," replied Jack.

*

The whole city was illuminated by lights, set against the dark background of the night. Ash wasn't entirely sure that the driver was taking the most efficient route to the Bellagio. Several times he could have sworn that it appeared to be only a few blocks away, and then the driver would make a turn. Of course everything in Las Vegas seems much closer than it actually is.

The limo pulled up to the entrance of the Bellagio. Ash peered out the window to have a look around; seas of people were flowing in and out of the casino. *How will I ever find Jack in all of this?* he wondered. The driver got out of the car and walked over to open the door for his passenger. Ash got out of the car and gave the driver three one-hundred-dollar bills. The man thanked him and handed him the pair of Maui Jim sunglasses. Ash put them on, pulled his hood over the top of his head, and made his way into the casino.

The Bellagio's lobby was incredible. An enormous colorful chandelier hung from its center and looked like thousands of luminescent glass flowers. The floors appeared to be made of marble and had an intricate pattern that reminded Ash of Italian or maybe Greek designs he had seen only in books. The lobby stretched into the distance for almost as far as he could see. A long check-in counter ran across the wall to Ash's left. To his right, the lobby opened into the casino floor. This was where he needed to go.

Ash spent the next few minutes trying to navigate his way around the gaming tables to look for Jack. He had heard how large the casinos were in Vegas, but experiencing it was something else entirely. There was no way he would be able to find him by simply walking around and looking. He decided it was best to cast another spell to see if he could discern more information about Jack's location.

It took Ash another few minutes just to locate a restroom, where he could do his magic in private. When he cast the spell, this time the image in his head revealed that Jack was on the move. He had missed him. Jack was in the backseat of a long car, surrounded by other people. From what Ash could see, he was headed down a street filled with lights and advertisements on all sides. Ash's wand swayed slightly back and forth in his hand. When he opened his eyes and compared the direction to his map, he knew Jack was headed roughly north.

Several casinos were located along this path: Caesars, the Mirage, Treasure Island, the Venetian, the Palazzo, and the Wynn. From the dossier, Ash recalled that Jack often frequented a club in the Wynn called XS. *That has to be where he's headed,* Ash thought.

He collected his things then attempted to navigate his way back to the lobby. This task proved to be much more difficult than he'd expected. The casino appeared to be designed like a maze that was meant to keep people from ever leaving. However, after a few minutes, he spotted the colorful chandelier in the distance and finally reached the lobby.

When he stepped outside and looked around for anything that could give him his bearings, he eventually spotted Caesars to his left. This gave him the rough direction in which he needed to go. As he headed toward the Wynn, he passed the massive fountain in front of the Bellagio. Suddenly an Italian symphony played out of several speakers hidden in the bushes along the path. The fountain erupted in a dazzling show of water and light. Hundred-foot-high water columns shot into the air and swayed to the rhythm of the music. As crowds gathered along the edge of the fountain to watch the show, Ash continued forward, easily passing through the herds of people.

Several times along the way, he stopped to confirm he was headed in the right direction, and in his mind, he eventually caught glimpses of Jack in a club. After a long hike, he finally reached the entrance to the Wynn. It soon would be time for him to ask Jack for his help. Ash was hoping Jack would simply collaborate, but something told him this evening wasn't going to end without incident.

*

The party was raging at XS. The loud beat of club music filled the air. Throngs of people were drinking and dancing.

In a private booth on the upper level, Smiling Jack was reclined in the middle of a U-shaped leather couch. Two scantily clad, very young women sat beside him, each resting under one of his massive arms. Smoke billowed out of a thick Cuban cigar that he held between his lips.

The table in front of him held an arrangement of high-end liquor bottles, including Stoli Elit and a Macallan 1939. Several members of his entourage occupied the other seats and were busy consuming drinks and talking. His bodyguards stood stoically near the door with their arms crossed as they surveyed the area, ready to jump into action should any uninvited guests try to enter.

Watching the crowd below, Bruce rested his hands on the railing at the edge of the booth. He obviously was enjoying himself as he swayed his head to the beat of the music. With some effort, Jack, having had enough lounging, got up and walked over to his friend. When he reached Bruce, he rested an arm around him and smiled widely. The two looked down below together; if there were winners and losers in this town, they were surely on the winning end of the spectrum.

After a few minutes of people watching, Jack spotted something in the crowd. "Well, I'll be damned," he said.

"What?" Bruce asked.

Jack pointed into the crowd. "You see that guy over there in the blue hood?"

"Where?" Bruce asked, as he looked where Jack was pointing.

"Right there!" said Jack, jerking his finger back and forth.

Bruce shrugged. "I don't see anything."

At that moment, Ash pulled the hood from his cloak down to his shoulders. To Bruce's eyes, a blurry figure slowly became clear and emerged from the crowd. He must have looked in that area a dozen times, but only now did he see Ash for the first time.

"Wait, I think I see him," Bruce said. "You mean that silly-looking blond kid, wearing the sunglasses?"

"Yeah, him," said Jack. "Go down there and invite him up here."

Bruce raised an eyebrow. "Seriously? Why?"

"Because he's here for me. He's one of *them*."

"Then…shouldn't we, like, get out of here?" exclaimed Bruce.

"Nah. This guy won't stop until he finds me. That's the way these people work. Better to do this here in public. He'll be less likely to try anything funky. Now go down and invite him up."

Jack turned to his guests. "All right, everyone. I have some business to attend to, so you'll all have to leave. Thanks for coming. Grab your drinks and head on out."

His announcement was met with frowns and boos, but this was Jack's private booth, and he was in charge. Slowly his companions gathered their belongings and made their way to the door. Bruce followed the crowd as they headed downstairs. The two girls who had been sitting with Jack remained seated, looked at each other, and giggled.

"That means you too, girls," said Jack, motioning his head toward the door.

With somewhat arrogant looks of disbelief, the two girls picked up their purses and drinks and waltzed out of the room. The bodyguards exited as well and closed the door behind them, standing guard outside. After everyone had left, Jack walked over to the couch, took a seat, and poured himself a glass of exorbitantly priced Scotch.

A few minutes later, the door opened, and in walked Bruce, followed by Ash. The two bodyguards peeked in their heads and looked over at Jack to make sure everything was okay. Jack gave them a nod, and they shut the door.

"Jack, do you want me to stay?" asked Bruce.

"I don't think that'll be necessary," he said, "but before you give us some quiet time, could you come over here for a second?"

Bruce walked over to where Jack was sitting and leaned his head in close. Jack whispered something in his ear. Ash tried to listen in but couldn't hear a word. Bruce nodded in acknowledgment then left the room.

"Pour you a glass of Scotch?" asked Jack.

"No, thanks. I'm good," replied Ash.

To read about Jack and now stand in front of him were two entirely different things. This man was ginormous and didn't seem the least bit intimidated by Ash. Instead he sat there calmly, wearing a smile. Ash's pulse rose slightly. He worried for a moment that nervousness would set in, but instead his mind focused, and a heightened sense of awareness rushed over him.

"Suit yourself," said Jack, as he poured himself another glass.

After his glass was amply filled, he plucked two cubes of ice from a tray and dropped them into his Scotch. He looked over at Ash and motioned to the seat across from him. "Well, at least take a seat then," he said.

"I'm fine standing," replied Ash. The two were silent for a moment, and then Ash asked, "Do you know who I am?"

"I don't know who you are, but I know *what* you are."

"That should make things easier," said Ash. "Do you know why I'm here?"

Jack brought his hand up to his chin and rubbed it a few times before responding. "I'd guess you're here for one of two reasons: one, you've come here to kill me, or two, you've come to ask for my help. Given that I'm still sitting here breathing and drinking this fine glass of Scotch, I'm thinking it's the latter."

"You would be correct," replied Ash.

"Then you're going to leave here disappointed, boy," said Jack. "In case you haven't heard, I don't do that anymore."

"Well, then I'll have to convince you."

"Son, you don't scare me," Jack said, before taking another sip of his Scotch then placing it on the table in front of him. "You know what scares me?" he continued. "Dark-hooded evil demons. The kind that haunt you in your dreams, the kind that stay with you when you're awake, and the kind that, if you don't cooperate with them, you wind up physically or mentally destroyed. And I'm not messing with that!"

"I'm not here about demons," replied Ash. "I'm here to find a girl."

"You aren't getting it!" Jack said, raising his voice. "If I use my ability to look more than a few seconds into the future, then I see him and he sees me. The last time that happened, I was out of commission for months, and I'm not doing it again!"

"Who are you talking about?"

"I'm sorry, but while he was busy murdering me, I didn't stop to ask his name. He scared the crap out of me."

"Look, Jack, I know you're scared," said Ash in a calming voice, "but there's a girl out there who needs our help."

Aside from helping save Bruce's life many years ago, Jack never had done anything with his ability except use it for his own personal gain. This private booth, this Scotch, the women he surrounded himself with—everything he had was a reflection of this. He could tell from the look on the boy's face, however, that he was being sincere, and although something inside him yearned to finally do something that was worthwhile and good, the risk was too great.

"I'm sorry. I really would like to help you, but this isn't going to happen," said Jack, as he reached into his pocket and secretly pressed the "call" button on his phone.

Within a few seconds, the door opened, and the two bodyguards, followed by Bruce, entered the room. They shut the door behind them and stood at the ready, awaiting word from Jack to take further action.

"I think it's time for you to leave," Jack said with a great big smile as he reached for his Scotch.

Ash took a look at the two large gentlemen then back at Jack. "All right, chubby, I guess we'll have to do this the hard way!"

He pulled down his sunglasses to reveal his bright-blue eyes. Jumping into action, the two bodyguards moved aggressively toward Ash. He quickly flicked his wrist, caught his wand, and pointed it toward them in one swift motion. Before they could reach him, he chanted, "𝔇ꙇ Ⱐᴄ (KI-UC)."

His eyes ignited in brilliant blue flames as an azure energy shot forth from his wand. The spell engulfed the two bodyguards, along with Bruce, and hurled them violently against the wall behind them. Ash raised his wand slowly, and with this action, the three incapacitated bodies rose higher into the air. Jack's whiskey glass fell from his hand and shattered on the floor. He was no longer smiling.

Ash looked at Jack and, with a cobalt stare, said, "Perhaps I forgot to mention that I don't have a whole lot of time."

"Okay! Okay!" pleaded Jack in a panic. "Just don't hurt them. Please let them down."

Ash lowered the three bodies to the floor before discontinuing the spell. The energy in his eyes died down slightly as he twirled his wand in his hand before returning it to its sheath. The two bodyguards and Bruce lay motionless, but still breathing, on the floor.

This was the first time Ash had ever used magic against actual attackers. Although his heart was pounding from nervousness and excitement, he didn't let the stern, confident expression on his face change. He reached into his cloak and pulled out the picture of Sinthia then handed it to Jack.

"I need you to help me find this girl, Sinthia Greyson," he said. "The file I have on you says you have the power of precognition, the ability to see the future. Now I don't have any idea how that's going to help here, but something tells me *you* do."

Jack lowered his head and sighed. "I do—a paradox."

"A paradox?" asked Ash. "Like in *Star Trek*?"

Jack raised his head and his eyebrows. "Great, I'm dealing with a nerd. Yes, just like in *Star Trek*."

With a slight look of embarrassment, Ash asked, "So how does this work?"

"There's no guarantee it actually will work, but I might be able to force myself to see a possible future where you and I go to see this girl. However, the only reason I would know where to go in that possible future would be because I would have already seen it by previously looking in the future—hence the paradox."

Ash tried to ponder what Jack was saying, but it hurt his head. The whole concept of alternate and potential realities was too far out there for him. There was a reason he had decided to study engineering rather than theoretical physics. Then again, over the course of the past few months, his views and understanding of the world had dramatically widened. Magic was real, and the possibility of what was and what could be was boundless. So if Jack thought it might work, they were going to give it a try.

"I don't think I understood a word you said, but if you think it'll work, let's give it a shot," said Ash.

"It won't be that easy," replied Jack. "You see, I've had a couple—okay, maybe more than a couple—of drinks tonight, and that dulls my abilities. We'll have to wait for the alcohol to completely clear my system before we can try this. You might want to take that seat now."

"I've got you covered," said Ash, as he shot his wand into his hand.

"Hey! Don't point that thing at me! Don't—" exclaimed Jack as he clenched up and covered his body with both arms.

Before Jack could utter another word, Ash had pointed his wand at him and chanted, "ᑐK ᒧR (IK-ARI)." Mild blue flames danced in Ash's eyes, and then, almost instantaneously, Jack felt all the toxins leave his body. For the first time since that fateful night with Stevie so many years ago, he was fully sober. It was if he'd awoken from a long, hazy, unending dream to finally see the real world once more. He didn't know how empty his cup had become until it was full again.

"Wow," Jack said exuberantly, as he looked over himself. "I feel fantastic!"

He lifted his sunglasses and looked down at the picture of Sinthia then raised his head with a smile. His eyes were taking on an ambient red glow.

"Now it's my turn," he said.

*

It had been years since Jack had stretched his abilities beyond the few seconds required to win at gambling. During his trance, his vision started off hazier than he had remembered it usually being. However, he could tell that it was dark outside and that he was in the passenger seat of a newer-model car. As his vision started to stabilize, he saw that Ash was in the driver's seat. The car pulled to a stop.

"This must be the place," Ash said, as he turned to Jack.

Knowing he was here to gather information about the location, Jack scanned the area. They had pulled over to the side of the road, across from an old, quaint, two-story house. The building was covered in brick siding and had a brown shingle roof. A small grass lawn was out front, separated from the street by a concrete sidewalk and driveway. Parked in the driveway was a black SUV. Perhaps he would be able to read the license plate or the number on the house when he got closer, but for now he didn't have much to go on.

"Well, we'd better get going," said Ash. "If your vision was correct, then we don't have much time!"

Ash and Jack exited the vehicle and made their way across the street; several similar but single-story houses were on both sides. Jack couldn't see any street signs and wanted to walk down the street to see if he could find anything but was worried about not doing exactly what he should be doing in this possible future. So he just continued to look around.

Behind the house were many tall cypress trees slowly swaying in the wind. As the branches parted, Jack caught a glimpse of something behind them. There was a bridge. A very tall bridge! He thought he recognized it but wasn't sure. The bridge was under construction, and there appeared to be a crane not too far behind the house.

As they walked up to the front door, Jack glanced at the license plate on the car. The numbers were fuzzy, and he couldn't quite make them out, but he saw a very distinct symbol on the left side of the plate. It was the symbol for the Saints, and here he'd thought that betting on football games would never pay off. He now knew they were in New Orleans, and the bridge he'd thought he recognized must be crossing the Mississippi.

This information was probably enough to go on, Jack figured. He tried to exit his trance, but something strange happened. Rather than waking up, he hopped a few minutes into the future. He and Ash were seated at a kitchen table. Steam poured up from two freshly brewed cups of coffee in front of them. A young woman with long, dark-brown hair was facing the counter. As she turned around, Jack recognized her from the photograph Ash had given him earlier. It was Sinthia Greyson.

He looked around the room for any more clues he could gather. On the fridge he spotted a calendar. Most of the days of the month had been crossed off, save for the last few. He tried to focus more closely without being too obvious about it. If that thing was correct, then he was seeing only a day into the future. This was tomorrow!

There was a knock at the door.

"I usually don't get so many visitors, especially at this time of night. Let me see who it is. I'll be right back," said Sinthia, as she headed toward the front of the house.

Jack leaned his head back to watch her. As she reached for the doorknob, things started to move in slow motion. As Sinthia slowly opened the door, it was flung open with such force that it knocked her to the floor. Jack saw two figures in black trench coats standing in the doorway. They appeared mostly human, but their skin was much paler than it should have been, and their eyes were pits of pure darkness.

Sinthia tried to crawl backward on her hands. One of the creatures stepped forward and stood above her. It reached into its coat and pulled out a dagger with a glowing, green, twisted blade. It then raised the knife into the air and gripped it with both hands in a ritualistic manner before thrusting it into Sinthia's chest. Blood splattered against the walls on both sides of her.

The creatures stepped farther into the house, and Jack saw there were at least a dozen or more behind them. Beyond the creatures, farther in the distance, he caught a glimpse of a man in a black cloak. His eyes glowed red from under his hood.

Jack turned toward Ash and yelled, "He's here!"

*

Jack awoke on the floor in the private booth at XS. He was breathing heavily, sweat dripping from his brow. Ash was kneeling next to him, holding his hand. While future minutes had passed for Jack, from Ash's point of view it had been only a few seconds.

"Are we at the stage in our relationship where we're holding hands now?" asked Jack.

Ash jerked his hand back. "Sorry. Your whole body was shaking, and I was worried."

"So I have some good news, some bad news, and some really bad news," Jack said, sitting up. "Which would you like to hear first?"

"I guess I'll take the good news first."

"Well, the good news is that I found Sinthia," said Jack. "The bad news is that we aren't the only ones looking for her. In my vision she was in danger. And the really bad news...well, you remember that demon fella I was telling you about earlier? He was there."

"Great," Ash said. "Well, at least that won't be my problem. I just needed to find her location and call it in. Can you describe it for me?"

"That's not the way this works. It's just like in *Star Trek*. You see, if we don't go together, then this whole paradox thing comes into play, and I'm not quite sure what will happen. You and I both need to see this through."

Ash shook his head. "I can't ask you to do that."

"Don't you understand?" replied Jack. "You already have."

*

They sat in the back of Jack's limo as a driver took them to the airport. Jack recounted the rest of the story in as much detail as he could remember. Ash took careful notes and searched for the girl's location with the map application on his cell phone. Using the street-view feature, he was able to a find a house near the Huey P. Long Bridge in New Orleans that matched Jack's description. This had to be where they needed to go.

Before they reached the airport, Ash also decided that he at least needed to let the Wizard know what he was doing and why. However, the phone number he was given went straight to voice mail. He left a message describing the situation and giving the girl's location. Hopefully the Wizard would get it soon and meet them there. This was the best he could do; the girl was in danger, and she needed his help.

"I hope we can still get a flight out of here at this time of night," Ash said, as they took the exit to the airport.

"Oh, I don't think that'll be a problem," replied Jack.

"Wait, didn't we just past the terminal?"

Jack nodded. "Yep."

"Where are we going?" asked Ash.

"I never fly commercial," replied Jack. "We'll take my private jet. It's faster, safer, and has much better food."

The flight from Las Vegas to New Orleans was far from smooth. A freak storm coming in from the northeast and passing over Texas forced Jack's plane to land in El Paso. He and Ash would have to rent a car and drive the rest of the way. Hopefully they would still make it in time.

CHAPTER 16
TAKE MY HAND

The turmoil from using the Seer's Gate left Aleister in a coma-like state. Several days passed before the other mages discovered his body in the storage chamber of Archmedea. A mortal's body would have given way to death over this period of time, but the constitution of the Blessed was inhumanly strong. He was found barely breathing and in desperate need of care.

Aleister lay unconscious in his bed. The Wizard had arrived only moments earlier but already had pulled up a chair and was sitting next to him. This wasn't the first time he had seen his friend in such a state. He clasped his hands and leaned in over Aleister. Though he was doubtful he could hear anything, it didn't stop him from trying to console him.

"Aleister, I don't know if you can hear me," said the Wizard. "Guess it doesn't matter, since you never seem to listen, but I have to say this anyway. You really need to quit messing with that thing. One day it'll make you go blind."

The Wizard smiled to himself for a moment. Something in him was hoping Aleister would smile back, but he didn't. His unusually pale, expressionless face just gazed at the ceiling. The stare of a dead man was in his wide-open gold-speckled eyes, and they didn't move or even blink. The shallow breaths exiting his gaping mouth, causing slight stirs of his dark-blond goatee, were his only signs of life. The Wizard hated to see his friend in such a state.

There was a knock at the door, and then it slowly swung open. The Wizard looked over and saw the silver hair of Sebastian as his head poked into the room.

"Do you mind if I come in?" asked Sebastian.

"Of course not. Please do." The Wizard motioned him in.

Sebastian entered the room and closed the door behind him. The hood of his dark-gray cloak was down, and his long hair rested on his shoulders.

"I heard that you'd arrived and expected you to stop by the Great Chamber, but you didn't," said Sebastian.

"You have my apologies," replied the Wizard, before looking back toward the bed. "I wanted to check on Aleister first."

Sebastian nodded in understanding. "Of course."

"I can see that his body still breathes, but I can't feel his presence," said the Wizard. "Is there anything more you can tell me about his condition?"

"You'll recall that many years ago Aleister was almost pulled into the Nether itself," said Sebastian. "Ever since, it's had a grip on his soul. When he was using the Seer's Gate, something happened that separated his soul from his body. We believe it's being pulled into the Nether at this moment. When it's entirely consumed, this mortal coil before us will die. Unfortunately there isn't much that can be done."

"I refuse to believe that," exclaimed the Wizard. "I won't sit here and watch my friend perish. There must be something we can do."

Sebastian seemed to ponder his response before he replied, "There is, of course, one possibility, but it's far too dangerous for us to consider."

"What is it?" asked the Wizard. "Please tell me."

Sebastian sighed before continuing. "While his mortal shell still breathes, it's tied to the soul by a silver cord. This cord can stretch to any length, no matter how far the body and soul are apart. It might be possible for one of us to enter Aleister's aura and follow this silver cord to his soul and, thus, the source of whatever or whoever is pulling it. However, in doing so, one would subject oneself to the same forces that are currently tearing at Aleister."

"But you've always told me that astral projection was safe," said the Wizard.

"It is on this plane," replied Sebastian, "but if one travels to the darker planes of existence, one opens oneself up to the energies that govern them. The areas near the Nether are particularly dangerous."

"I understand, but I'm going nonetheless," said the Wizard. "More than my friend's life is at stake here—his very soul may be lost forever. I know he would do the same for me. The risk is mine to take."

"That it is," replied Sebastian. "I would like to try to convince you otherwise, but I've known you for far too long and know your stubbornness has no bounds. I'll watch over your bodies, but I must warn you, should you not return, I won't send in another soul to retrieve yours."

The Wizard nodded. "I understand."

He stood up and pushed his chair aside. Then he lay on the floor next to Aleister's bed. He pulled out his wand and held it in both hands as he crossed them in front of his chest. After closing his eyes, he chanted, "ᗰᔕ ᔕᐯ (MA-AVA)." A deep purple energy emanated from the jeweled tip of the wand then slowly crawled over the Wizard's body, forming a shell around him. When his body was entirely encased in the field, it went limp, for his soul had gone elsewhere.

*

The shock of trying to pass through the Seer's Gate had blasted back Aleister's soul. He knew it was risky, but he did what he had to do. At the very least, he had managed to save Detectives Valle and Kent and hopefully delayed the demon's plans. He hadn't expected the experience to leave him unscathed. However, what happened next was completely unpredicted.

Rather than waking up back in his body, he saw only darkness and felt something pull him upward. He floated for what seemed forever, and then suddenly he stopped. Some distance away, a brilliant light emerged in front of him. As the rays hit him, a calmness and peace came over him. *This is what it must be like to die,* he thought.

He slowly drifted toward the light, fully ready to accept what was to come, but then something wrapped around him and tugged at him. He looked down to see what was pulling him back. To his shock, the forms of two demonic female figures were gripping him with their clawed hands. They were nude and had blood-red skin decorated with a myriad of arcane black tattoos. Their long black hair floated back and forth, as if they were underwater. As they looked up at him, he saw they had the faces of beautiful young girls, save for their eyes, which were empty and black.

Fear overcame Aleister; his heart was pounding as if trying to escape from his chest. His eyes widened, and he threw open his mouth to yell, but no sound came out. He struggled to pull himself free. However, the strength of the demons seemed to increase with each motion he made. They gripped him tighter and tighter. He continued to fight but felt himself being slowly pulled downward by the demons. He realized their aim wasn't to kill him — at least not for now — but rather to take him somewhere. Somewhere he probably would rather not go. In a panic, as if he were drowning, he repeatedly thrust his hands upward, gripping the emptiness.

Time has little meaning in the void that is the astral plane, but to Aleister it felt as if he were fighting the demons' downward pull for hours or perhaps even days. His will was waning, and he didn't know how much longer he could hold on. Down below he saw a swirling crimson vortex. An unrelenting raw evil emanated from it, and a deep coldness came over Aleister's astral form.

Several more female demons emerged from the vortex. They flew upward and crawled all over Aleister, eventually engulfing him. He could no longer see and could only feel the tearing of their claws into his being. Ripping pain shot through his shaking body as they dug in. His eyes snapped shut and held tight as his teeth clenched in his open mouth. Every cell in his body screamed in agony. It was almost unbearable. There was little fight left in him, and the pull was getting stronger and stronger. With his last bit of effort, he thrust his arms upward one final time.

To his surprise, a hand wrapped around one of his and held it tightly. Then he felt it pull him out from the grip of the demons. He looked up, and as his head cleared the swarm of demons, he saw the form of the Wizard.

"Giving up so easily?" said the Wizard.

"I was just waiting for someone to give me a helping hand," Aleister said with a smile.

He willed himself upward as the Wizard pulled, but the demons weren't giving up so easily. A few of them flew toward the Wizard and wrapped themselves around him. Their claws dug into him, tearing at him and beginning to pull him down. As the Wizard struggled, he too felt them gain strength with each motion he made. It was as if they were feeding off his fear and panic.

"Their power grows the more we struggle!" yelled Aleister.

"If one path is blocked, one must try another," replied the Wizard.

"This isn't the time for riddles," Aleister said, pushing his foot against the head of one of the demons.

"Demons gain their strength by feeding on the lower emotions of mortals," yelled the Wizard. "Let go of your fear. Ignore the pain of their claws. Stay as calm as possible and think of the most pleasant memory you can remember. Think of how it raised your being and lifted your spirit."

Aleister closed his eyes and followed the Wizard's instructions. He pictured a scene from his childhood. He took in the sheer joy of being young again, when the world was still new and the thoughts of future struggles, yet to come, weren't even memories waiting to be formed. A peace rushed over him, and the present conflict, though he still felt it, started to feel as if it were happening to someone else far away.

At first he felt himself being pulled down even faster, but he didn't let these thoughts allow him to fall into a panic. Then he felt the strength of the Wizard's hand. His friend was here with him and would help him through this if he just trusted in him. Slowly he felt the spindly fingers of the demons slip off him, followed by a rush of what he could only describe as air whizzing past him as he flew upward.

The Wizard looked down at him and said, "Open your eyes, Aleister. We're almost there."

*

The elderly mage, Sebastian, was watching over the bodies of the Wizard and Aleister when suddenly Aleister jumped up. He'd been jolted back into his body and instantly awoke. He glanced around the room, trying to get his bearings. A few moments later, the Wizard's eyes opened. It had worked! The Wizard had retrieved Aleister's soul from the brink of being sucked into the Nether.

Sebastian smiled at Aleister. "Welcome back," he said.

Aleister was still frantically looking around the room for the Wizard when he replied, "Where is he?"

"Down here," the Wizard said from the floor, then pulled himself to his feet.

Pure joy coursed through Aleister's veins. "Thank you for coming for me! I don't know how much longer I could have lasted without your help."

"Anytime, my friend," replied the Wizard. "Of course, now that makes two you owe me."

Aleister managed to muster a smile and nodded.

"I swear the two of you find yourselves in more trouble than any of the other mages," said Sebastian. "I warned you not to tamper with the Seer's Gate, Aleister."

"I'm sorry, Master, but I couldn't stand idly by," asserted Aleister. "Too much is at risk, and I wasn't brought into this order to be a bystander."

"I suppose not," replied Sebastian reluctantly. "But hopefully you've at least learned something from this experience."

"I've learned much, but I don't think they're the lessons you think they are," Aleister said. "I now know how the Seer's Gate can be used to travel between places. I alone wasn't strong enough to operate it, but the council could!"

"Then you've learned nothing! We'll take no such risk!" exclaimed Sebastian, "That thing will be locked away forever."

"The two of you need to calm down," interjected the Wizard with a slightly raised voice. "I'm sensing there's more that Aleister has to tell us."

Aleister nodded. "There is. When I was peering through the Seer's Gate, I saw a demonic creature. It was using the Sangrian Map!"

"That isn't possible," stated Sebastian. "It's well known that only an angel or one of the Blessed can operate it."

"I swear! I saw it with my own eyes!" exclaimed Aleister.

"Calm down, Aleister," said the Wizard. "Can you tell us what sort of creature it was?"

Aleister nodded again. "It had pale white skin, deep-black wings, and razor-sharp claws. I encountered a similar creature when I was first trying to retrieve the map from the antique dealer, but this one was much larger and much more powerful."

"These creatures don't sound like the offspring of demons. They sound like full bloods," said the Wizard.

"As disturbing as this truth may be, I'm inclined to agree," said Sebastian.

"There's more," Aleister continued. "It also knew my name and could detect my presence through the Seer's Gate."

"If it knew your name, then it must have been Nihalus himself," exclaimed the Wizard.

"Though I didn't dare think it at the time, I believe you're right," said Aleister.

The Wizard let out a deep sigh. "I knew he would one day show his face again. It was only a matter of time."

"Aleister, did you see where the location on the map was pointing to or whom Nihalus was trying to locate?" asked Sebastian.

"I think I interrupted him before he could complete his work, but I can't be sure," answered Aleister.

"He surely must be seeking out the Blessed One," said the Wizard.

"Or perhaps he's looking for the girl," Sebastian said, rubbing his chin.

"She needs our protection! We must go to her!" exclaimed Aleister, as he sat up and appeared to be ready to jump out of the bed.

"Not to worry, Aleister," said the Wizard, laying his hand on his friend's chest. "I've sent my initiate to track her down. He's extremely capable, and I'm sure I'll hear from him soon."

"You sent your initiate?" Aleister scoffed. "And that's supposed to make me feel better?"

"You must trust me. He has power unlike any I've seen before. He won't fail me."

The Wizard lifted his hand from Aleister's chest and started to walk toward the door. Both Aleister and Sebastian looked surprised to see he had suddenly decided to leave.

"Where are you going?" asked Aleister.

"When the elders designed this place, I don't think they had modern technology in mind," answered the Wizard, as he opened the door. "I need to check on Ash, and there isn't exactly good cell reception down here."

CHAPTER 17
RECOVERING SIN

Alone and in the dark, Nihalus hung from the ceiling of an abandoned building. When his eyes opened, they ignited in red flames of anger and hatred. Several days had passed since he had sustained his injuries at the hands of Aleister and the detectives. His wounds finally had healed, and his powers had returned in full. For a moment, his thoughts drifted to revenge and the many ways he could exact pain upon them, but then he quickly returned to the task at hand. He had the map that would lead him to the boy, and once he had dealt with the Blessed One, there would be no one to stop him. The mortals would kneel at his feet, and the world would be his.

Nihalus dropped from the ceiling and spread his wings. He flew over to a dilapidated table and spread the Sangrian Map upon it. With a clawed fingernail, he sliced open his palm and let his blood drip onto the corner of the map. The blood spread across the surface, causing the continents of Pangea to drift into their present locations.

As he chanted, "◑ᒉ ◑ɴ (ONA-ON)," the lines on the map ignited in brilliant flames.

Nihalus stared intensely at the map. "Show me the location of the Blessed One!" he proclaimed.

From within the corner circle, a blue flame emerged. It moved around the map as it had before. Nihalus waited until it eventually stopped. After a few moments, its glow intensified as it hovered over a spot in the state of Louisiana.

"New Orleans," said the creature with a hiss in its voice. "I have you now!"

*

It was already dark when Ash pulled up the rental car along the side of the road, across the street from a house that matched the description and location from Jack's vision. The neighborhood was filled with small single-story houses, and this was the only two-story house in the area. The house was made of brick, as Jack had described, and a black SUV was parked in the driveway. Behind the house, Ash saw a large collection of trees moving in the wind. The full moon hovered in the cloudy sky, far above a tall bridge farther in the distance.

Ash turned to Jack and said, "This must be the place."

The two got out of the car and made their way across the street and up to the front door. Ash looked around, and when he couldn't find a buzzer, he knocked. A few moments later, they heard someone coming to the door. The door cracked open slightly, and the face of a young woman peered out. She had long dark-brown hair, fair skin, and a unique set of very deep-blue eyes. Jack and Ash immediately recognized her as the girl from the picture.

Sinthia looked at the two men. Ash was dressed in his blue-and-black cloak, and Jack was wearing his all-black Giorgio Armani suit.

Both were wearing sunglasses. While they appeared extremely odd, they didn't look threatening. Sinthia opened the door a little farther. She was wearing a white spaghetti-strap tank top and an old pair of jeans. Based on her attire, Ash fully expected a Southern accent to come from her lips but was surprised when he heard something else entirely.

"Hello," said Sinthia in a soft French accent. "Can I help you?"

"Hello," replied Ash. "Are you Sinthia Greyson?"

She raised a thin eyebrow. "Yes. Who wants to know?"

"My name's Ash, and this is my friend Jack," Ash said, before pausing with a dumb look on his face.

It suddenly had dawned on him that he had no idea how to continue this conversation. He knew he needed to convince Sinthia she was in danger and he and Jack were here to help, but what he needed to say to get her to trust him was beyond him. As he stood there thinking, she did it for him.

"Oh, are you here about renting the room?" asked Sinthia.

Ash realized this was exactly what he needed. "Yes."

"You do know I only have one small room available, right?" said Sinthia.

"That's all I need," replied Ash. "My friend Jack just gave me a lift over here."

"Well, then, why don't you two come in?" said Sinthia, as she fully opened the door and stepped to the side. "I was just about to make a pot of coffee. Would you like some?"

"That would be great," said Ash, as he walked into the house, followed by Jack.

"The kitchen is just down the hall," said Sinthia. "Afterward I'll show you the room."

Ash and Jack made their way to the kitchen. The dim hallway looked freshly painted in sandy brown, with russet crown molding running along the top. An oil painting of a bouquet of sunflowers hung on the wall near the entrance. They walked past a wood-railed staircase along the right wall, which led upstairs, and an open doorway to a dimly lit room on their left. Ash peeked into the room as they went by. He saw a small beige sofa and two chairs in front of a low espresso-colored coffee table. On the wall behind the sofa was another painting. This one depicted a serene scene of brightly colored water lilies floating on a calm reflective pool of water. Except for comic books, Ash never had really been into art, and since he didn't recognize any of the pictures, he imagined perhaps Sinthia was an artist and these were hers. He might have been somewhat disappointed if he ever found out that they were prints of famous works by the French Impressionist Claude Monet and that Sinthia spent her days wearing an apron and waiting tables at a nearby bistro.

As soon as they reached the kitchen, the first thing Jack did was look at the calendar on the fridge. It matched his vision exactly. The demons would be arriving soon, and Sinthia's life would hang in the balance.

Sinthia followed them into the kitchen. "Please take a seat. I'll get the coffee started," she said.

Ash and Jack sat down and watched as Sinthia walked over to the counter. She reached up and removed a jar of coffee from one of the upper cabinets. Then she grabbed the pot from the coffee maker and headed to the sink.

As she filled the pot with water, she turned toward Ash. "I hope you don't mind my asking, but the two of you two don't seem to be from around here. May I ask where you're from?"

"I don't mind you asking, Sinthia," responded Ash. "I'm from Boston."

Her eyes lit up. "Oh, I visited Boston many years ago. It's a great city. And please call me 'Sin.'"

"Okay, Sin," replied Ash. "Your accent doesn't sound like you're from around here either. Can I ask? Where are you from originally?"

"I thought the accent would be a dead giveaway." The corners of her lips quirked upward, causing her cheeks to slightly dimple. "I'm originally from Paris."

The pot was almost full, and Sinthia returned her attention back to the coffee. She finished filling the pot, walked over to the coffee maker, and poured the water into it.

She turned her head back toward Ash. "So what brings you to New Orleans?"

"I'm here for work," he said.

Sinthia thought his answer was a bit short and wondered if she should pry any further but decided not to. She looked back at the coffee maker and placed the pot below. Then she took a paper filter and a few scoops of coffee and put them into the reservoir. After she switched on the machine, she turned around fully toward Ash and Jack.

"Okay, boys," said Sinthia. "It should be ready in a few minutes."

Ash and Jack glanced at the coffee machine as it started to brew. The coffee slowly dripped into the pot beneath. They watched it intensely, as if they were watching the ticking of a clock. This wasn't far from the truth, for when it was full, they would almost be out of time.

Unable to control her curiosity any longer, Sinthia asked, "So what do you do for work, Ash?"

This will be the turning point in the conversation, thought Ash. He needed to get straight to the point if they stood any chance of saving her. There was a good chance that she wouldn't believe him, but he had to try. Whatever happened from this point forward, he knew he would be changing the future that followed.

"I protect people," Ash said matter-of-factly. "And today I've been sent here to protect you."

The smile faded from Sinthia's face, replaced by a look of fear. For a moment, her eyes drifted toward the staircase in the hallway then back again. Slowly she took a step away from Ash and Jack. Her hands reached behind her to search for a knife or perhaps something else she could use as a weapon.

"Protect me?" she said with a slight stutter. "Protect me from what?"

Ash wanted to stand but thought that might scare her even more, so he remained seated.

"Sin," said Ash in a peaceful voice, "I need you to stay calm and listen to what I have to say. We don't have much time. In a few minutes, there'll be a knock at your door. Some people are looking for you, and they're coming here with ill intent."

"What people?" Sinthia said hysterically. "What do they want?"

At least she's asking the right questions, thought Ash. This meant she was starting, even if only partially, to believe him. Now, if he stood any chance of saving her, he needed to figure out how to turn her belief into trust.

"I don't know," he said. "But I do know they'll do anything to get it. Please let us get you out of here, and I'll tell you everything once you're safe."

"Why should I believe any of this?" said Sinthia.

Ash thought for a second then decided to take a gamble. He reached up and slowly pulled down his sunglasses. As they lowered, Sinthia saw that his brilliant blue eyes swirled with wisps of energy.

"These eyes don't lie," said Ash.

As Sinthia stared into his eyes, she said, "Okay, I'll go with that. Let's get the hell out of here."

"Great," said Ash. "Let's leave through the back door before they get here."

"I can't leave without my—" Sinthia said, before she was interrupted by a knock at the front door.

Nihalus and his henchman had arrived sooner than expected. Ash and Jack sprang into action. Ash stood up and extended his arm. His sapphire-tipped wand shot into his hand. With his other hand, he grabbed Sinthia's arm and started to pull her toward the rear door. Jack got up as well and moved to follow them.

Sinthia tore from Ash's grip and ran down the hall as she yelled, "I'm not leaving without my son!"

She has a son? Ash thought, then looked over at Jack. "I got this!" he told him. "You've already done enough. Now get out of here!"

Jack had been running his entire life, and this was his one moment he could finally do something to help someone other than himself.

"No! Save the girl," yelled Jack. "I'll hold them back!"

Ash didn't think Jack stood much of a chance against what was coming, but this was his choice, and there was no time to argue. He dashed after Sinthia, who was already halfway up the stairs. Jack ran past the staircase toward the front door and braced himself against it. There was another loud, insistent knock.

A raspy voice came from behind the door. "Step away. We aren't here for you."

"Are you here for a lozenge?" replied Jack.

The demons apparently didn't appreciate his sense of humor, as he heard them snarl and move back. Then he felt an enormous force smash against the door as something charged against it. Were he a mere mortal standing there, the door surely would have caved in. But they hadn't counted on the man behind it being one of the Touched—and close to three hundred pounds at that. Although it was a struggle for him, Jack's strength and immense girth held the door in place.

"Better hurry," Jack yelled up the stairs. "I'm not sure how long I can hold them."

Upstairs, Ash followed Sinthia to a bedroom at the end of the hall. She quickly switched on the lights in the room. Lying in bed, snuggled in sheets decorated with robots, was a boy, perhaps seven or eight years old, with a floppy mane of light-brown hair. His blue eyes opened slightly, squinting against the light in the room.

"Mommy," said the boy in a half-awake state. "What's going on?"

"Shh, Daniel. We need to be quiet. We have to go."

Sinthia scooped him up then turned around toward Ash. She moved toward the door until she saw Ash shaking his head. Without saying a word, he gestured toward the window, and she knew exactly what he was thinking.

Downstairs, the demons charged at the door again. This time the hinges started to tear from the frame, and Jack struggled to hold it in place. He knew that on their next push there would be nothing more that he could do. While fear filled his heart, he met it with vigilance and determination. He didn't owe anything to Ash, the mother, or her child; he owed this debt to himself, and he was ready to pay it.

He heard the demons pull back and prepare for their next charge. The clamor of their feet resonated like a dozen drums as they ran forward then struck the door. With what strength Jack had left, he tried to hold his ground, but it wasn't enough. The door separated from the frame and smacked him clear across the floor. One demon hopped onto the door and snarled in his direction, while others poured in from behind him.

Although the demons wore human clothing—black trench coats—their features were far from normal. Their skin was inhumanly pale, and their faces were animalistic in form. Fangs protruded from their mouths, and in the place of their eyes were deep black pits.

Like shadows crawling against the wall, two of the demons slithered up the stairs. Another leaped through the air and landed on Jack's chest. A large shadow filled the room as a cloaked figure made its way to the doorway.

The creature on Jack's chest reached into its coat and pulled out a glowing green dagger with a devilishly twisted blade. It gripped the knife with both hands and held it above Jack, ready to bring it down and end his life. He had seen this in his vision, except it was Sinthia who was lying below the blade. Thinking he knew exactly what would happen next, Jack closed his eyes, ready for what was to come, but the creature stopped. Its reptilian-like nostrils flared in and out. It smelled something familiar.

"Never our own kind," said a raspy voice from the doorway.

After hearing those words, the creature hopped off Jack's chest and joined the others running up the stairs. There were a dozen or more of them. This wasn't an attempt to capture a girl or a boy—it was an onslaught meant to end this war this very night.

Upstairs, Sinthia was leaning out of the window, holding the end of a bedsheet she had tied around Daniel. She had just finished lowering him to the ground. Ash stood in the doorway, watching the hallway. Suddenly a loud crash resounded from downstairs. Something had burst through the door and was coming for them. Feeling their demonic presence approaching, he held is wand outstretched and at the ready.

"Sin, you're going to have to jump," yelled Ash. "They're coming. I'll hold them back as long as I can."

"I don't think I can," said Sinthia in a panic.

He quickly turned back toward Sinthia. "Then I'll help."

He pointed his wand at her and chanted, "√κ ⊙ι ⚡ι (IK-OHIV-SI)." She felt something come over her and allowed the spell to take its effect. Then she felt herself grow lighter and lighter. Her feet rose from the floor.

"I'm flying," said Sinthia with amazement.

"Yes, you're flying…Now go!" yelled Ash.

"Thank you," she said, as she pushed herself out the window and slowly floated to the ground.

"Thank me when it's over," replied Ash, as he turned back toward the hallway.

Two demonic creatures emerged, slithering up the stairs. When they spotted Ash, they sprung up and dug their vicious clawed fingernails into the sides of the walls. They scurried along the walls as if it were the floor, never taking their hollow black eyes off their target.

Ash stood his ground with his wand at his side. When the creatures got closer, they leaped off the walls and attacked with their claws extended. As they flew through the air, Ash pushed his wand forward and chanted, "⚡ι ⑤S (KI-NAS)." His eyes ignited in brilliant azure flames as his wand shot forth a swirling blue ray of energy. As the beam struck the two demons, it thrust them against the walls, and they exploded in a bright majestic cobalt flash. Their shadows burned into the plaster, and wisps of blue smoke poured from the scorch marks they'd left behind.

Before Ash could congratulate himself or even take a breath, he spotted the shadows of a demonic horde still coming up the stairs. There were too many of them, and there was little chance that he would be able to defeat them all. He glanced at the window, then back at the hallway, then back at the window. There was only one way out of this. Ash ran toward the window then leaped out.

As he was falling, he turned his body around, pointed his wand at the window, and chanted, "ᔑ/Ϛ ℨ| (MA-RIM)." A blue energy beam shot from his wand and flew toward the open window. When it reached it, the energy spread out and formed an azure barrier over the exit. He saw the demons enter the room and rush toward the window. The field of energy jolted them and repelled them backward.

As the ground raced toward him, he quickly twisted his body again, pointed his wand downward, and chanted, "ᔑ/Ϛ ⊘| (MA-OHIV)." With catlike grace, he landed safely in a crouched position several feet from the house. He stood up and looked at the window. The demons were still being held at bay. Of course, he had no idea how long his field would be able to hold them. He also assumed they weren't complete idiots and eventually would find their way out.

Ash turned around to see if he could spot Sinthia. The moonlight shot through the trees, and he saw the silhouette of a woman, holding the hand of a child, running toward the bridge. He sprinted toward them, faster than he ever thought he could, for he moved with the strength and speed of the Blessed. As he ran, he retracted his wand back into its sheath.

The three of them reached a clearing, where they saw the Huey P. Long Bridge in the distance. They were out in the open, and the bridge was more than a hundred feet tall. Fortune, however, smiled upon them, and the bridge was under repair; a large crane hung over the top of it.

"Guess we'll have to climb," said Ash.

"We aren't climbing that thing!" exclaimed Sinthia, as she pulled Daniel closer to her. He quivered slightly as he clung to her and looked up at his mother with a wide-eyed stare.

"We have no choice," Ash replied.

Then they heard the rustling of trees as something tore through them and rushed determinedly forward. Ash turned around and peered into the forest. The trees were violently swaying; the creatures had to be getting close. He swiftly swung around and, in one motion, lifted Daniel up, put him over one shoulder, grabbed Sinthia's hand, and ran toward the crane. With little choice or resistance, Sinthia allowed herself to be pulled into a run by his side.

As they reached the crane, the creatures approached the edge of the forest. They snarled and hissed as they lifted their reptilian noses into the air to smell for their prey. Quickly they caught their scent and raced across the field, running on all fours like animals.

Ash released Sinthia's hand and put Daniel down. Then he flicked his wrist and shot his wand into his hand. He pointed it at the crane and chanted, "ᗰᗩ ᑕᑌ (MA-CU)." The crane turned then lowered, forming an inclined ramp that touched the top of the bridge. Ash hoisted Sinthia up, and she climbed onto the top of the crane's cabin. Then she reached down, and Ash handed Daniel to her. His little hands held tightly to his mother's as she pulled him up.

RECOVERING SIN

"Go, Sin!" yelled Ash.

"Are you crazy? I can't climb that thing!" she said, gesturing toward the crane.

"You can do this. I know you can. Now go!"

"Hold on to Mommy's back," said Sinthia, as she leaned down and looked into Daniel's eyes.

He nodded, and then she turned around. He crawled onto her back and wrapped his small arms tightly around her neck. With only a second's pause and a big gulp, she started to climb the crane.

Ash pulled himself up onto the crane's cabin. He followed them at a distance since he likely would have to engage with the demons and wanted to give Sinthia and Daniel ample time to get away before the beasts closed the gap. He kept his eyes on the creatures as they bounded toward the crane. Despite Sinthia's hesitation, she appeared to be an excellent climber. Even with the weight of Daniel on her back, she was making good time. But there was little chance that she would be able to reach the top before the demons were upon them.

When the creatures neared the base of the crane, Ash stopped climbing. He hooked his feet between the lattices and turned around. His wand shot into his hand, and he was ready to make his last stand. His position was poor, and he was outnumbered, but he would hold them back for as long as he could.

Then suddenly, just before he had lost hope, a blinding flash exploded below. Purple and gold beams shot toward the horde of demons, blasting them back. They dug their claws into the earth, trying to withstand the force, leaving long fingernail trenches. The demons struggled to stand up and get a good view of their new attackers. As the light cleared, the Wizard and Aleister were standing there with their wands at the ready. The Wizard apparently had gotten Ash's message.

The Wizard looked up at Ash and yelled, "Save the girl. We'll deal with these beasts!"

Ash nodded and withdrew his wand into its sheath. He unhooked his legs, turned around, and rapidly ascended the crane. His movements were inhumanly graceful and fast. He would reach Sinthia and Daniel soon.

As the battle ensued below, Ash, Sinthia, and Daniel reached the bridge. Cars raced past them, but there was a small, unoccupied pedestrian walkway over to the side. Ash turned around. He saw that, despite the mages' efforts, a handful of demons had made their way through and were rapidly clawing their way up the crane.

He looked over at Sinthia and yelled, "Run!"

Sinthia put Daniel down, gripped his hand tightly, and ran down the walkway, dragging him behind her. Ash ran behind them, constantly looking back to see if the creatures had reached the top. He could still see purple and gold flashes coming from beneath the bridge. The Wizard and Aleister were putting up the fight of their lives.

The trio were nearing an area of the bridge that was over the water when three of the creatures reached the top. They hopped onto the bridge's railing in hunched-over positions and raised their reptilian noses in the air. After taking a few deep sniffs, they swung their heads toward Ash, Sinthia, and Daniel. Then the demons jumped down on all fours and scuttled down the walkway.

"We need to jump!" yelled Ash, as the trio continued to run.

Panting, Sinthia yelled back, "We'd never make it!"

"I got us." He shot his wand into his hand. "Just like before."

By the time they reached the section of the bridge over the water, they heard the scraping of the demons' claws against the concrete walkway close behind them. A large casino barge had just started to pass beneath the bridge. Sinthia climbed onto the bridge's railing and pulled Daniel up next to her. When she looked back, the demons were less than twenty feet away.

"They're almost here!" she yelled.

Ash dove forward then grabbed Sinthia and Daniel under his arms as he cleared the railing. As they fell, he quickly chanted, "ᗰᘐ ᗩ� (MA-OHIV)." Their descent turned into flight, and they headed toward the passing barge. From under Ash's arm, Sinthia was still facing the bridge and saw that the demons were perched on the railing above them. They were getting ready to jump.

As the demons leaped off, and just before Ash and Sinthia had reached the barge, Ash chanted, "ᗰᘐ ᘓR (MA-SER)." In an instant, Ash, Sinthia, and Daniel vanished from sight. The demons, assuming the trio had landed on the barge, jumped onto the ship.

Screams of terror filled the night air, as the pale creatures rampaged through the ship's guests searching for them. They paid no regard to subtlety, hurling some of them through the air and running their glowing, green twisted daggers through others. Several passengers jumped from the boat into the water and started to swim to shore. One of the demons leaped off to follow and quickly brought them to their end. By the time the fiends had cleared the top floor, it lay littered with mutilated bodies and splattered blood. Survivors hugged their loved ones as they cowered in fear and horror.

The demons continued their relentless hunt for the trio into the interior of the barge, but they wouldn't find them, for being on that boat was never part of Ash's plan.

Once they were invisible, Ash changed their direction and floated them safely across the Mississippi River and onto the bank on the other side. With a lot of luck and the help of some extraordinary friends, they narrowly had escaped.

CHAPTER 18

A STORY OF SIN

Ash, Sinthia, and Daniel made their way to the Knights Inn in Metairie on Orlando Drive near Route 61. Ash still had plenty of money left from the cash the Wizard had given him and paid a little extra to get two adjoining rooms. The rooms were nothing special but were in much better shape than they'd expected, given the motel's worn exterior.

After Ash had opened the double doors separating the rooms, Sinthia took Daniel into one of the rooms, and Ash went into the other. Ash heard Sinthia's calming voice as she tucked Daniel into bed. He had trouble making sense of everything that had happened and could only imagine what was going through their heads, but at least they were all safe at the moment.

Ash sat down on the floor, crossed his legs, and closed his eyes. He was worried that the demons might be able to track his magical energies, as they had before. The Wizard once told him it was possible to pull energies back into oneself to avoid detection. Ash never had tried this before but thought he should give it a shot. He began to clear his mind as he regulated his breathing. When he felt himself enter a trance, he imagined his magical energies being drawn back into his being. The brilliant azure glow of his eyes gradually receded.

When he opened his eyes again, Sinthia was leaning against the doorway between the two rooms, watching him with her mesmerizing blue eyes. Her long dark-brown hair hung down along the sides of her face. Her white spaghetti-strap tank top and jeans were now covered with specks of dirt.

"You were really great back there, and I wanted to thank you for what you did," said Sinthia in her soft French accent.

"I'm just glad we made it out safely," Ash said. "I can only hope my friends fared as well."

"I was so focused on Daniel's safety that I forgot about them," said Sinthia in an apologetic tone. "I'm sorry. I hope Jack and the others are okay."

"Best not to worry about it right now, I suppose."

"Are the others your friends as well?"

"One of them was. I didn't recognize the other."

Sinthia sighed deeply. "What are we going to do?"

"We should get some rest. It's been a long day." Ash stood up. "With any luck, the Wizard made it out of that mess okay and will try to contact me."

"You're probably right," Sinthia said, as she started to lower her head. Then she slowly lifted her eyes, looked at Ash, and said, "The thing is, though, I'm not that tired."

"Neither am I."

Sinthia nervously twirled her hair between her fingers. "Mind if I come over to your place? Maybe we could talk?"

243

"Of course." Ash motioned toward a loveseat near the window. "Please come in."

Sinthia entered the room, walked over to the loveseat, and took a seat. Ash followed and sat next to her.

"What would you like to talk about?" he asked.

"I don't know where to start. Maybe you could tell me more about those things? What the hell were they?"

"To be entirely honest, Sin, I'm not exactly sure," replied Ash. "My master told me of beings on this earth that are the offspring of demons and mortals, but he never described anything like what we saw. They didn't appear to be human at all."

As the words escaped his lips, he realized almost instantaneously that he might have said a bit too much. Sinthia looked uneasy. Her eyes widened, and her lips quivered slightly as she spoke.

"Do you think they'll find us here?" she asked.

"I think we're safe for now." Ash leaned over and placed a hand on top of hers. "I promise you I'll do anything in my power to protect you and Daniel."

"I know." Sinthia turned her hand around to hold his. "I trust you."

"Now the real question is 'Why they were after you in the first place?'" asked Ash.

Sinthia shrugged. "I honestly don't know. I'm no one special."

"I'm sure you're special to someone," Ash replied.

Sinthia looked up into his eyes and smiled. "I like your eyes better this way."

"Thanks." Ash smiled back at her. "I was once told that the eyes are the windows to the soul. They reflect who you truly are and what you truly want."

"And what do my eyes tell you?" asked Sinthia as she stared at Ash.

Ash looked deep into her piercingly dark-blue, mysterious eyes. He was neither a seer nor a fortuneteller, but as he looked into her eyes, he became lost in her gaze. It wasn't a spell or arcane effect, but there was something amazingly comforting and familiar about them. Something he couldn't entirely describe. He also watched and noticed a slight quiver in them. She was still scared and worried.

"They tell me I'm meant to be here with you," said Ash, before shaking his head and correcting himself. "I mean, they tell me I'm meant to be here to protect you and keep you and Daniel safe."

Sinthia smiled and looked more at ease. "I'm still a little shaky," she said. "I think I could use a drink. Would you mind if I checked the fridge?" She was hoping a previous occupant might have left something behind.

Ash smiled. "Go right ahead. I doubt you'll find anything, but have a look."

Sinthia let go of his hand and got up. She walked over to a mini fridge next to a table with an old television on it. As she bent over and opened the fridge, she saw that it contained a half-empty bottle of Smirnoff lying on its side, a small can of unopened cranberry juice, and two bottles of Budweiser. She looked back at Ash. "It looks like we're in luck…and I'll be having some vodka. There are two beers in here too. Do you want anything?"

Ash really wanted—and was more than ready for—a drink, but he knew his mind needed to be clear for what was to come.

He rubbed his face with his hands. "I'll have to pass tonight."

"Your call, but I'm still having one," replied Sinthia, as she removed the bottle of vodka and can of cranberry juice from the fridge.

She grabbed a glass and mixed her beverage. Normally she would have preferred to have ice in her drink, but there didn't appear to be any around, and she didn't feel like leaving the room. She meandered back over to Ash, taking the first sip of her drink on her way. After she had taken her seat, she rested the hand that held her drink on the arm of the loveseat and put her other hand on her knee, placing it closer to Ash than it had been previously.

"Sin, please don't take this the wrong way," said Ash. "But I have a feeling there's something you aren't telling me."

Sinthia looked away from him and took a big sip from her drink. There indeed was something she wasn't telling him. She took a deep breath then slowly turned her head back toward him.

"What if I told you that today wasn't the first time I've seen eyes like yours?" she said.

"I guess I'd say I wouldn't be entirely surprised," Ash said, placing his hand on hers again. "Do you want to tell me about it?"

"Perhaps some other time. It was a long time ago, and it didn't end well."

This might be the clue he needed. If she had met a mage before, perhaps that was why the demons were after her. Although he wanted to press her further, he could tell by the look in her eyes that this wasn't the time. She needed to feel safe, and surely digging up bad memories from the past wouldn't help. So he decided to let it go for now.

"I understand. We don't need to tell our sad tales tonight," Ash told her.

She held his hand tightly, as if to say, "Thank you."

"Do you mind if I ask you something else?" said Sinthia.

"I'm at your disposal, madam," replied Ash, immediately after which he wondered why he had responded in such a ridiculous manner.

"Have you always been like this?" asked Sinthia. "I mean, have you always been able to cast spells and do all those amazing things?"

Ash was hesitant to tell her the truth—that this was his first mission and that a few months ago he was just a geeky kid at MIT. Sinthia already was worried, and telling her the truth probably would just make her worry even more. He thought it might be better to lie or at least avoid answering the question directly. But something inside him told him she would be able to see right through him and know he was lying. There was something so familiar about her, as if she knew him.

"To be honest, this is all probably almost as new to me as it is to you," answered Ash. "A few months ago, I was just a normal kid, worried about college and grades. Then I had this weird experience and met this strange man. I know him only as the Wizard. He taught me about magic and the nature of things."

"Was he a good teacher?" asked Sinthia.

"Yes," answered Ash, smiling lightly. "I haven't always been the best student, though, but I think I'm getting better at it."

Ash lifted his hand from Sinthia's then lowered the hood from his cloak. His blond hair fell forward, revealing the two ebony streaks that ran down the sides of his head. Sinthia placed her drink on the table next to her and leaned forward before running her fingers through the dark portions of Ash's hair. Ash watched her hand as she did this. He had almost forgotten about the black streaks.

"That's a very unique hairstyle," said Sinthia with an intrigued look. "Do you moonlight in a punk band on the weekends?"

The memories of Ash's encounter with Miss Murder rushed into his head. He tilted his head down in shame.

"Not so much," he replied.

She brought her hand closer and rested it at the side of his face. Her soft touch against his skin soothed him and helped him keep his unpleasant thoughts at bay. He brought his hand up and placed it on hers.

"It's a reminder of a mistake I once made," he said.

"You don't have to tell me about it," said Sinthia in a sympathetic tone. "Like you said, we don't need to tell our sad tales tonight."

"We probably should get some rest now," said Ash, releasing her hand and letting it slowly fall back to her knee.

Sinthia nodded. "You're right, but would it be okay if I finished my drink first?"

Ash smiled. "Sure."

For the next few minutes, the two sat in silence as Sinthia finished her vodka and cranberry. She sipped gradually, as if she felt that when the glass was empty, this moment they were sharing would end. When she finally finished her drink, she placed the glass on the table and got up without saying a word. She walked slowly towards the doorway and ran her fingers along the bed as she passed it. Ash was watching her the whole time.

As her fingers reached the end of the bed, she stopped and, without turning around, asked softly, "Would you mind if I stayed a little longer?"

Ash felt his heart lift. He didn't want her to leave.

"Maybe just a few more minutes," he said.

Sinthia turned toward the bed and crawled into it while staring at Ash. She lay with her body extended and held her head up with her arm.

Ash got up, removed his cloak, and rested it along the edge of the loveseat. Then he walked over to the bed and lay down on his back next to Sinthia, tucking his arms behind his head. As soon as he was comfortable, Sinthia inched forward, placed her head on his chest, and wrapped her body close to his. He lowered his right arm and held her. They both closed their eyes.

"You make me feel safe," she said, running her fingers along his chest. "I think I'm ready to tell you my story now."

Ash nodded, then listened as she launched into her tale.

"I was just sixteen and still living in Paris," Sinthia began. "I'd just received my baccalaureate a few months earlier, after graduating from lycée or what you would call high school. My parents wanted me to go straight to university, but I convinced them that I needed to take some time to think about what I wanted to do. They always supported me in any way they could.

"While I was in lycée, I worked part-time at a popular café called Café Kléber. They agreed to bring me on full-time. I rented a small one-bedroom apartment on Avenue Fremiet near the Pont de Bir-Hakeim. It wasn't much, but it was the first time I'd had a place of my own.

"I was an avid runner and woke up early each morning for a run along La Seine. If you've never taken a stroll along La Seine, I'd highly recommend you go someday. There are few things as beautiful to start your day. One morning I noticed that a man was sitting on a bench near my apartment, reading a newspaper. The next morning and those that followed, he was there again. He never said a word or bothered me in any way, but I felt like he was watching me.

"One morning, before I started my run, I walked over to the bench. I was pretty bold back then. I placed my finger on the top of his newspaper and lowered it until he could see me and I could see

249

him. He was an attractive young man, perhaps in his mid to late twenties, with short blond hair and a goatee. His eyes appeared a bit strange. They were mostly brown but also had specks of yellow or perhaps gold in them. He seemed very surprised, almost as if he hadn't expected anyone to know he was even there.

"I just came out and asked him, *'Vous me regardez?'*

"He responded in a British accent, 'My apologies, mademoiselle, but I don't speak French.'

"I had taken several years of English in school and had plenty of opportunities to practice at Café Kléber with all the tourists, so my English was pretty good. I was about to repeat exactly what I had said in English, but since the man appeared much more handsome and far less threatening than I'd imagined, I changed my tune.

"'Good morning, sir,' I said. 'You know, if you want to ask me out on a date, there are better ways.'

"He seemed taken aback by my boldness, and it took a few moments for him to respond. 'Okay,' he said. 'Would you like to go to a café?'

"'Not right now,' I told him. 'I'm going for a run, but perhaps if you're here when I get back?'

"'I'll be waiting right here,' he replied.

"I went for my run as usual. At that time I was running between seven to eight kilometers per morning, but I decided to make it a little shorter that day. When I returned, the strange man was still sitting there, so I walked over to him.

"'You ran off so fast that I didn't even have a chance to introduce myself,' he said, as he stood and extended his hand. 'My name is Aleister.'

"Though something told me he already knew my name, I shook his hand and replied, 'Please to meet you, Aleister. My name is Sin.'

"'It's a pleasure to meet you, Sin. Is there a café nearby?' he asked.

"'This is Paris,' I replied with a smile. 'There are cafés on every corner and many in between.'

"He smiled in return. I guess, technically, that cup of coffee was our first date. I found him so mysterious and intriguing. He seemed hesitant to see me again, but for some reason, I kept spotting him around the city, and eventually, after several cups of coffee and many long conversations, we started to see each other. Before long, he was spending many of his nights with me in my apartment.

"One day he gave me a necklace as a gift. The locket hanging on it was a silver loop surrounding two overlapping symbols made of jade. The first looked like an inverted *S* and the other like a curved bolt of lightning. Though the chain fell apart years ago, I still carry the pendant on my keychain. He said the strangest thing about it. He said it would protect me from the eyes that can't see. I didn't know what to make of that, but the necklace looked quite old, and I thought it was very pretty.

"Aleister and I were happy for quite some time, but then one night everything changed. I awoke to find him screaming in his sleep. His body was convulsing, as if he were possessed by something. I was frightened and didn't know what to do. I tried shaking him several times to wake him.

"His speech changed into a language I'd never heard before, and then suddenly his eyes flung open. They were glowing bright gold, as if they were on fire. He looked at me, but it was if he couldn't recognize me. Then I felt myself being lifted into the air. My body felt paralyzed and not under my control.

"I yelled, 'Aleister, please stop!'

"'You can't have me!' he screamed in return.

"The glow in his eyes intensified, and then I was thrown across the room. My body smashed into a large mirror above the dresser, sending pieces of glass flying everywhere. I fell onto the dresser then rolled onto the floor.

"It took me a few moments to pull myself up. As my head reached the level of the bed, I looked over and saw Aleister with his hands over his face, sobbing. He looked back at me with tears in his eyes.

"'I'm so sorry, Sin,' he said.

"I got up and held him. I told him everything would be okay. He continued to cry in my arms until he fell asleep, but I couldn't go back to sleep because I knew right there and then that I needed to leave him.

"Aleister often left on business trips out of the country for several days at a time. It was before one of these trips that I told him I could no longer be with him. He seemed heartbroken but said he understood. I gave him a kiss good-bye, and after he left, I packed my things and moved back in with my parents. However, this wasn't the last that I saw of him. A few weeks later, I caught glimpses of Aleister out of the corner of my eye every now and then. I felt like he was following me.

So one day I had a talk with my parents, and they helped arrange a trip for me to America, where I would stay with an aunt of mine who had moved there many years ago. After I left, I never saw Aleister again."

At the end of the story, Ash and Sinthia lay there quietly, holding each other as they slowly drifted off to sleep. Later, when Ash awoke in the middle of the night, Sinthia was no longer in the bed with him. He got up and walked over to the doorway between the rooms. There he saw Sinthia and Daniel fast asleep, holding each other's hands. He smiled as he watched them for a few a minutes then returned to his bed.

*

The next morning, Ash awoke to the sound of the television in the other room. Sinthia and Daniel apparently had found something they were watching entertaining because he heard them giggling. He reached into his pocket and removed his cell phone. With Nihalus and his minions still in the area, using telepathy as a method of contact was out of the question, and this was likely the only way the Wizard had to reach him. When he tried to turn on his phone, he realized the battery had gone dead, so he jumped out of bed and grabbed his cloak.

He walked over to the doorway, poked his head into the other room, and said, "Sin, I need to leave for a few minutes. Will you two be okay?"

Sinthia, who was sitting on the couch with Daniel, turned toward Ash. "Is everything all right?"

"Yep. I just need to find a charger for my phone. I was going to ask at the front desk."

"Okay, we'll be right here," said Sinthia, as she turned back toward the television and hugged Daniel.

The man at the front desk did, in fact, have a charger that fit Ash's phone; a previous guest had left it in one of the rooms. However, seeing that Ash was a bit desperate, he took advantage of the situation. He said he would sell it to him but quoted him fifty dollars, much more than what a new charger would cost. The price, however, didn't really matter to Ash. He was more concerned about getting in contact with the Wizard than haggling. So he paid the man and took the charger back to the room.

As he walked in, Sinthia asked, "Did you find what you were looking for?"

"Yeah, it cost me a small fortune, but I got one," Ash said, dangling the charger from his hand.

He closed the door behind him and walked over to the seating area of his room. He scanned the walls for an outlet and quickly found one. After plugging in his phone, he rested it on the table next to the loveseat. It would be a few minutes before it had enough power to even turn on.

He walked back over to the doorway and looked into the room where Sinthia and Daniel sat watching TV. She heard him approach and leaned her head back.

"Do you think your friends will call?" asked Sinthia.

"With any luck the Wizard already has."

Daniel turned away from the TV, rested his chin on the back of the couch, and asked, "Aren't you a wizard?"

Ash smiled. "Yes, Daniel, I suppose you're right. I was talking about my friend, who's also a wizard. I'm hoping he'll try to contact us so we can meet up with him."

"Can we fly again?" asked Daniel, lifting his head and grinning eagerly.

Sinthia patted Daniel's head. "No more flying for now, honey." She turned back to Ash. "I'm not sure if wizards need to eat, but we're hungry. Do you think we could get some food before we meet up with your friend?"

"I don't know about the rest of them," Ash said, "but I'm starving!"

"Last night I saw a diner close by, down the street," said Sinthia. "Perhaps we could go there."

"Okay," Ash said. "We just need to wait for my phone to get enough charge so I can check my messages."

At that moment a beep sounded from his phone.

"Which…I guess would be right now," Ash said, as he walked over to his phone. "Get your things together, and we'll head out soon."

"Oh, darn," Sinthia said sarcastically. "When we left, you forgot to tell us we needed to pack anything."

Daniel giggled loudly.

Ash missed the humor of the statement, as he was busy looking down at his phone. There was a text message from the Wizard. It read, "This line is no longer safe. We have to leave town tonight. Meet me on the fifth floor of the airport's short-term parking lot at 8:00 p.m. Bring the girl and her son."

Something about the message struck Ash as odd, but he couldn't put his finger on it. Perhaps it was just that he would have expected a call rather than a text message, especially given the gravity of the situation. Ash picked up his phone and the charger and placed them in his pocket. When he turned around, Sinthia and Daniel were entering his room.

"Message from your friend?" she asked, as she held Daniel close to her.

She looked worried, and he was worried too. The message from the Wizard gave him an uneasy feeling, and he still had no idea what had happened to Jack or even if he was still alive. But he knew he needed to put these thoughts and concerns aside for the moment and say something to comfort Sinthia and Daniel and lighten the mood.

"Yes, but we'll have to get to that later," he replied, "because right now we have a more important mission ahead of us. We need to find some pancakes!"

BLOOD AND ASH

The boy laughed, and his mother smiled.

CHAPTER 19
INTO OBLIVION

After eating a full breakfast at the diner, Ash, Sinthia, and Daniel walked down the street until they found a small shopping center. They were all in desperate need of some new clothing, as their attire had been dirtied and worn by the previous night's ordeal. Ash was pleasantly surprised that Sinthia and Daniel were both quick shoppers, and within less than an hour, they all had found something.

Their next stop was back to the Knights Inn. It was still early in the morning and well before checkout, so they went to their rooms for a quick shower. Sinthia asked Ash when they were meeting up with his friend. He told her it wasn't till later in the evening, so they had all day. She suggested she show him around the city, and he agreed.

The day was blissfully normal. The city of New Orleans had so much to offer. They walked through the New Orleans City Park for a couple of hours and later visited the Audubon Zoo. Ash normally wouldn't have enjoyed either of these activities very much, but there was something about being with Sinthia and Daniel that made them fun. For a while he forgot about all the turmoil of the past few days.

As it got later in the day, Ash told Sinthia they were to meet the Wizard in a garage at the airport at 8:00 p.m. She desperately wanted to go back to her house and pick up some items, but he convinced her otherwise. Although he told her not to worry and said everything would be okay, he still felt something wasn't quite right about the meeting.

The sun hadn't yet set, but the time for their rendezvous with the Wizard was approaching, and they didn't want to be late. They hailed a taxi along the corner of Walnut and Magazine and headed to the garage. The traffic was heavier than Ash had anticipated, and they arrived just a few minutes before eight o'clock.

The parking garage was seven stories high, and the Wizard was supposed to meet them on the fifth floor. As they made their way inside, an uneasy feeling came over Ash. The garage was far from empty, but there didn't appear to be many people around. As they headed to the elevator, he held Sinthia's hand, and she held Daniel's.

As the elevator ascended to the fifth floor, Ash felt a presence grow stronger and stronger with each level they passed. It wasn't the same feeling he'd had when he was around the Wizard. This was something entirely different, and it sent a chill up his spine. Something definitely wasn't right here.

When they got off the elevator, Ash turned to Sin. "I want you and Daniel to wait here."

"Why?" asked Sinthia with a look of worry. "Is something wrong?"

"I'm not sure, but something doesn't feel right." He pointed to one of the large columns supporting the building. "Wait right there.

If I'm not back in five minutes, take Daniel and get as far away from here as possible."

"I'm scared," said Sinthia.

"I won't let anything happen to you or your boy. You have to trust me," said Ash.

"I do." Sinthia, still holding Daniel's hand, moved behind the column. "We'll be right here, waiting for you."

"Here, take this," Ash said, handing her his remaining cash.

After she took the money, she grabbed his hand, pulled him in close, and gave him a light kiss on the lips. "Be careful," she said.

Unexpected warmth rushed through him. He held her hand for another few moments then replied, "I will."

Ash disappeared around the corner of the column and walked down the long pathway of the garage. He stopped and peered back a few times, spotting Sinthia peering back at him from behind the column. Each time he waved his hand for her to stay hidden. When he eventually looked back and couldn't see her anymore, he felt she had gotten the message, and he continued on.

The sun had just finished setting, and many of the lights on this level were either entirely out or flickering at best, making the light in the garage poor. The large columns and high walls formed shadows around every corner, making it difficult to see. Ash heard only his own footsteps, intermingled with the sounds of traffic from below. As he neared the end of the garage, he noticed a figure standing in the darkness several feet in front of him. He couldn't tell who or what it was, but it had the silhouette of a man in a mage's cloak.

Ash stopped walking and addressed the figure. "I'm here."

"Did you bring the girl and her son?" asked the figure in a voice that sounded vaguely like the Wizard's.

The presence Ash had detected earlier was emanating from this figure. He felt its cold, dark energy filling the space.

"They're safe," replied Ash, "but you aren't the Wizard!"

"You're correct, young one," said the figure, as it stepped out from the shadows.

The figure was wearing a long, dark cloak with a hood that obscured the upper portion of its face. It had a black goatee surrounding its mouth and sharp fangs. As it lifted its head, Ash could see it had deep-black eyes that blazed with the crimson glow of fire.

Its voice changed to something sinister and raspy as it said, "Please allow me to introduce myself. My name is Nihalus, and I can tell by your stench that you're that annoying boy from Massachusetts. Obviously Miss Murder's reports of your demise were overstated. I'll have to a have a little talk with her when I'm finished here."

"Where are my friends?" asked Ash in a confident, demanding tone.

"The fat man and the mages," replied Nihalus, as he slowly paced back and forth. "They're still alive—for now. I might even be inclined to allow them to continue to be so…if you and I can reach an understanding."

"Are you offering me a deal?" asked Ash.

"I'm considering it, but I don't think you'll like the terms," replied Nihalus, as he pulled down the cloak from his head.

Though the features on Nihalus's face weren't entirely human, he was unexpectedly somewhat handsome. Every feature appeared as if it had been perfectly chiseled out of pure white stone. To Ash's surprise, his nose didn't look anything like those of the previous creatures he had encountered. Instead it was quite human, save for the fact that it came to a fine point at its end. His long deep-black hair was pulled back into a tight ponytail. Trails of red energy swirled around his black eyes.

"You see, I care little for their lives," continued Nihalus. "They're meaningless half-breeds and of no consequence to me, but I know you feel otherwise. I can see you care for them. I also see the fear building in you and can almost taste your displeasure with me."

Nihalus pulled open his cloak and let it fall, exposing the rest of his form. Although his chest was bare, the lower portion of his body was covered in a black kilt that hung to the ground. His pale chest was chiseled and very muscular, and across it were two dark leather bands, as if he had something strapped to his back. On each of his hands was a black metallic gauntlet, each of which had a large deep-red ruby embedded in it.

"You know," said Ash, "if we're just going to get naked, I might have better places to be."

Nihalus looked directly at him and snarled. His rage made his red eyes ignite more brightly. He reached his left arm over his head and behind him, then pulled out a large shiny copper torus. He raised it in the air and held it above him.

"Do you know what this is, boy?" Nihalus asked sternly.

Ash pretended to think for a moment then replied, "The world's largest inedible doughnut?"

Nihalus didn't look the slightest bit humored by Ash's response. "It's known as a Seer's Gate. Not many people know the tale behind it or the true power it holds. It was once wielded by the strongest of the angels and was a powerful weapon. Ages ago, it was split into two, and what you see before you is only half of its whole. Yet it still holds unspeakable power—the power to rip through the weak fabric of this mortal realm into dimensions far beyond your comprehension. Would you like to see how it works?"

"Not really," responded Ash. "But something tells me you're going to show me anyway."

Nihalus placed the Seer's Gate on the ground in front of him. Then he backed up and stretched out his arms. He looked down at the torus and chanted, "◯R ◯R (OR-NER)!" The Seer's Gate erupted with a glowing column of blood-red energy that shot up and spread out against the ceiling. Ash jumped back and shielded his eyes with his arm. The light quickly subsided as the column solidified into a flowing, reflective red liquid.

"Beautiful, is it not?" said Nihalus, as he slowly walked around the Seer's Gate until he stood in front of it. He pointed back at it and continued, "What you see before you is a direct passage to the oblivion known as the Nether."

"Going back home?" asked Ash.

Again, Nihalus didn't look humored and responded angrily, "What do you know, half-breed? It was never my home!"

At this point, Ash was pretty sure he was being set up for something, and though he wasn't entirely sure what that was, he was almost certain it wasn't good. He thought perhaps it would be best just to whip out his wand and face the demon before things got worse. However, he still didn't know where his friends were and decided instead to keep Nihalus talking. Perhaps he could get him to reveal their whereabouts.

"This is all very interesting, Mr. Nihalus," said Ash. "And I'm sure you've just been dying to tell someone about your devious master plan for taking over the universe, but I just don't care. What I do care about is my friends. So, I'm just curious...are you ever going to quit your babbling and tell me where they are?"

"Your kind are always in such a rush, never savoring the actual details that matter. Your kind aren't worthy of this world," Nihalus snarled. "But that won't be a problem for much longer. My bargain is this. Once the Blessed One steps through this gate, I'll release your friends."

"I won't surrender myself so easily!" exclaimed Ash.

"Such beautiful arrogance—" Nihalus started to say, then stopped in midsentence and turned his gaze away from Ash.

Ash felt something approach from behind him. He glanced over his shoulder to see Daniel watching them from around one of the pillars. He had stepped out farther to get a better view, when Nihalus had spotted him.

"There you are," said Nihalus in a pleased, raspy voice.

The demon threw his hand forward, and a beam of red energy emerged from his gauntlet and hurtled toward Daniel. Ash reacted almost instantaneously, as if by sheer instinct. He flicked his arm out, shot his wand into his hand, then twisted it under his other arm, pointing it in Daniel's direction as he chanted, "ᔑᓵ ᔕᓵᛁ (MA-RIM)." Just as the red energy was about to wrap itself around Daniel, a glowing field of brilliant blue emerged in front of him and deflected the blast.

Sensing that Sinthia was close behind Daniel, Ash yelled, "Sin, get him out of here!"

Nihalus made a fist with his other gauntlet and raised it in the air. Immense glowing red energy swirled around it. Then he pointed it at Ash. In the form of a red dragon, a fiery blast shot toward him.

Ash turned his wand straight up and chanted, "ᔑᓵ ᔕᓵᛁ (MA-RIM)." Another blue shield materialized in front of him, blocking the attack from Nihalus just in time. However, the blast was extremely powerful and pushed him back several feet as he struggled to maintain the two energy fields. His eyes burst into azure flames.

"Sin, I'm not sure how long I can hold both of these," yelled Ash, as he tried to strengthen the two fields by pushing his wand forward.

Sinthia ran toward Daniel and pulled him behind one of the concrete pillars just as the blue shield in front of him gave way. The red energy shot past them and smacked against a wall several feet away.

With all his energy now unified, Ash pulled back his wand then gave it a strong push forward. The red energy beast pushing against the field in front of him was repelled. Nihalus was taken by surprise as the energy surged back toward him. His hands ignited in flames as he roared into the air. He stood there for a moment with his arms at his sides as smoke drifted into the air from both his gauntlets.

Ash dissipated his shield and held his wand at his side. He stared at Nihalus with determination, and Nihalus stared back at him.

"You're indeed powerful, young one," said Nihalus, "but no half-breed can prevail against me. I'll slay you where you stand."

"Let's dance!" replied Ash.

Both of Nihalus's gauntlets glowed and swirled with massive amounts of red energy. He pushed his hands forward, and a wave of crimson shot toward Ash. Unsure whether he could deflect or withstand such an enormous amount of energy, Ash rolled over to the side, dodging the blast. Concrete shards erupted from the ground and flew into the air as Nihalus's spell missed and struck the floor of the garage.

"You'll have to do better than that!" exclaimed Ash.

Nihalus was outraged.

The two continued to shoot spells back and forth at each other. Their power and skill seemed to be almost equally matched. A brilliant display of red and blue energies flew across and filled the garage. Their eyes burned with power. They dodged or deflected each other's onslaughts then countered with their own. Sinthia and Daniel huddled behind the pillar as the battle raged on. Neither combatant was letting up.

Then a well-placed spell from Nihalus nearly struck Ash's legs. Ash instinctively chanted, " (MA-OHIV)" and flew into the air, but he misjudged the height of the garage and smacked against the ceiling. He fell hard to the ground. Nihalus thought he had an opening and flung another blast at Ash's prone body, but Ash tucked and rolled out of the way. Then he quickly countered by chanting, " (KI-NAS)," trying to dispel the demon's body. The blast struck Nihalus's side and pushed him back toward the Seer's Gate.

It was then that Ash noticed that as the demon got closer to the red energy emanating from the gate, it appeared to be drawing him in like a strong magnetic field. Nihalus struggled to pull himself from its grasp.

Ash stood back up and said, "Is that all you got?"

"You fool," yelled Nihalus. "I draw power directly from the Nether itself. I'll show you what true power is!"

Nihalus held his arms outstretched at his sides. Streams of red flowing energy poured from the Seer's Gate directly into the rubies on his gauntlets, causing his entire hands to glow with intense energy. Ash was about to regret taunting the demon, as it pushed both hands forward and shot forth a crimson blast of concentrated magical energy.

Ash tried to raise a shield of magical force by holding his wand in front of him and chanting, " (MA-RIM)." Though he managed to raise it in time, this attack was several times more powerful than any of Nihalus's previous spells. It shattered the field in front of Ash, knocking him back and sending his wand flying out of his hand. Ash watched as his wand whisked through the air then fell and slid across the ground. The glowing sapphire tip of the wand slowly grew dimmer and dimmer as it got farther and farther away, eventually disappearing into the darkness.

Ash dove behind one of the concrete pillars directly across from the one shielding Sinthia and Daniel. He held his side as blood dripped from his wounds. With his wand lost, so was all hope.

Nihalus laughed a wicked laugh. "So sad. The Blessed are nothing without their toys. You should have known that you can't defeat me. You're not the One. You're just a boy playing a game he can't hope to win."

Ash looked over at Sinthia, who was holding Daniel tightly in her arms. She looked at him with fear and tears in her eyes. It was then that something came over Ash, and he had a moment of clarity. This was never about him. Every sin, every benevolent act, every mistake, every right move, every chance meeting, everything he'd ever done had led him to this moment. He finally understood his purpose and what he had to do.

"Sin, you take good care of Daniel. He has a special destiny," said Ash, as he pushed himself up against the pillar behind him.

"No! What are you doing?" yelled Sinthia, reaching one of her hands toward him.

"What I was meant to do," replied Ash, stepping out from behind the pillar to face Nihalus.

Nihalus stared back at him. "If it's a glorious death you seek, I'll grant you your last wish, and then I'll walk over your cold corpse and take the boy. You should know by now that you can't hope to kill me."

INTO OBLIVION

A smirk rose on Ash's face. "I don't have to kill you, demon. I just have to delay you until he is ready," and then he ran directly toward Nihalus.

Nihalus thrust his hands forward, causing hundreds of blazing fireballs to shoot from his gauntlets toward Ash. Ash raised his hand in front of him and screamed. His eyes ignited with an intense, brilliant flow of blue energy as an azure field of energy emerged before his hand. Without a wand and without using the ancient tongue, by his sheer will he had cast a spell. Blasts of flames ricocheted off the shield as he raced forward.

"Impossible!" screamed Nihalus.

Ash rammed his energy shield straight into Nihalus and knocked him backward, toward the Seer's Gate. As Nihalus struggled to resist, Ash continued to push with all his will and might. As they got closer, the gate reached out to them and started to pull them both in. Nihalus reached forward and grasped Ash's wrist, thinking Ash wouldn't risk letting himself be sucked into the Nether, but he was wrong. With one final push, he threw both their bodies into the portal. The blood-red liquid wrapped around them.

There was a brilliant explosion of energy as they fell into the Seer's Gate, and then the gate almost instantaneously collapsed to the ground. The red liquid-like energy from the portal spread across the concrete floor of the garage then quickly dissipated into the air. The two had passed into oblivion, and the gate had been sealed.

Sinthia had been watching the battle in horror. As the portal collapsed, she let go of Daniel and raced toward the Seer's Gate. When she reached it and realized there was nothing she could do, she fell to her knees.

"Ash!" she screamed, as tears streamed down her face.

Daniel walked up behind her and rested his hand on her shoulder. She reached back with her hand and held his. Then she leaned her head on their clasped hands.

"We have to go, Mommy," he said.

"I know, honey," she replied. "Just give Mommy a minute."

Sinthia continued to cry as Daniel slowly pulled his hand away and walked over to the Seer's Gate. He rested his hands upon it for a few moments then turned his gaze in the direction that Ash's wand had flown. The boy walked over to the area where he thought it might be and soon found it lying on the ground near the edge of the garage. He stared at it for a few moments, admiring its silver body and elegant blue-sapphire tip. Then the very structure of the garage trembled and shook. The lights hummed then illuminated brightly. The wand slowly wobbled back and forth, and then it rose from the ground and flew into his hand.

EPILOGUE

Battle worn, the Wizard and Aleister stood in the Great Chamber of Archmedea, located beneath the Pyramid of Khafre in Egypt. Across a large dark oak table sat Sebastian, his elbows resting upon it. Christopher and Robert stood at his sides.

"I'm happy both of you are still alive," the elderly mage said. "As you know, I was against using the Seer's Gate to teleport you to the girl, but as it turns out it, it was the correct call. Aleister, you have my apologies for doubting you."

Aleister nodded in acknowledgment.

"Now can you please tell me what happened after you arrived in New Orleans?" asked Sebastian.

"We arrived just in time to assist Ash and Sinthia in their escape," replied the Wizard. "There were hordes of full-blooded demons on their tails. Aleister and I managed to hold them at bay until Nihalus himself arrived.

"He flew down from the sky and hovered in the air with outstretched wings. Then he unleashed a rain of fire upon us, with complete disregard for his own minions. His power was immense, and even the combined force of our shields and spells were no match.

"As we lay there, wounded on the ground, the demons swarmed and overwhelmed us. They knocked us unconscious, and when we awoke later, we found ourselves in captivity, along with Smiling Jack.

"The three of us were in a nearly pitch-black room, encased in a glowing red magical field. Our wands and other items had been stripped from us. As we looked out into the blackness beyond our prison, we saw the glimmer of dozens of glowing green eyes stalking around. Even if we could have managed to bring down the field, they would have surely destroyed us. There appeared to be no escape.

"I noticed a pain in my left shoulder and felt a small open wound there. I surmised that Nihalus or some other creature had drawn a small amount of my blood from it. This is similar to what happened to Aleister when we first encountered Nihalus. The creature seems to be able to extract information by ingesting the blood of others. It was my best guess that he was using this information to continue his pursuit of Ash and Sinthia."

"And how did you manage to escape?" asked Sebastian.

"It wasn't by our hand," replied the Wizard. "Aleister and I tried everything we could think of to penetrate the field, but without our wands, our options were limited. Hours passed, and the growls of the creatures outside grew, as if they were getting hungry. Then suddenly they screamed in agony. Aleister, Jack, and I moved closer to the edge of the field to get a better look at what was going on.

"In bursts of green flames, one by one they faded from existence. Then, to our continued surprise, the red field slowly opened from the top then collapsed to the ground, freeing us."

"So they just let you go?" asked Sebastian. "Do you have any idea of the cause?"

"We know that pure-breed demons normally can't enter this world," said the Wizard. "And when they do, they're generally anchored to the object that brought them into this existence. It's my belief that they were brought in through the other Seer's Gate, and when Nihalus was defeated, someone else took possession of the object. This caused the demons to be sucked back into the Nether. The field itself bore the signature of Nihalus and faded when he was banished."

"And what was the fate of Smiling Jack?" asked Sebastian.

"We let him go, Master," replied Aleister.

Sebastian raised a wiry eyebrow. "And why did you decide to let one of the Touched go?"

"It's simple," replied the Wizard. "Contrary to the belief of this council, not all of the Touched are bent on destruction, and he wasn't our enemy in this conflict. In fact, if it weren't for him, Sinthia likely would be in the hands of Nihalus."

*

Bruce's encounter with Ash at the club had left him with a few cuts and bruises, but otherwise he was okay. Over the past few days, he barely had left his house, which was located a few miles outside of Las Vegas. He was worried about his own safety but more so about his friend. Jack had been missing for several days, and Bruce had called nearly everyone they knew.

Bruce was sitting on the couch, twirling the contents of a glass of Scotch, when he heard someone enter through the front door.

Instantly his eyes turned to a pair of decorative samurai swords hanging above the fireplace. He'd never even swung a sword before but thought it was better than no defense at all. So he grabbed one of the swords, unsheathed it, and held it tightly in both hands.

From around a corner, he saw a shadow enter the room. It was a very large shadow. He raised the sword into the air and yelled, "Beware! I'm armed!"

He then heard the familiar, sarcastic voice of his friend. "Please don't hurt me. I've had a rough couple of days."

Bruce dropped the sword to the floor and ran around the corner. Jack was standing there in the same expensive, tailor-made suit he'd worn the last night Bruce had seen him, though it appeared a little worse for wear: one sleeve was missing; the other was torn at the elbow; and the pants were covered in dirt. He gave Jack a huge hug. Jack winced a little, obviously in pain.

"Careful there, buddy," said Jack. "But damn is it good to see you!"

"Man, I was so worried. I almost thought I'd never see you again," Bruce said, releasing his friend.

"Honestly, I wasn't sure I was going to make it back."

Bruce fired several questions in rapid succession: "What happened? Where were you? What happened to that dude from the club?"

"Slow down," said Jack, making a pushing motion with his hands. "I'll tell you everything, but first I need a—"

Bruce interrupted, "A drink? I'll go make you one right now. What would you like?"

Jack shook his head. "I was going to say a shower. In any case, I'm giving up drinking."

"Really? But you love to drink. It's, like, your favorite hobby."

EPILOGUE

"Yeah, I used to, but this whole experience over the past few days has shown me something. I've been wasting my abilities and basically just getting by. There's so much more that I could be doing. The time has come for me to make some changes, and those changes start today."

"Well, that's great, but would you mind if I had a drink?" Bruce asked, with a look that indicated he was seeking approval.

"Go right ahead, my friend. I said I had an experience, not that I became a Mormon preacher," Jack said, with his trademark smile.

Bruce smiled back. "Got it. Are you sure I can't convince you to tell me about your adventure right now?"

"All right, but can we at least sit down?"

The two walked into the living room and took seats across from each other. Bruce reached over, grabbed his drink, then eagerly looked at Jack.

"So I headed to New Orleans with that kid from the club to look for this girl..." started Jack.

*

"I see," said Sebastian, as he rubbed his whiskery chin. "While I don't agree with your decision, I understand why you made it. However, should we become aware that Jack is using his abilities for ill intent, the two of you will have to deal with him. Am I understood?"

The Wizard and Aleister nodded.

"Let's move on then," said Sebastian, "The other Touched involved in this mess, Miss Murder...do you have any information on her?"

"Nothing new," replied the Wizard. "After she attacked my apprentice, she seemed to have just disappeared."

"I'm sure she'll show up again," said Sebastian.

*

Sarah was seated at the bar in a dive called the Paradise Lounge along Route 90 in Madison, Wisconsin. She was wearing black cowboy boots, a very short pair of jean shorts, and a tight white T-shirt that exposed her midriff. A dark pair of sunglasses covered her eyes. Unseen by mortal eyes, her demonic pets, Jinx, Kynx, and Lynx, sat on the table next to her, dangling their legs over its edge.

The jukebox was playing her favorite song, "Witchy Woman" by the Eagles, and she was enjoying a bottle of Corona with a lime. A small group of rugged-looking men, seated at a table a few feet away, were busy talking among themselves. They couldn't stop staring in her direction.

Finally one of them, a tall man dressed in a blue flannel shirt and blue jeans, got up and walked over to her. He rolled up his sleeves and adjusted his short dark-brown hair as he approached.

"Hey, there, beautiful," he said, as he leaned his elbow on the bar and looked over at her. "Now what's a nice girl like you doing in a place like this?"

"Who says I'm a nice girl?" she responded, without even taking the time to look at him.

The man was unsure whether she was flirting with him or just trying to shut him down. But it didn't really matter. She was the most attractive thing he'd ever seen, and unless she slapped him in the face, he wasn't going to give up.

"Can I buy you a drink?" he asked.

She turned her head slightly toward him and took a sip from her beer. "Thanks, but I already have one."

"Come on, sugar. I'm trying here," he said, as he put his hand on her arm.

EPILOGUE

Sarah slowly looked down at his hand. He could tell she wasn't pleased by his advance, so he quickly pulled it back. She looked back up and took another sip from her beer.

"You know," she said, "I might not be good for you."

*

Sebastian lowered his head and reviewed some papers in front of him. The room was silent for a few moments, and then he raised his head and looked back at the mages.

"Do you know anything about the fate of Sinthia Greyson?" asked Sebastian.

"After we escaped, we returned to Sinthia's home, hoping she would return there, but she never did," replied Aleister. "We attempted to use our scrying incantations to detect their whereabouts, and though their ties to some of the objects in the house were strong enough to allow us to perceive that they were still alive and on the move, we were unable to track them."

"Them?" asked Sebastian with a puzzled expression.

"Yes," replied the Wizard. "It appears that since we last encountered Sinthia Greyson, she bore a son."

"It's interesting that we weren't aware of this. What can you tell me about this boy?" asked Sebastian.

"Unfortunately, not very much," responded the Wizard. "It was dark when we arrived, and we only saw him at a distance. I can say he was perhaps seven or eight years old."

"I see," said Sebastian, before pausing in thought for a few moments then looking at Aleister. "I would ask why you were unable to track them, but as I recall, she carries with her a medallion that prevents us from detecting her whereabouts, which, if I also remember correctly, you gave her."

"Yes, Master, I did. I thought it was a good idea at the time," replied Aleister. "I was sent to watch and protect her. I gave it to her to obscure her detection by the Touched. I never thought we would be the ones she would be running from."

"So she and her son are lost to us then," said Sebastian.

"At least we know they're still alive. That's what is important," replied the Wizard. "And I get the feeling that when the time is right, we'll see them again."

*

A light breeze blew through the midnight air. Under the light of the moon, Sinthia and Daniel wandered along the side of Interstate 10, just outside of New Orleans. She wore a look of confidence and determination as she held her son's hand tightly. A large bag was slung over her left shoulder. As the lights from cars and trucks approached from behind, she held out her thumb, trying to hitch a ride. She didn't really care where they were going, just as long as it was as far away from New Orleans as they could get.

There weren't many cars on the road at this time of night. Vehicle after vehicle passed them until finally a red semi pulled over to the side of the road. Sinthia tugged on Daniel's hand as she picked up their pace to reach the front of the trailer. When she got there, the driver reached over and opened the passenger-side door. He was an older man with a scruffy beard. He wore an old flannel shirt and a well-worn black cowboy hat and was chewing a mouthful of chaw.

The man leaned over and in a strong Southern accent said, "Howdy, ma'am. Where are you and your boy headed?"

Sinthia held Daniel under her arm and in her French accent replied, "How far are you going?"

"Well, this trailer is headed all the way to San Francisco City."

"Then we're headed to San Francisco," said Sinthia.

"Hop right in then. I could use the company."

"Much appreciated," said Sinthia with a smile. "Thank you so much."

She lifted Daniel into the seat then pulled herself up. Then she rested her bag on her lap and closed the door. The driver gave two pulls on the horn before continuing down the highway. This made Daniel smile.

"You don't see too many hitchhikers nowadays," said the trucker, "especially ones with children. Is everything okay?"

Sinthia nodded. "Yeah. We just needed a change of scenery."

"I hear that," the man said. "You're traveling kind of light, though. Would you mind if I ask what's in the bag?"

Before Sinthia could respond, Daniel said, "It's a magical gate."

"Right," said the trucker with a broad smile. "Well, you don't have to tell me if you don't want to."

*

One of Sebastian's advisors leaned over and whispered something in his ear. The elderly mage nodded a few times then continued with his inquiry.

"Were you, by any chance, able to recover the Sangrian Map?" asked Sebastian.

"No," replied the Wizard. "As you know, the map was last in the hands of Nihalus. We can only assume it disappeared with him."

*

After an extensive search, Detectives Valle and Kent finally had a new lead in the alley murder case. They had managed to track down a small cabin near the town of Willard along the Finger Lakes in Upstate New York, owned by Professor Albrecht. Though they didn't have a search warrant, they figured with what they'd seen, even if he were still alive, there was no way the professor would be filing any complaints with the department.

The residence was filled with occult books and collections of ritualistic paraphernalia. Several shelves contained vials of essential oils of various colors and jars of rare herbs. Walls were lined with intricately etched medieval daggers and swords. Half-melted candles surrounded incantation circles drawn in white chalk on the floor. Chalices made of all manner of materials, from wood to glass to metal, lay next to elaborate altars. They spent hours searching through every last crevice of the cabin when finally Kent stumbled upon what appeared to be an old diary. As he flipped through the pages, he found a section that described various properties around the country.

"Hey," said Kent. "I think I found something."

"Well, what is it?" asked Valle.

"There's a list of addresses here. Maybe they're hideouts Albrecht was using. There's one here that's not too far from the seventh precinct."

"Good thinking, Kent," said Valle. "If we wounded that creature, then maybe it had to retreat there. Let's check it out."

Later that night, in a run-down, boarded-up building, the detectives found the Sangrian Map on an old broken table. It had reverted back to its inactive state and displayed the supercontinent of Pangea once again. With this and the diary they'd found in the cabin, they were back on the case.

*

"Well, I think that concludes all the questions we have," said Sebastian. "Now I believe congratulations are in order. We can already feel the shadow of darkness receding from this world. It stands to reason that your theory that the demon Nihalus has been banished from this realm is correct. You've done well."

"It wasn't without incident," replied the Wizard. "And the one you should be thanking is no longer among us. I feel that his presence has left this world as well."

"You speak of Ashley Drake, your troubled apprentice," said Sebastian.

"Yes, he wasn't without his flaws, but in the end, it appears he confronted Nihalus and ultimately sacrificed his life defeating him," the Wizard said sadly.

"We'll mourn his loss," said Sebastian in an equally somber tone. "Now the two of you should get some much-needed, much-deserved rest before we send you out again."

Aleister looked at the Wizard, who nodded.

"No rest is needed, Master. We're ready now," said Aleister.

Sebastian sat in thought for a moment before replying. "Then let's get to it. It appears the demon Nihalus was very busy with his time in this world. He was reaching out and bringing together groups of Touched throughout the globe. Now, with his demise, they're disorganized and vulnerable. We're going to take the offensive and track them down. This war could soon finally be over."

"Where do we start?" asked Aleister.

"I'm sending you both to Madrid. There's been a disturbance there that I want you to look into," replied Sebastian. "We have a contact in the city who'll give you more information when you arrive."

"We'll be on the first flight," said the Wizard.

"Flight?" The elderly mage shook his head. "Thanks to Aleister, we now have mastery of the Seer's Gate. We've set it up in a more permanent location here in Archmedea and will use its power to send the two of you to Madrid."

"Then we'll be on our way," said the Wizard.

As the Wizard and Aleister were leaving the room, Aleister leaned toward the Wizard and asked, "Do you think we've seen the last of your apprentice?"

"One never knows," replied the Wizard.

*

Covered in blood, Ash fell forever. He had his redemption, and just before the darkness engulfed him, he smiled.